DON'T GO
away mad

BESTSELLING AUTHOR
LACEY BLACK

BURGERS & BREW
Crüe

Lacey Black

Don't Go Away Mad

Burgers and Brew Crüe, book 2

ISBN-13: 978-1-951829-12-4

Lacey Black

Jasper

"I'm out of caramelized onions! Where the hell are the onions?" I bellow into my busy kitchen, ready to jump up my assistant's ass for the second time today. She knows today's special is the meatloaf burger, or "Paradise by the Dashboard Light" as the menu depicts, and one of the main ingredients is freshly caramelized onions over a grilled meatloaf patty.

She knows this, and yet I have no fucking caramelized onions.

"They're right here," Petra says, flustered, tossing a fresh batch of the vegetable into the metal bowl.

"Keep 'em coming, Pet. We've got five more orders behind these," I state, making two of the gourmet burgers my restaurant is known for.

Burgers and Brew, that's what we're called. The bar and restaurant my three friends and I opened just five years ago. What started as a pipe dream shared over a lot of cheap beer, transformed into what you see today featured in foodie magazines and websites all over the United States. We've turned hamburgers into an art, thanks to unique and delicious topping combinations and clever names.

Case in point: "Paradise by the Dashboard Light."

It's my take on a classic meatloaf sandwich. Fresh ground beef, a secret blend of spices, a bit of breadcrumbs, with a ketchup and homemade barbecue sauce glaze. Top it with those caramelized onions that are so hard to keep stocked, and a lightly toasted Kaiser bun, and you have a delicious take on a Sunday evening family favorite entrée.

I catch movement out of the corner of my eye and find Isaac heading to my office, a stack of papers in his hand. Isaac is the brains on this particular operation. We call him Numbers or Newton, after Isaac Newton, and he keeps our budding business in the black. It was Newton's solid business plan that helped us secure the loans needed to start Burgers and Brew. He's probably the one who works just as many hours as I do, making sure our bills are paid and everything runs smoothly.

Well, as smoothly as it can, considering we staff over two dozen employees and are opening our own brewery.

My friend, Jameson, took on that project. He serves as head of security on the bar side of the business but is overseeing the transformation of the empty warehouse next door to the future Crüe Brewery, an ode to our favorite band from college. We're still a ways out from being able to produce our own beer, but we're all pretty excited about it. Jameson has been working on recipes at home, when he's not here.

He also plays a mean guitar. In fact, he's our house musician on Friday and Saturday nights, packing the place with crowds from Stewart Grove and many surrounding communities. I'm not sure when Jameson learned to play, but I know he's always had a guitar in his hand since I met him in college.

The man behind the bar is Walker. He makes sure the alcohol flows at a steady pace and the patrons are enjoying themselves. He even has this crazy tradition that every Saturday night, he plays a Mötley Crüe song on the old jukebox and dances on the bar. The first time he did it was during a successful opening weekend and a few too many celebratory shots, and ever since that night, everyone screams for more. Even his girlfriend, Mallory, seems to egg him on.

I'll tell you, seeing my friend around Mallory has been something to witness. We all saw his feelings for her way before he acknowledged them, and it was fun as hell to tease him about it. The icing on the domestic bliss cake is Mal's three-year-old daughter, Lizzie—or Lizard, as we like to call her. Cutest little thing I've ever seen, and she definitely livens up this place when she's here.

Finally, there's me. I run the kitchen with an iron fist, but if you want to be the best, you have to actually *be* the best. And that's me. I've always wanted to be a chef, though I never saw myself serving hamburgers all day long. When I was in culinary school, I thought I'd be at a three-star Michelin restaurant, preparing cuisines to jet-setters around the world. Yet, when my friends and I had a little too much to drink and we started brainstorming this place, it grew on me.

A lot.

Now, I can't see myself anywhere but here. Running my own business with my best friends is exactly where I want to be in this life.

"Order up!" I holler, making sure the plates look as appetizing as they'll taste.

"I'm coming, hold your horses," Mallory states as she swipes the freshly prepared plates onto her tray.

"I have no horses, Mal. You know this," I tease. Mal works as a server in the restaurant, which is where Walker met her. She's one of the newest employees but is one of the best. She's attentive and quick, and the customers love her.

"I'm well aware of your shortcomings in the patience department, Jasp," she sasses as she pushes through the swinging kitchen doors.

"Is that a smile I see?" Patrick, my dishwasher, asks.

"Get back to work," I growl without any heat behind the demand.

He laughs as he stacks clean plates on the shelf in front of my face. The kid is one of the hardest workers I've ever encountered. At just twenty, he couldn't afford college post-high school, so he opted to find a full-time job. He uses the money to help support his disabled mom, who has been in a wheelchair since an automobile accident almost a decade ago. He's kind, reliable, and does a great job, even pitching in where needed if we're ever in a pinch. Patrick has shown a little interest in cooking lately, so I make sure to pull him over to the grill every once in a while, usually after the lunch rush has already gone.

Patrick's also one of the only employees to stick out my mood swings. Working in the kitchen of Burgers and Brew isn't for the faint of heart. It takes someone who pays close attention to detail, can keep up with the demand of a high-intensity job, and thick skin. They need the latter to put up with me on a day-to-day basis.

I know I'm a son of a bitch. I've been called it plenty of times over the years. You don't think I haven't heard the grumblings by the kitchen staff or the whispers of the serving staff? Oh, I've heard it all.

But this is my business, my legacy, and I expect it to be done right or not at all. What goes out those swinging doors has my name on it, even when I'm not behind the grill. Therefore, every step in the process must be executed perfectly or the whole thing could crumble.

I won't let that happen.

Gigi, our server manager, comes through the door and delivers a tray of dirty dishes. She's been with us since the beginning, having waitressed for two decades before. Gigi's very grandmotherly and an important part of the team. Plus, she doesn't put up with my crap and calls me on it often. She's one of the only people alive I'll allow to walk into this kitchen and give me hell. Anyone else would be fired, but not her.

"We've got a table of seven seating now," she hollers, as she sets the dirty dishes on the counter for Patrick.

"You need him to bus?" I ask, without taking my eyes off the task at hand.

"Not yet, but I'll let you know," she adds before heading back out.

"All right, team, let's get ready to kick it into high gear. Patrick, get those plates through the washer. We'll need to stay on top of them. Mark," I say, turning to the man working the burger prep station, "grab more cut fries from the walk-in. Petra, prepare the buns to be toasted. We've got burgers to make," I demand just as more orders start to come in.

An hour later, we've finally slowed down enough that I can take a breath. I love being busy. Not only because it means we're making money, but because it's just in my DNA. Keep moving, make the burgers. It's what I do. If I'm not here—that's not very often— I'm running the trails out at Grove Park or I'm racing up the 102 in my Mercedes. She doesn't like to sit still either. My two-year-old SLC 300 Roadster loves to stretch her legs as often as I'll let her.

I make four fresh hamburger patties and doctor them up to each of their preferences. I throw piping hot fries on their plates, load them on a tray, and head for the door. "I'll be in the bar if you need me, Petra," I say to my assistant, who'll take care of any orders that come in while I'm in my weekly Monday afternoon owners' meeting.

When she waves her understanding, I push through the swinging doors and head for the bar. The guys are already there, laughing at something Walker is saying. "Lunch is served," I announce as I approach the table.

Jameson jumps up quickly and starts helping me hand out the plates. "My mouth's been watering ever since I saw today's special on the sign," he says, handing off meals to our friends. When the food has been distributed, I set the tray on the empty table behind us and take my seat.

"Before we start, I need to use someone's garage or spare room for a decent-sized box," Walker says, shoveling fries in his mouth.

"What's in it?" Jameson asks before taking a bite of his burger.

"A recliner."

That causes us all to stop and look his way. "A recliner?" I ask.

"Yeah, one for little kids. A few months back, we saw them at the furniture store down the block. Lou fell in love with it, and all I've been able to think about since is getting her one," Walker replies, referring to Mallory's daughter, Lizzie. He started calling her Lou not too long after he met her for the first time, short for Lizzie Lou.

"You can use mine," I tell him, taking a bite of a fry. "I have plenty of room in the garage or spare room."

"Thanks. I'm picking it up when I leave here, so I'll run it over before I head home," he confirms.

"You know the code," I state, even though I don't need to. All three of them know the security code to my house, like I have keys and know the codes to theirs. There's no one I trust more in this world than the men sitting around this table right now.

"While we're eating, and before we jump into an update on the brewery, I found out who purchased the small empty building across the street. It's going to be a bakery," Isaac informs us.

"A bakery?" I ask, my interest piqued, taking a few fries and popping them in my mouth.

"Yeah. The paperwork filed with the city was completed three months ago by a Lyndee Gibson," Isaac says casually.

I choke on my fries.

Flashbacks explode in my mind.

Air is sucked completely from the room.

A fiery little pixie with dark hair, brown eyes the color of milk chocolate, and an attitude bigger than the Grand Canyon. She was my favorite sparring partner in culinary school, and if I'm being honest, my biggest competition. There was something about her that got under my skin from the very beginning. Day one, when she walked in, gave me a little smile, and proclaimed herself as the best in the class.

I'll admit, she was damn good. Lyndee Gibson kept me on my toes during the day and wide awake at night. While she was this little spitfire with dark flames burning in her eyes, that spunk also seemed to fuel a certain fire deep inside of me. Specifically, down in my balls.

"You all right?" Walker asks, reaching over and slapping me on the back as I choke on my fries.

"Fine," I gasp, reaching for the glass of water sitting in front of me. After a few sips, I feel the burn in my throat subside. "Went down the wrong pipe."

"Do you know her?" Isaac asks, his all-knowing eyes locked on mine.

"What?"

Jameson starts to laugh. "I'll take that as a yes. He's avoiding like a mother."

I huff out an exasperated breath. "Whatever."

"No, he's right. Something's up. What is it? Did you sleep with her?" Walker asks, a look of pure amusement on his face.

"No," I growl, grabbing my burger and taking a big bite, hoping it will help change the subject.

"No, you didn't, but you wanted to?" Jameson asks with a laugh.

"Shut up."

He barks out a big boisterous laugh. "That's a yes."

I can't dispute it, because he's absolutely right. Back in school, she was this sexy little thing in black leggings and lasers shooting from her eyes. There was something about getting her all worked up that turned me the hell on. It became our *thing*. I used to push every single one of her buttons, just to watch her detonate.

It's how I got through school unscathed.

"Well, we should anticipate the opening of her bakery within the next few weeks. I don't foresee it having any impact on business here," Isaac states. "Do any of you?"

Both Jameson and Walker shake their heads, but I know better. I learned the hard way not to underestimate Lyndee. I did that exactly one time during a particular sautéing project that first year and ended up with a failing grade and a burnt piece of whitefish.

I decide to keep my mouth shut until I have an opportunity to find out what's going on. If Lyndee is opening a bakery directly across the street from my restaurant, it's for a reason. She's probably trying to capitalize on our success, using our name and product to worm her way into *our* customer base with a friendly smile and the prospect of a sugar rush.

I may not have seen Lyndee in a decade, but I know this isn't a coincidence.

Can't be.

Nothing is ever coincidental where Miss Gibson is concerned.

"If there's nothing else then, let's talk about the brewery," Isaac says, pulling us away from the new business across the street and right into our sister company being constructed next door.

It's a pleasant change of topic, one I enjoy hearing about. Jameson and Isaac are working their asses off on our new brewery, everything from logos and brew names to potential distribution options after we're finally producing our own beer. I love hearing their excitement, feeling their energy with each detail they share.

"We're starting with four recipes we'll serve in-house. The plan is to incorporate seasonal brews starting next summer. A summer ale and something for fall. I've been testing at home and think I almost have a good recipe down," Jameson informs us.

"I think that's it for today," Isaac finally says, after we've gone over questions and concerns.

"Leave the plates, and I'll take them back to the kitchen," I tell my friends, watching as they place their empty dishes on the tray.

Isaac and Jameson take off for the office upstairs, while Walker practically runs to the bar when he sees Mallory over there placing a drink order. I grab the tray to haul it back to the kitchen, but my legs carry me in the opposite direction. Instead of heading to my domain, I find myself lingering at the front windows of the bar, where I have an unobstructed view of the building across the street. It has white paper across the windows, which is why we weren't sure what was going in, but because of its small size, we knew there was a limited number of options.

Now that I know it's a bakery, I'm looking at it with a more critical eye. The awning is a light blue, the brick façade freshly painted white. It's bright and cheery, and I'm sure resembles the same on the inside.

Lyndee Gibson.

Hell, I wasn't expecting that one.

The woman I butted heads with daily in college is going to be right across the street from me. My cock actually seems to like that idea, giving me a happy little jump in my pants. Unfortunately for him, there's no way her opening a business across from us will have the results he's hoping for. Nothing good could come from this.

This has bad written all over it.

Lyndee

I set the paintbrush in the pan and smile. After four hours of painting with both brush and roller, it's finally complete, and I couldn't be happier with the final project.

Glancing around, a sense of pride fills my entire being. This is it. All my hard work and determination, my sleepless nights and ramen noodle budget has paid off. I'm a week away from opening Sugar Rush, my very own bakery in the heart of Stewart Grove, Ohio. After nearly two decades of hoping and wishing for this day, my dream has finally become a reality.

Ever since I was a little girl and had my very first homemade scone from a small bakery in my hometown of Wellington, Ohio, I knew what I wanted to do with my life. The flavors burst to life on my tongue, sweet and buttery and oh so perfect, and before long, I was saving my pennies to purchase homemade breads and pastries for my family. We weren't exactly poor, but we definitely didn't have the extra cash to spend at the bakery.

My mom did the best she could, but it wasn't easy. As a single parent, she worked day and night, sometimes as many as three jobs, to make sure me and my brother, Dustin, had a roof over our heads and food on the table. That's where I learned how to cook the basics. Mac and cheese, hotdogs, and meatless spaghetti were a few of the basics I made on those nights Mom worked. Dustin wasn't picky, as long as it was soft enough or cut up enough he could eat it.

When I was fourteen, I taught myself to use the oven. Using my grandma's old recipe books and ingredients I purchased from the dollar store, I tried my hand at fresh breads, cookies, and cakes. I fell in love with baking, the sugar in the air and the flour in my hair. It was my solace when the stresses of real life started to suffocate me.

What could a fourteen-year-old possibly stress about, you ask?

Besides having a mom who worked herself to the bone, we were taking care of Dustin. My brother is four years younger than I am and was born with cerebral palsy, though is considered higher functioning. He can talk pretty well, feed and bathe himself with little complication, but still uses a walker or wheelchair to help him get around. He has the use of his extremities, but becomes weak when he overuses them. When Dustin was younger, it wasn't too bad. Even without having a dad around, we made it work. We were a team, Mom, Dustin, and me.

Until it all came crashing down around us.

With me graduating culinary school and working at that very bakery I discovered my passion for pastries, Mom was able to slow down a little bit. She found a full-time position at a physician's clinic that provided enough income, and partnered with mine, we were doing just fine in our cozy three-bedroom house in Wellington.

We didn't need the man who ran out on us when I was just six years old. If he wasn't able to handle being a parent to a boy with a disability, then I didn't want him there. Even at a young age, I could see the disconnect in him. He never wanted to hold Dustin and would often leave him in his crib to cry, until I'd go in and take care of him. I bathed him, fed him, and changed his diapers. I know his departure in the middle of the night when Mom was at work was tough, but it was a blessing in disguise.

Then, four years ago, we lost Mom. I'll never forget opening the front door and seeing those two police officers standing there. A drunk driver crossed the centerline when she was on her way home from work on Friday evening. By the time the accident was called in and the emergency personnel arrived, she was already gone.

"That looks great," my brother says, pulling me out of my melancholy.

I blink up, taking in the light-yellow wall, and smile. "Thanks." I beam proudly, glancing around at the brightly colored room. Three walls are yellow, with the wall that separates the customer side of the bakery with the kitchen a lovely lavender. I wanted this part to be cheerful and fun, to give the customers a little slice of sunshine while they're here.

"I think those multi-sized and colored shelves will really pop on the yellow," he says, maneuvering his electric wheelchair through the room, careful to avoid the stacked tables and chairs in the middle.

"I agree," I reply, glancing at the pile of newly painted blue and green shelves. Dustin and I found them at the secondhand store and bought all they had. They're all different lengths and styles, and we painted them a sage green color and a light blue that matches the awning out front. I plan to use them to display cute canister sets, fun kitchen gadgets, and even books that patrons can grab and read while they enjoy a cup of coffee and a breakfast pastry. The local secondhand stores have been a gold mine for finding fun treasures to decorate my bakery at a fraction of the cost of purchasing new.

Even the tables and chairs I'll be using came from there. I found two gorgeous wingback chairs and a round end table too that will be perfect in the corner by the front window, opposite the entrance. The rest of the tables are small bistro-style, some perfect for two chairs and others will fit four, but it's the chairs that I really adore. No two chairs are alike. I had to hit both secondhand stores in town, but also made a trip to a nearby city to get enough. My inspiration for the design hit me one night while watching an episode of *Friends* on television. Monica and Rachel's four chairs were all different, and I fell in love with the look instantly.

"I'm ready to start moving tables," Dustin says with a chuckle.

"We have a long way to go before we can do that though," I tell him, glancing at the torn apart front counter and display. The shell is positioned against the purple wall and will need to be reassembled and put in their final positions. But they're heavy. When I purchased them off a buy, sell, or trade group on social media, I paid them an extra hundred bucks to deliver the pieces to me. It took three guys a good half an hour to get them inside the bakery, so moving them on my own isn't going to be easy. Not at all.

That'll be a bridge I cross when I need to.

"The kitchen is set up," Dustin proclaims, proud of the hard work he put into helping finish the heart of my business.

"Show me," I reply, wiping my paint-splattered hands on my leggings.

My brother leads me into the newly finished kitchen and waves his hand dramatically. "All of the pots and pans are washed and ready to go on the shelves," he says, motioning to the big stack of new, clean kitchen products.

I move around him and start to move the gorgeous equipment onto the industrial shelves. I can feel my brother's eyes on me every step of the way, making sure it's easily accessible by both me and him. Dustin isn't a baker like me, but he knows his way around a kitchen. Over the last four years, I've spent a lot of time in the kitchen. It helps calm me when I get upset or stressed, and Dustin has picked up a few things. At first, he was afraid to bother me, but over time, we learned to work together. Having him beside me, kneading dough, actually helped my mood more than hampered.

"Perfect," he states as I slide the last stack on the shelf.

Taking a step back, I smile proudly and agree. I look around the entire kitchen, from the stainless-steel double ovens, the massive refrigerators, and the dishwashing system. This room took the biggest hit on my start-up budget, but it is all necessary to do business.

"What else is on the list to do today, boss?" I ask, stretching my achy back.

"The kitchen is pretty much done. All that's left is that big case out front. How are we going to move it?" my brother asks, concern filling his brown eyes.

"I've got a plan," I tell him.

I have no plan.

"Do tell," he says skeptically, turning his chair and facing me.

"I would, but then it won't be a surprise," I reply, trying to hide my grin.

Dustin laughs and shakes his head. "So, you have no clue how we're going to do it."

I don't argue, because he's not wrong. I'm going to have to ask for some assistance moving the large pieces. Our neighbor to the left is a bank, while the one on the right a gifts and boutique store. I could possible ply some of the male loan officers next door with fresh goodies if they'd come over and assist with the move. There's also the option of asking for assistance from the men across the street. I've seen a few come and go from the restaurant, but the biggest activity comes from the warehouse next door. Rumor has it there's a brewery going in there, and I'm sure there a few able bodies there who would appreciate some sweet rolls as payment for helping a neighboring business.

"I figure we can ask for help from a neighbor," I finally acknowledge.

"Have you met them yet?"

"Well, the bank next door gave me the loan," I reply with a chuckle.

"What about the one across the street. That restaurant has a steady stream of customers in and out all day, not to mention the ones who go into the bar side." Dustin's words cause me to pause and turn.

"How do you know that?" I ask, glancing toward the front windows that are covered with white paper.

"I have eyes, Lyn. Every time I've been on the sidewalk, I've witnessed it. They're very busy for a burger joint."

I lean against the large center island I'll use as my prepping station and relax. "I've been told it's a nice one though. Not like the McDonald's down the road. Maybe we should order to-go one of these nights before we head home," I suggest.

"Sounds good," he replies.

I've slowly been learning about our new town over the last few months. Dustin and I rented a small two-bedroom condo that is wheelchair accessible and only two blocks off the main artery through town. We've been able to walk to and from the bakery, but we know the weather won't hold much longer. It's almost Christmas, and every day the temperature drops colder and colder. When that happens, we'll resort to using my old Chevy Malibu and either his walker or the other wheelchair that's a bit more compact. Dustin's able to get in and out of my car with a little assistance, but I always hate how using the walker slowly takes its toll on him throughout the day. With his motorized chair, he has the freedom to move around all day, which I know he appreciates.

In the four months we've been in Stewart Grove, we've stuck pretty close to home. I've been on a budget, especially since I'm opening the bakery, but we've enjoyed eating at a few local restaurants. Unfortunately, Burgers and Brew hasn't been one of them yet. Maybe this Friday night we'll treat ourselves to dinner at the place known for its gourmet hamburgers and homemade fries. Just thinking about it causes my stomach to growl.

"When does the new girl start?" my brother asks, referring to the part-timer I hired last week to help.

"She'll be here Wednesday through Friday this week for training," I reply, excited to actually get started doing what I love. But that's just two days away and I'm not set up yet. I'm going to have to bite the bullet first thing tomorrow and ask for help in moving the counter and display case. Once that's set, the rest will fall into place and we can add the final touches.

"Well, then let's get all this finished so we're ready for her," Dustin proclaims, turning and heading for the dishwasher.

He gets up out of his chair and works the new system easily. I turn on the radio, finding a local country station, and continue setting up the kitchen. The first order of supplies will be delivered Friday, and I'll be able to start prepping for Monday's grand opening over the weekend. I really don't have any idea how much to make. I don't want to overshoot my quantities, but I don't want to be short either. Though, I suppose running out of a certain product would be a good thing, right?

Daisy will serve customers at the front counter, while Dustin and I focus on the baking and restocking. Well, I'll technically fill in wherever needed. It's my business, and for the first several months, we'll be operating on minimal staff. I'll arrive at four in the morning to prepare the first batch of goods. By the time we open at six, I'll have hot coffee and the pastries flaky and fresh. Daisy will work six to eleven, leaving her time to get to her other job at noon. The rest of the day, Dustin and I will handle the front counter and kitchen until we close at two.

Someday, I hope to expand and offer lunch options too. Paninis, soups, and salads. Quick, healthy, and delicious lunch options to dine in or carry out when you're on the go. Fresh lemonades, teas, and smoothies, and maybe even ice cream. But that's all a pipe dream. First, I have to make my business plan profitable as it stands, then maybe someday, I'll be able to expand.

We work the rest of the afternoon on the kitchen, making sure it's ready. I even grab the broom and mop to clean the flooring up front. It's hard when I have big stacks of chairs and tables in the way, but at least I get it clean enough to not track dirt throughout the rest of the building. Every completed task is a step toward opening day, and with each check I tick off my list, a fresh wave of pride overcomes me.

Just as I place the broom and mop in the storage closet, I hear the back door open. Dustin has been on top of taking out the trash, so it's probably just him. I step out of the small space and head for the employee bathroom to wash my hands. We got lucky all the bathrooms were already ADA compliant, which is perfect for my brother. He doesn't have to worry about shimmying into a tiny bathroom or having to use the one up front for customers.

An old George Strait song plays on the radio, and I instantly start to hum along. Once my hands are washed and dried, I head into the kitchen, my eyes cast down as I pick at a big run of yellow paint smeared across my stomach. "Did you get it taken care of?" I ask Dustin, feeling his presence in front of me.

"Lyndee Gibson."

That voice.

I'd know it anywhere.

Warm, rich, and smooth as honey and exactly as I recall it from my dreams. A voice I haven't heard in more than a decade, not since we completed culinary school, but one I'd never forget.

Jasper Kohlmann.

I look up, my wide eyes meeting his chocolate brown ones. I'm instantly transformed back to a time where my biggest worry was whether or not I'd be able to pass applied mathematics and whether or not my scholarship would cover everything I needed it to.

"It's been a while, Lyn," he says, his voice gravelly and low.

"It has. How are you?" I ask, still trying to wrap my head around the fact Jasper Kohlmann just walked through the door of my bakery.

"Oh, I'm doing well," he replies, casually leaning a hip against my island. I can't help but notice the way his polo shirt molds to muscular arms and stretches tautly over an equally firm chest. My throat is suddenly too dry, my eyes unable to move from the physique in front of me. The years have definitely been good to Jasper.

He takes a step forward, breaking the trance I seem to be under. My eyes fly upward, his narrowing as he advances. I take a step back, my butt hitting the refrigerators and keeping me from farther retreat. My eyes widen as he steps directly in front of me, his musky cologne infiltrating my senses like a bomb filled with remembrances of a time long past.

A flashback plays out, one with him advancing, his sweet scent hitting my nostrils. I swore he was going to kiss me that night, I saw it in his eyes. But the ding of a timer broke the spell we were under, causing us to jump apart. The moment we shared was never repeated, though it did many times over the years in my dreams.

He studies my face, taking in the bags under my eyes and the stress lines marring my forehead. I can imagine what he sees when he looks at me. The fatigue, the tension, and the apprehension that comes along with opening a new business in an unfamiliar town. I'm sure it's all there in spades.

Suddenly, his eyes narrow even more, that familiar wariness filling his gaze. It takes me right back to school, where he was a constant nuisance and my biggest competition. Familiarity wraps around me, warm and comforting, just like it did back then. A tingle races down my spine, and I feel the interrogation looming.

"What do you have planned, Lyn? Why are you opening up a bakery right across from my restaurant?"

Jasper

She gasps. It's the sweetest sound that goes straight to my groin, much like it did back in school. The reminiscence about my body's reaction to the noise is short-lived, however, when her dark eyes fill with fire. "Excuse me?"

"You heard me, Lyn. What are you up to?"

"Up to? What the hell are you talking about? What restaurant?" she asks, seeming a little flustered by my line of questions.

"Burgers and Brew." I cross my arms over my chest and hold my ground, refusing to give even an inch.

Her eyes—the ones that are still the most beautiful shade of brown—narrow into slits moments before they widen, almost comically. "*You* own Burgers and Brew?" She inhales sharply.

"Yes," I reply quizzically. Why would she ask that if she already knew I was the owner?

She turns to look toward the front, but with that white paper, it prohibits her from seeing out. I just stand in my place—which is entirely too close, considering I can smell the fruitiness of her hair—

and watch as she processes something. She glances around from the front to her feet, her eyes searching, her mind wondering.

"Where's Dustin?" she finally asks, knocking the wind out of my sails.

Dustin? Who the hell is Dustin?

Something blooms in my chest, hot and uncomfortable as hell. Is that...jealousy? I've never felt anything of this sort before, not even in high school when my girlfriend would flirt with other guys to make me envious. Suddenly, the thought of someone serious in Lyndee's life doesn't sit well at all. In fact, I fucking hate it, which is stupid.

I don't know this woman, not the one she became. I knew her ten years ago when we were both young and dumb kids, anxious to graduate school and embark on the world before us. We were fueled by competition and a hint of sexual tension, though we never acted on the latter. There was that one time, the night I almost kissed her, but the moment was interrupted, never to nearly happen again.

Yet, the thought of this *Dustin* makes my blood run cold and an ache form in my chest. Of course, she'd have someone. Lyndee is a gorgeous, feisty sprite of a woman, and any man would be lucky to have her.

Wait, what?

No, she's not. She's a pain in the ass, or at the very least, a big thorn in my side. A hot as hell thorn, but a nuisance just the same.

Before I can ask any questions, she moves, pushing slightly against my chest and scurrying past me. "Dustin?" she hollers, heading for the front of the bakery. I'm instantly drawn to how bright and colorful the room is. It's nothing like our restaurant, but it seems fitting for the type of business she's opening.

"Who are you looking for?" I ask, coming up behind her and looking around.

Suddenly, we hear the back door slam. Lyndee brushes past me a second time, her body pressing against me as she rushes by. "There you are," she sighs, stopping as she reenters the kitchen area. "Where did you go?" she asks the man who is using a walker to get around the space.

"I took the trash out and then needed a little air. The temperature is really dropping," he replies, breathing labored just a bit.

"Why don't you sit down? I don't want you to overdo it," Lyndee advises, moving across the room toward the motorized wheelchair I missed earlier.

"I'm okay," he insists, yet moves toward the chair. She hovers nearby as he shifts the walker to the side and carefully sits down, taking a deep breath and relaxing once he's settled.

"Do you want something to drink?" she asks, already heading for the massive refrigerator along the wall.

"Just a little water, I guess," he says, finally turning his attention to me. His light brown eyes observe me with open curiosity, his cheeks pink from the cooler outdoor temperature, and his dark hair is in disarray. "Who's this?" he asks, taking in my appearance in the doorway.

Lyndee hands him a bottle of water before glancing my way. "This is Jasper. I went to college with him."

The eyes of the man I assume is Dustin light up. "Really? You knew Lyn back when she was all awkward and ugly?"

The comment surprises me greatly, as does the laughter spilling from his lips immediately after he says it. "Who are you calling ugly?" she gapes, hands on hips and staring at the man in the wheelchair.

He turns to me and says, "Notice how she didn't dispute the awkward?" He smiles before taking a drink from the bottle.

"Well, even I will admit, I was a tad awkward when I was younger," Lyndee grumbles, crossing her arms and giving the other man the stink eye.

He chuckles heartily before tucking his water into his side and moving my way. He stops directly in front of me and extends a hand. As I reach down and shake it, he says, "Dustin Gibson, Lyndee's brother."

His introduction catches me off guard. Admittedly, I wasn't expecting the sibling connection, but now that I know, I see the resemblance. The same hair and eye color, the shape of their face, and the slightly upturned nose. They're definitely related, which seems to ease the discomfort I've felt in my chest since the moment I heard Lyndee asking about Dustin.

"Jasper Kohlmann," I state, returning the hand gesture. "I own the restaurant across the street."

His eyes light with delight. "Really? Lyn and I were just talking about ordering out later this week."

I give him a smile. "Tell me when and I'll prepare everything personally."

"What kind of burgers do you make?" he asks, leaning forward just the slightest as he eagerly awaits my reply.

"All kinds. We have a wide menu of specialty hamburger options, and our fries are hand cut and seasoned."

"I can't wait to try one. Lyn, let's get burgers tonight," he tells his sister with a huge, hopeful grin.

"We'll see, Dustin," she replies, glancing at me with narrowing eyes. The way she stares, it's as if I've somehow opened my mouth when I shouldn't have.

Why are women so damn confusing?

She's the one who started a business directly across from mine, yet she makes me feel like I've done something wrong here. Crossing my arms, I pin her with a look of determination. I'm not going to let her swoop in and threaten my livelihood, my business.

"I'm going to head back," I state.

"Thanks for stopping by," she quickly replies, clearly a little eager to get me out of here.

"Hey, Jasper?" Dustin asks, stopping me before I can move for the exit. "Do you know anyone who can help move that counter and display?"

"Dustin," Lyndee chastises, her mouth moving but no words coming out. She pins him with a wide-eyed look. "I'm sure Jasper has more important things to do, like run a business."

"Yeah, but you said you were going to ask the guys across the street for help," he says, confusion written all over his face.

"Or the ones at the bank next door," she argues, her fight losing steam rapidly.

"But Jasper is here now. I bet he has a few friends who can help," her brother suggests, unable to understand why Lyndee is so against asking for my help.

Deciding to cut her out of the conversation, I turn to Dustin. "I can help. I have three friends who co-own the restaurant with me. I can ask a few to help. When do you need it moved?"

"Tomorrow morning would be best," Dustin replies. "We're going to finish setting up the front tomorrow but need those big pieces in place to complete the job."

"What time?" I ask, completely ignoring Lyndee as she stammers and tries to interject herself into the conversation.

"Eight or nine? We're at your mercy," he says, "so you pick."

"Isaac and I are both there by eight. I can get Jameson or Walker there too if I give a little notice."

"Lyndee was going to make treats."

"Hello," she finally says, catching our attention. "Do I have any say here?"

"Of course," her brother assures. "But you said we needed help for that part, and Jasper is willing to help."

She eyes me skeptically. "Yeah, but—"

"No buts, Lyn. My friends and I would be happy to help a neighbor in need," I inform her, crossing my arms over my chest and leaving no room for argument. "Plus, I'm anxious to taste your...sweets." My voice drops low and borders on dirty, and I can't help feel a touch of satisfaction when she blushes.

"Well, I'll be sure to bake a few things for your friends," she replies, intentionally leaving me out of her statement.

A wolfish grin spreads wide across my face. "I'm sure they'll appreciate it as much as I will," I add, sliding a pair of sunglasses on. "Dustin, it was a pleasure meeting you. I'll see you at eight tomorrow morning."

He offers me a wave. "Nice to meet you, Jasper. See you."

I turn my attention back to Lyndee. "And I'll see you tomorrow too," I proclaim, heading for the back door. As I move past her, I add in a whisper, "Don't forget my...payment."

She makes a noise, a combination of a gasp and a growl, and I can't help feeling a slice of excitement sweep through my veins. Lyndee Gibson, right across the street on a daily basis. Lord help me, I'm actually looking forward to it. I've never sparred with anyone like her, and the prospect of going toe to toe with Miss Gibson again has me all sorts of enthusiastic. I may not know what brought her here after all these years, but it'll be fun finding out.

Suddenly, I can't wait until tomorrow morning.

By the time I head home for the night, snow flurries are falling. As the sun dropped, so did the temperatures, just enough for light snow that won't even stick. We've been fortunate to have fairly mild temperatures for mid-December, but it appears winter has finally arrived.

I head out to my warm car, thanks to automatic start, and slide inside. The dinner rush is well past, and the bar side of the business is starting to come to life. Even for a Monday night, we have a steady stream of customers stopping by to unwind after a long day.

I pull out of the back parking lot and turn left on the main roadway through town. I can't help but take a quick glance as I pass, noting the bakery lights are all out, indicating Lyndee and Dustin have already gone home for the night. Not surprising, since it's past eight. Lyn was always more of an early bird, like me. I imagine operating a bakery would require more early hours than late ones, though I can predict she'll have both of those the first few months.

I know we did. When we started Burgers and Brew, the four of us worked our asses off, seven days a week. Often, I opened, cooked lunch and dinner, and then closed down the kitchen too. Partly because I thrived on the thrill of knowing everything was done to my exact specifications and demands, but also to help save money. We put a lot into the start-up, and those first six or eight months were the hardest to get through.

But we did it.

We were able to turn a profit fairly quickly, and as business continued to pick up, we added more employees. Walker hired more help behind the bar, and Isaac and I brought in even more kitchen and serving staff. We had enough to get by, but with a rapidly growing business, we needed more and fast.

Five years later, we're still evolving.

I pull into my driveway, pressing the button for my garage door opener. Once the door is closed behind me, I slip out of my car and head for the entrance off my kitchen. I purchased this house just a few years ago, an older four-bedroom Tudor home built in the early nineteen-hundreds. It's undergone a few renovations over the years, but the key elements in a Tudor home are still there. Steep gabled roofs, decorative timbering, and embellished doorways, it's all part of the charm.

On the inside, the previous owners have kept the elaborate woodwork, fortunately. I removed the nasty floral wallpaper when I purchased it and had to refinish some of the flooring due to slight water damage but tried to keep the house true to design. All except the kitchen. That's the only room I modernized to my taste. Sure, the cabinets are still classic, the trim original, but the counters and appliances were updated. It's a combination of old-school and contemporary and perfect for my favorite room in the house.

I remove my shoes in the mudroom off the kitchen and set my bag on the kitchen island. I don't have any necessary work to complete, but I always bring my laptop and bag home, just in case.

Mostly, I like to make notes or examine recipes, especially at night when insomnia gets the better of me.

First up is a shower. After spending all day in front of a grill and near a deep fryer, I always take time to wash the day off my skin. As I strip off my work clothes and toss them in the hamper, a certain little pixie filters through my mind, and I'll be damned if my cock doesn't start to harden.

Dammit.

As much as I try, I'm unable to push away thoughts of Lyndee and seeing her in person for the first time in so many years. She's exactly as I remember her, yet with new, unfamiliar curves to her petite body. I'm rather annoyed I even noted the swells of her breasts and her hourglass hips. Oh, I always notice those attributes on women, but this isn't just any woman.

This is Lyndee.

My intent was to take a quick shower and head down to make something for dinner, but the moment the jets hit my back and chest, my body starts to relax a little and I feel myself letting go of the day's stress. Well, all except one particular element, but I refuse to think her name. Or of those luscious tits I'd kill to get my hands on. Or the way her paint-splattered leggings molded to her round ass.

"Fuck," I groan, leaning my forearms against the cold tile. The shock of cool on my skin does nothing to alleviate the fire suddenly racing through my veins. I try to ignore it, but there's a familiar throb in my groin that won't let me forget.

I take my hard cock in my hand and give it a squeeze. My balls draw up, anxious for release. I move swiftly, the water making it easy to slide along the rigid length. I can feel precum beading on the tip as the familiar tingle sweeps up my spine. I try to think about anyone else, but I just can't do it. Lyndee is front and foremost, the fantasy of her pouty lips wrapping around the head of my cock, her warm tongue dancing down my burning flesh. When I close my eyes, she's all I see, all I feel, as if she were literally on her knees in front of me.

Unable to hold back any longer, my orgasm barrels through me like a tornado, ravishing and destroying everything in its path. I call out the only name on my lips and mind, both a blessing and a curse. I come harder than I think I ever have, my legs wobbly, my body sags against the wall for support. It's hard to breathe.

"Shit," I grumble, reaching for the bar of soap and rewashing my body, as I wait for the guilt to slide in. It doesn't, however. I'm left feeling sated and rejuvenated, ready to tackle every obstacle before me.

Except Lyndee.

That's one hurdle I need to avoid like the clap.

Nothing good can come from befriending her once more, not that we were ever really *friends*. We never got to know each other personally, outside of school, and were more adversaries, both in the kitchen and out of it. We kept our battle friendly, pushing each other's buttons without letting it turn bitter or nasty, and at the end of those years, walked away without so much as a backward glance. Oh, I've thought of her over the years, dreamed of her narrowed brown eyes when she'd dispute something I did and remembered the smile she'd give when she got the highest grade on a lesson. Yet, I've always been able to push those remembrances to the back of my mind, locking them up behind a thick wall.

Now, she's here. In Stewart Grove. Directly across the street. There's no way to hide from her. Not that I'd want to. I won't let her wield that kind of control over me.

I'll do my thing and let her do hers. It's not like we run in the same circles or anything. I'll go on with my life, running and continuing to build my business, without giving the small bakery across the road any thought. That means not letting her gorgeous face infiltrate my private, dirty thoughts in the shower, or out of it.

Except, I know that won't happen.

What is the saying? Keep your friends close and your enemies closer. Should be easy, considering I'm helping her set up her front area tomorrow morning. I've got this.

Lyndee Gibson, prepare to be brought closer than ever before. If you have something planned, I will figure it out and won't let you get away with it.

Lyndee

I slept horribly last night. I was plagued with images of Jasper standing in my kitchen, staring at me with those consuming dark eyes and condescending smirk. The exact same grin he always wore back in school. The one that said he was better than everyone else there, including me.

In some ways, he was.

I've never seen a more naturally skilled chef than what I witnessed when Jasper was in the kitchen. He was calm, collected, and under complete control of his environment. Witnessing him work was like watching the sun setting over a crystal blue ocean landscape. It was gorgeous and serene, a sight to behold. I can only imagine what he's like now, as an adult.

Back then, he was driven to be the best, which pushed me to be even better. He used to focus his culinary skills on appetizers and entrées, while I worked on perfecting desserts. Oh, he gave them his best shot, but he could never top me in that department. Especially his pecan pie. It was the one dish that I was able to best him at.

Glancing out the window, I see the light dusting of freshly fallen snow covering the ground. I knew it was coming but had hoped it would hold out just a little longer. As pretty as it is, I'm more of a spring kind of girl. Bring on the scent of impending rain and blooming flowers. Sure, the snow is pretty for a short time, but then it turns dingy and dirty. Not to mention I have the coordination of a baby deer learning to stand for the first time each and every time I try to walk in it.

It's not pretty.

"Dustin," I holler in the hallway, just outside his bedroom door. "Do you want to go with me now, or would you prefer I come get you later?"

His door opens immediately, and he appears at the threshold with a smile. "I want to go now," he says, using his walker to exit his room. "I really liked Jasper. I was hoping to talk to him more," he adds, stepping past me and heading down the hall.

My heart hammers in my chest. I want to shield my brother from Jasper, but I know I can't. He might be my little brother, but at twenty-eight, he's still an adult. And, I think he's lonely. Sure, we're close and spend all of our free time together, but there was no missing that flash of excitement and longing in his brown eyes. He hasn't made any friends since we moved to Stewart Grove, and that's my fault. I should have done better introducing him to people in the area. A fresh wave of guilt settles in, making me feel like I'm failing him.

When he reaches the end of the hallway, he stops and glances back. "Do you think he likes baseball?"

His question saddens my heart. Dustin loves baseball, even though he was never given the opportunity to play. When he was younger, Mom couldn't afford a lot of the physical therapy he required to make him stronger. Often, we were without insurance, the cost well outside of her monthly budget as a single parent. So, he had to watch from the bleachers or couch. When he was seven, he decided Cincinnati was his team and has been cheering for them ever since.

"I don't know, Dust," I answer honestly.

"I'll ask him," he replies with a shrug, turning back and moving through the condo. When he reaches the kitchen, he stops in his tracks, his eyes widening with worry. "What if he's an Indians fan?"

I bark out a laugh. "Well, I guess you'd have someone to dispute favorite players and weird stats with."

He makes a face, one of annoyance. "It's not weird, Lyn, it's great. Plus, we all know Frank Robinson is the greatest Reds of all time."

Smiling, I shake my head. "If you say so."

"Come on, a thousand and nine RBIs in five thousand five hundred twenty-seven at bats. Three hundred twenty-four home runs, Lyn, with a .303 batting average. How amazing is that?"

"Pretty amazing," I mirror, unable to hide the hint of boredom in my voice. I've never gotten into baseball, have always found it fairly boring. Actually, sports aren't really my thing. I'd rather curl up with a good book and hot cocoa underneath a fluffy blanket or sit on the back porch as the sun starts to drop below the horizon. *That* sounds like a good time to me, not spending hours watching men swing at a ball with a stick.

But I do it.

Regularly.

For Dustin.

"Anyway, let's go!" he exclaims, hightailing it for the door that leads to the garage bay housing my car.

I may not hold his enthusiasm for seeing Jasper, but I am fairly excited to go to the bakery. Especially since after Jasper and his friends are done, the front half of my new business will be almost set up. I'll be able to add the final touches, bringing my dreams, my vision to life.

Grabbing the basket of goodies on the counter, I slip my purse over my shoulder and meet my brother in the garage. Once inside, I crank up the heat, even though the inside of the car isn't super cold and we're only going a couple of blocks. However, I get cold easily, and there's something about the snow that makes me want to feel warm and toasty.

The drive is short, yet slow on the freshly fallen snow, but that doesn't stop my brother from talking about baseball the entire trip. I pull into the alley, noticing the slightly gathered snow by the back door. "I'm going to let you get out here, so you don't have to go through the snow with your walker."

Dustin rolls his eyes. "I'll be fine. It's not even that deep."

"I know, but humor me, huh?" I ask, stopping my car anyway at the back entrance to Sugar Rush.

He doesn't argue, just gets out while I unlock the door. Once he's inside, I move my car across the alley, where employees for the bank next door park. The spots are full right now, but I imagine when I start getting here at four in the morning, I'll have my pick of any spot.

Pasting a grin on my lips, I grab my belongings and head for the back door, careful not to slip in the wet slush covering the alleyway. As I approach the small concrete landing for my space, I feel my foot start to slip out from under me. I don't have time to reach for the wall, the doorknob, anything to grab on to. I'm going to fall.

But I don't go down.

I'm wrapped in a pair of strong arms and pulled against a hard chest. "Careful, Lyn," Jasper whispers against my ear.

The breath leaves my lungs, but it has nothing to do with the cold air hitting me. It's caused by the fresh scent, the waves of musky aftershave washing over me as I'm held in someone's arms. Warmth races through my veins, and my body begins to heat, as if I were lying directly on top of a furnace vent. Not to mention, the comfort that surrounds me like my favorite blanket at home.

"Why do women always fall at your feet?" a man says somewhere behind me.

I jerk as realization sets in. Not only are we not alone, but we're not...together. There's no reason to feel anything but appreciation to the man who kept me from falling on my ass in the slushy snow.

Pushing myself out of his grasp, I stand up and turn around, adjusting my purse strap and the basket in my shaky hands. "Hello," I croak, staring at the three very handsome men in front of me.

Jasper chuckles. "I see you're still light on your feet," he teases, that cocky grin plastered on his face. I narrow my eyes, which only makes him laugh. "You going to invite us in or leave us standing out in the cold snow?"

Sighing, I reach back and grab the door, careful not to drop the basket in my arms. "Let me," the tall man with tattoos peeking over the neck of his shirt says. He holds the door as I slip inside, followed by the others. "I'm Jameson," he adds, reaching his hand forward, dark tattoos stretched across the skin.

"Lyndee," I reply, giving him a friendly smile.

At first glance, he's a little scary. No, not scary, but maybe a bit intimidating. Hard eyes, dark hair, and an I-don't-give-a-shit attitude rolling off his broad shoulders. Though, there's something else in those deep eyes. A friendliness I wasn't expecting. Standing there in combat boots, worn and tattered blue jeans, and a Nirvana T-shirt under a beat-up black leather jacket, he gives off a strong vibe to keep your distance, but that's not what I catch a glimpse of in his eyes. There's a sadness there, one that makes my heart ache just a little.

"And I'm Isaac," the other says, shaking my hand as well. This one's like night and day different than Jameson. In black dress slacks, a blue button-down, an impeccable black silk tie, and a designer peacoat, I can tell he puts a lot of time and money into his appearance. His hazel eyes are friendly, his dark hair professionally styled. This man probably gets regular haircuts, and possibly a professional shave.

"Nice to meet you," I state with a nod.

"Hey!" Dustin proclaims, joining us in the kitchen.

"Dustin, good to see you again," Jasper replies, giving my brother a warm smile.

"You too. I see you brought some friends to help move the counter," he says, the roll of the walker wheels echoing through the room.

"I did. This is Jameson and Isaac. Walker would have been here too, but his girlfriend's daughter has a dentist appointment this morning she was nervous about," Jasper responds, heading to where my brother stands. "Are you ready to show us where you want this stuff moved to?" he asks Dustin, completely leaving me out of it.

Annoyance spreads through my veins as I watch the two walk off, chatting, and leaving me behind. Jasper's friends follow, taking in the kitchen as they go. Isaac glances back. "You have a great space here."

"Thank you," I reply, my heart swelling with pride as I give the room a onceover. I've put everything into this building, my life savings and then some. I took out loans and have lines of credit that make my palms sweat with anxiety, but all of those are necessary evils to obtain my dream.

"I have a great relationship with several local vendors. If you ever need help or get in a pinch, let me know. We'll help however we can," Isaac states, his words striking me like a blade.

Tears prickle my eyelids, but I blink them away. I'm not sure why I want to cry, other than in gratitude for the generosity he's offering. As a new business, and a new transplant to town on top of it, the vendors were a bit nervous when I set up accounts. No one wants to give credit for their product to someone they don't know, even if that product is flour and sugar.

"Thank you," I tell him, swallowing the emotions that come with seeing it all fall into place with one week until opening.

I step into the front lobby area, and quietly observe as they get a game plan together.

"This big display case goes here," Dustin informs, motioning with his hands where we want it, "And the counter beside it."

Jasper scrunches his eyebrows together in question. He turns to me and asks, "Why this way? The display would be closer to the kitchen if you flipped them. Easier to move product from the back to the front."

His righteous tone heckles my nerves. "I don't want it there."

Jasper crosses his arms and narrows his eyes. "That's dumb. It makes more sense the other way."

"No, it doesn't. This way, the patrons see the display first. They're more liable to make purchases based on products that catch their eyes right away. They can see the cakes, cookies, and donuts before they even get to the counter to place their order, mouth already watering. It might be a few more steps for me to deliver baked goods to the case, but it's better for the consumers." By the time I finish my spiel, I'm breathing hard. What is it about Jasper Kohlmann that elevates my blood pressure and gets me all riled up?

He seems caught off guard by my little outburst, but I can tell he's considering it. His head cocks to the side ever so slightly and he nibbles on his bottom lip in contemplation. My eyes zero in instantly on the lip action, and my legs squeeze together to try to alleviate the sudden ache. "I can see your point," he concedes, his eyes focused on the pile of cases, shelves, and counters.

It's dead silent for several heartbeats before Jameson busts out laughing. He faces his friend, biggest shit-eating grin on his scruffy face I've ever seen, and asks, "Did you just admit you're wrong?"

"No," Jasper states quickly. "My plan is the most logical."

His friend just nods, laughing his ass off. "Sure, Jasp."

The other one, Isaac, turns to me and smiles. "I agree with your way of thinking," he whispers, keeping his voice down, probably so Jasper doesn't hear him.

"Are we gonna move this stuff or what?" Jasper asks, ignoring the razzing from his friends and heading for the display case.

The guys discuss the best way to move it without scratching the floor before they get into position. Jameson takes one side, pulling, while Isaac and Jasper get behind it and prepare to push. Jasper looks over at my brother. "You make sure you guide us, okay?"

"Yeah, definitely!" my brother proclaims, eager to help any way he can.

The case glides across the floor, the men moving it barely breaking a sweat. I don't even have to jump in to make sure it's where I want it. My brother is on it, knowing the exact place I envision its position.

As soon as it's set, they head for the counter. It's bigger, more awkward, and will probably cause a little more strain than the other piece. It does, and I instantly feel guilty at how hard they're working on my behalf. Good thing I baked extra goodies last night when I couldn't sleep to make up for their help today.

When it's in place—to never be moved again, that's for sure—all three lean back against it and sigh. "Damn, that's heavier than it looks," Isaac groans.

"It took five guys to get it off their trailer," Dustin informs.

I move quickly, heading back to the kitchen to retrieve bottles of water from the fridge and the basket of goodies. When I return, my arms are full, and Jasper rapidly jumps to help me. As he takes two bottles from under my right arm, he brushes his fingers across my chest unintentionally. Well, I think it's accidental. The wave of lust streaking through my blood is overshadowed by the shock and flash of desire he tries to hide in those brown eyes.

"Thank you," he replies smoothly, handing the bottles off to his friends. He even takes a fourth one to my brother.

"Oh, I made goodies too," I state, setting the basket on the newly positioned countertop.

"Goodies?" Isaac asks, the first to pull the cloth back to see what's inside. "Holy mother of sweetness."

I chuckle as Jameson practically pushes Isaac out of the way, reaching for a chocolate iced éclair. One bite in and he's moaning in pleasure. "Marry me, Lyndee. Marry me right now."

While Isaac chuckles and I smile at the unusual—but not my first—marriage proposal, Jasper seems to have the opposite reaction. He reaches over and smacks Jameson in the back of the head. "Quit joking around," he practically growls at his friend.

Jameson, seeming a touch amused, just holds up his treat. "Who's joking? Have you tried one of these?" he asks, waving the éclair under Jasper's nose.

"No." He arches an eyebrow at Jameson, who only seems to find humor in the situation.

"Well, you're due," the tattooed man says, practically shoving the éclair in Jasper's mouth.

"What the hell," he grumbles, reaching for a napkin to wipe the smashed chocolate, pastry, and cream filling from his face. I do catch the slip of his tongue sneaking out and licking the treat off his lips.

Apparently, Jameson saw it too. "See? Good."

"Not bad," Jasper concedes, making me laugh when he appears none too happy about his admission.

"You'll have to get in line though. I've already called first dibs."

I should be offended, but to be honest, I'm completely amused by their interaction, and I know Jameson isn't serious about his proposal. It's the sugar talking.

"I need to get back to the restaurant," Jasper states, grabbing his water bottle and heading for the back door.

"Thanks for your help," I holler just as the door shuts a little harder than normal. My wide eyes fly to Isaac and Jameson, both on their second pastry. "Is he okay?"

A look is exchanged between them, one I can't decipher. "He's fine," Isaac assures me, finishing off his second pastry. "These are amazing. I think you're going to do great here." He waves his hand around, referring to my location.

"Thank you," I whisper, worry mixing with the sense of pride I always feel when I think about this undertaking. "And those are all for you. Take them back with you."

"We could share them with Walker," Isaac says to Jameson.

"Fuck Walker. He didn't help, he gets nothing," Jameson replies gruffly, though I can tell he's joking. He gives me a sheepish grin. "Sorry about the language."

I wave him off. "No worries. I've heard them all and use them frequently."

He gives me a smile in return. "Then we'll get along just fine."

I laugh.

Dustin asks Isaac and Jameson about baseball—he's happy to hear Jameson watches and roots for the Reds—and the restaurant. Before I know it, they've been here another thirty minutes, just hanging out and chatting, sharing information about their business and those around us.

"We should head back," Isaac finally says, wiping his hands on a napkin.

"I can't tell you how much I appreciate your help. Truly. I don't know what I would have done to move those pieces."

Jameson reaches for the basket that's several pastries lighter than it was when I brought it here. "Anytime. You need anything, just let us know." He gives me a big grin. "And thanks for these. I might just hide them, so I don't have to share."

"Here," Isaac says, handing me a business card. "My cell is on the front, but I added Jameson's, Walker's, and Jasper's to the back. Call anytime."

"Oh," I start, surprised by their generosity. "Here, let me give you mine." I jot it down on one of my new cards, the ones I just had printed last weekend. "Again, thank you so much."

"You'll be seeing us often, Lyndee. Welcome to the neighborhood," Jameson says.

They head for the back door and slip out, offering waves before disappearing at the end of the block. If the paper was down off my windows and front door, I'd be able to watch them return to their business, not that I need to see them go. It's just nice to know I have allies in the area.

"You ready to set up shop?" I ask Dustin, a new wave of energy encompassing me, as I take in the counter and display. I'm ready to fill them, to see customers lined up in front of them and seated around the room.

I'm ready to open Sugar Rush.

Jasper

I'm irritated as fuck and can't stop pacing the kitchen. Even whipping up some of my favorite dishes is no match to settle the uneasiness I feel in my entire body. Tension. Like I touched a fork to an electrical socket. I did that once when I was a kid, just to see what would happen. It was only the briefest touch, but it was enough to brand the shock and pain into my thick skull for life.

That's how it feels being near Lyndee. There's a hum, an electricity I can't seem to get past, and if I'm being honest with myself, that's why I'm so pissed. No one has ever affected me the way she does. She's under my skin, and I can't shake her.

I've had girlfriends in the past, yet when our relationships ran its course, I had no problem walking away. When it was done, it was done. Period. I never got worked up, never drowned my sorrows in liquor. But with Lyndee, I'm tempted to head to the bar and down shot after shot of something hard and smooth, something that'll ensure I wake later with a killer headache and a bad attitude.

Why her?

Why does she affect me the way she does?

I guess if I knew the answer to that question, I wouldn't be wearing the tile down in my kitchen.

Needing a little space, I head to my office and shut the door. Petra is here, preparing for lunch, and humming a happy little tune. I just need quiet. Peace. Solitude. For five fucking minutes. White walls that don't scream bright and chipper, all sunshine and happiness.

I shiver at the thought. I don't mind color, and don't deny her walls were cheerful and welcoming, but there's something about bold and dark that screams professional. I guess that's the difference between her business and my own. The yellow and purple was fitting in her bakery, while the dark woods and deep blue hues are perfect for us. Of course, that's in the main restaurant. In my domain, it's white. Crisp, clean white and industrial steel. I can see every splatter, every imperfection in my kitchen and on the plate. I have no room for messes back here.

I think back to Lyndee's kitchen. It actually does somewhat resemble my own. White, clean, and shiny. It's all new and ready to be used. A memory flashes through my mind, one of a certain brunette covered in flour and kneading dough. She used to love getting dirty, of getting right in the thick of whatever she was making, not even caring she was getting just as many ingredients on herself as she was her cooking surface.

That night I almost kissed her, she had flour in her hair and granules of sugar on her cheek.

I push the recollection from my mind and adjust my pants. Yes, I'm hard. So fucking hard it hurts. Just seeing her, thinking about that night does it to me every time, and now I'm just pissed. Pissed she still has this effect on my body. Pissed I still let her get under my skin. And even more pissed I stormed out of there in front of my friends. No way are they going to let it slide just how much she gets to me.

Fucking hell.

I wipe my hands over my face and drop into my desk chair. I quickly boot up my laptop, prepared to start a new vendor order, when a single click brings up the internet. From there, I type her name into the search engine.

What am I doing?

I ignore the inner voice in my head telling me to knock it off and get to work, but when the search results start popping up, I find myself falling down the rabbit hole of online information on one Lyndee Gibson.

First up is her social media pages. There are a few posts, a handful of pictures, but nothing too recent. The last photo shared was one of her and her brother at a Reds game. Dustin looks ecstatic, all decked out in his crimson shirt and ball cap, while Lyndee is wearing the appropriate shirt and smile, looking like she'd rather be anywhere else. It's in her eyes. She's bored out of her mind but is putting on a good game face for her brother.

There's another one of them together, standing on a beach with an older woman. Their mom. Sure, I quickly scan her bikini-clad body from head to toe, but that's not what catches my eye. It's the light in her eyes. The happiness pouring from the photo from all three, as if no one has a care in the world and they're just excited to be together. The caption reads, St. Pete Beach, first time visiting the ocean. It was posted over five years ago, and even though she's aged a bit since it was taken, she still has the same youthful and innocent gleam in her brown eyes.

Closing out of her social media, I click the next link. This one takes me to an obituary dated four years ago. Her name jumps out at me like a neon sign, listed with Dustin's as some of the only survivors. There's an aunt and uncle listed too, but that's it. Jesus. She doesn't have any family nearby. The ones included in the obituary live in Kansas.

My mind races to my own family. Mom and Dad happily married and two younger sisters, one married and the other engaged. They all live in Westville, Ohio, which is a short one-hour drive from here. Close enough to jump in my car and go for a visit or meet halfway and have dinner somewhere. We're not exactly right down the road, but close enough. I know they'd be here in a heartbeat if I needed them. In fact, my parents make a trip here monthly to have dinner and catch up, sometimes bringing my sisters and their significant others.

I also have the guys. We became tight in college, but even closer while pouring everything we had into this place. Sure, we've butted heads on several occasions, but there's no one else I'd trust more than them to embark on this journey with.

Lyndee has no one.

No one but Dustin.

Well, I can't say that. She might have friends or even a…boyfriend. That thought sends my heart straight down to my Italian loafers. I'm not sure why the prospect would bother me so much, but it does. She's gorgeous, with the most alluring brown eyes I've ever seen. She's funny, sassy, and compassionate. That fact shows with every interaction with Dustin I witness. Anyone would be lucky to go home at night to someone like Lyndee. You know, if you're into that sort of thing.

Which I'm not.

But if she has a boyfriend, why didn't *he* help her move that case and counter?

I ponder that question as I click on another link featuring her name. This one from our own local newspaper and dated for today. It's an article regarding the bakery and its upcoming opening. As I scan the editorial, I realize the author wrote a fluff piece full of warm and fuzzy feels meant to make you want to become a patron of Sugar Rush the moment it opens. She talks about Lyndee's education and experience, as well as her vision for the newest business in Stewart Grove. The writer even got to sample a few pastries that'll be on the menu when it opens next Monday and gave them rave reviews.

Oh what does he know about cream fillings?

I bet his only reference is the Bavarian cream donuts sold at the gas station on the edge of town. He clearly has no clue how to tell if there's the perfect mixture of sweet and tart.

I read the rest of his piece, boasting about the varieties of breads and coffees to be served, but it's one specific mention at the bottom of the article that catches my attention.

Award-winning pecan pie.

Oh. Hell. No.

I remember that damn pie. It's what got her the top grade on our final exam senior year. We were neck and neck until that damn project. How we both ended up baking the same product is beyond me, but all I know is hers came out on top. It was bullshit, of course. No way was her pecan pie better than mine. I'd been perfecting my recipe all year, knowing it was going to crown me champion and top student.

Until those results came in.

She barely squeaked by, earning a half a grade point higher than my own ninety-nine.

I read the rest of the article, about how she put the small bakery she was working for on the map with those fucking pecan pies. She won local contests, as well as a few national ones. She was featured in *Foodie News* magazine, and even though there have been dozens of offers to purchase her recipe, she refuses to sell.

My blood pressure is high. I can feel it swooshing in my ears like waves on a sandy beach during high tide.

She won awards.

Fucking awards.

They should have been mine.

Before I can even stop myself, I click on the Send a Message to the Editor button at the bottom of the article. I let my anger get the best of me, telling the newspaper how very wrong they were about the bakery and Lyndee. I spew lies about the cleanliness of her bakery, specifically the kitchen, and make up some big story about how she was fired from her previous job for failing to pass basic health department inspections. I even allude to the fact she slept with the inspector to keep it out of the media.

When I'm done composing the email, I let the mouse hover over the send button. After a few long seconds, I finally release the clicker, sit back in my chair, and take a deep breath. I should feel better after trashing the bakery she hasn't even opened yet and her reputation, but...I don't.

At all.

I rake my hand over my face and slide my fingers into my hair.

"What the hell am I doing?" I ask myself. No way would I actually send this email. I may not be a fan of my new neighbor across the street, but I'd never stoop this low. If her business is going down, it's not going to be my fault.

I click on the little X at the top right corner of the email and shut down the browser. Jesus, what the hell is wrong with me? I can't believe I even composed that pile of garbage, let alone considered sending it. What kind of asshole am I?

Don't answer that.

Thank God there's no one in the room with me to add their two cents. There's probably a list a mile long of people who'd jump in and share tales of my assholery over the years.

I jump out of my office chair and pace the checkered tile floor, the same way I did in the kitchen earlier. I'm losing my mind. Lyndee is driving me absolutely insane from all the way across the street. I can't see her, but I know she's there, smiling and laughing and being all...happy.

And I'm the sad asshole across the street, who what? Is wishing I could see that smile, feel the warmth of her laughter? Wants to watch her come alive in the kitchen, the dough between her fingers and the flour in her hair? The one who grabs her ass when she walks by and kisses her goodnight at the end of a long day?

The startling realization is the resounding yes to all of those questions.

I was wildly attracted to her back in school, and turns out, ten years later, she still checks all the attributes I find appealing. So I can play this two ways. Pretend she doesn't exist, as I convinced myself I was going to do early this morning. You know, before I saw her again. Seems like the logical thing to do, but after just a short twenty minutes across the street, that's proving to be damn hard. I can't stop thinking about her.

Which leaves me one other option.

Fuck her out of my system.

I know that sounds harsh, but you have to admit it has merit. I can't stop from getting hard whenever she's near, and if the way her nipples pebble against her top and her breathing hitched both times I brushed past her is any indication, the feeling is mutual.

Maybe we just need to...you know.

A few casual screws and we can both move on without so much as a glance back. Seems perfect, actually.

Of course, now I just need to convince Lyndee to go along with it. She doesn't seem like the casual relationship kind of girl, but I can show her how rewarding it can truly be. No strings, no expectations. Just sex.

It's actually brilliant. My dick is already on board with the idea.

Settled with how I'm going to handle the whole Lyndee *situation*, I just have to figure out how to approach the conversation with her. I need to have my ducks in a row, so to speak, and have solid talking points. Resolute reasons why us having sex is a perfect solution to our pesky attraction problem.

Then we can both move on.

Shouldn't be too hard, right?

It's midafternoon when Isaac finally makes his appearance in the kitchen. "I have those orders we discussed yesterday for you to review," he says, taking a bite of something in his hand.

"What are you eating?" I ask, curious because he didn't come down from his office to order something for lunch.

He smirks, powdered sugar sprinkled on his lips. "Jelly donut. It's the only treat I could steal away from Jameson. He only let me have it because he doesn't like jelly. The bastard hid the basket."

"I could make you lunch, you know. It would be a hell of a lot better than some jelly donut," I chastise, wiping my hands on the clean towel and reaching for the papers in his hand.

"Better than this?" he asks, shoving the donut in my mouth. For the second time today, I'm taking a bite of one of Lyndee's treats. "Good, huh? We might be in trouble having her across the street. It's going to be too tempting to run across the street for something sweet."

Don't I know it.

Only I don't think we're talking about tasting the same kind of *sweets.*

"These look fine," I state, handing the orders back to him.

"Okay, I'll get them submitted shortly." Isaac doesn't move, though. He stands there, finishing off his donut, and watches me.

"What?" I ask, knowing full well he's got something to say and won't leave until he says it.

Now, he smiles. "So...Lyndee."

I roll my eyes. "She was in my classes during culinary school. Pain in the ass, actually. Hardly remember her."

He laughs. Actually laughs. Like full belly, bent over to catch his breath laugh. "No? She seemed to remember you."

I shrug. "What can I say? I'm a memorable guy."

"Oh, don't I know it. I field half a dozen in-person visits every week from women who are looking to reconnect," he quips, referring to the handful of women who have stopped by to see me on occasion. It doesn't happen as often as he's insinuating, but it has occurred from time to time.

"Whatever. Do you have a point to your jabbering?"

"No, not really. I guess it's good to know you're not into her. Especially since Jameson was talking nonstop about her when I went to confiscate the basket."

That catches my attention.

"Was he?" I ask casually, though I feel anything but off-the-cuff.

"Oh, yeah. He was talking about maybe heading over after work today and seeing how the setup was coming along. You know, see if she needed any more muscle over there."

I see red. "The fuck he is!" I bellow, just as the man himself walks into my kitchen.

"What's going on in here?" Jameson asks, walking over to make himself a burger.

"You are not dating Lyndee," I demand, unable to contain the wrath threatening to explode from my chest.

He arches a single eyebrow upward. "What?"

Just as I go to open my mouth, Isaac bursts into another fit of laughter. "You should have seen how pissed you got," he laughs, slapping me on the back. Turning to Jameson, he adds, "I told our man Jasp you were heading across the street to woo our new neighbor. He was just voicing his displeasure."

"That's not what I was doing," I argue, but it falls on deaf ears.

"You don't think she'd say yes if I asked her out?" Jameson asks, clearly very amused by the conversation.

"Whatever. I'm just saying you're both very different," I backpedal.

"And she'd be more suited with someone else. Someone like you, right?" Isaac asks, smiling so wide I can see his molars.

"Shut up. Get the hell out of my kitchen," I maintain, reaching for the spatula in Jameson's hand.

Both of my friends laugh so hard they can barely breathe. "Call me when my burger's done," Jameson adds humorously, heading for the swinging door.

"Make me one too?" Isaac asks, hot on Jameson's heels.

"Yeah, yeah," I grumble, throwing two more patties on the grill. If I'm making burgers for those two knuckleheads, I might as well prepare one for Walker too. "Assholes."

They are, assholes that is.

But they're my assholes. My best friends. And even though I played right into their hands a few minutes ago, I know their teasing was in good fun.

It also made me realize something.

If I'm going to get her out of my head, I'm going to have to kick my plan into gear quickly. I need to pitch my idea to her and hope for the best. The sooner I sleep with her, the faster I'll be able to stop thinking about all the things I want to do to her. For her. With her.

The list is long and itemized.

But after one or two times, three times tops, I'll stop thinking about that list and how she plays into it. No more late nights. No more shower fantasies. No more waking up hard, wishing she was crouched between my legs and taking my length down her throat.

I'll be cured of the curse that is Lyndee Gibson.

Easy peasy.

Lyndee

Friday night.

Just another day of the week to me.

When I was in school, I wasn't a partier. I was too focused on getting through school and helping my mom where I could. That often meant working extra shifts as a waitress at a barbecue joint not far from campus. Friday and Saturday nights meant late ones, but for a whole different reason than other college students.

After I graduated, I went home and worked in a bakery. For nine years, I devoted myself to the business. I watched as employees came and went, most using it as a stepping-stone until something bigger and better came along. What could possibly be greater than the scent of baking breads and scrumptious sugar desserts?

Nothing.

I loved my job. The owner, Mrs. Edwards, was a widow who had been so supportive during the loss of my mother. She gave me the time I needed off and allowed me to grieve at my own pace. She stepped into the role my mother had been in my whole life, giving me a shoulder to cry on and accolades when I deserved them. She was even amazing with Dustin, not saying a word when he would come to the bakery and just hang out for hours on end.

Until one day, a year ago, she blindsided me with the news she was selling. Her niece was purchasing the business but didn't have the same vision Mrs. Edwards had. Within a month, the bakery became a sandwich shop, serving deli fresh meats and cheeses and fresh bread using Mrs. Edwards' recipes.

I tried to stick it out. I really did, but it just wasn't in my blood. Sure, I helped baking bread every day, but it wasn't the same. In fact, I hated it. I wanted to make sweet jams and the creamy frostings. I wanted what was in my heart and soul.

Dustin was the first one to suggest we move. At first, I brushed off his comments, scared to step out of the comfort zone of home. Yet, on a Friday night, one not too dissimilar from this one, he came to me and said he needed a change. He was sad living in the house without Mom. He wanted a fresh start, something we could build on together.

That was when I realized he was right. I wasn't happy at the sandwich shop and the house just didn't feel the same. It was empty, and even though we had thousands of memories keeping us comfortable within those walls, it didn't feel like it was ours anymore.

It took us a week to settle on our new location. Dustin stumbled upon a book about Stewart Grove at the library. This town was built on a feud between two men, both claiming they were the founding settler of the land. Dustin absorbed every word written in that book, often reading sections of it aloud to me at night. I don't know what it was about it, but I was intrigued and excited to know more. We started looking at rental options on the internet, pleased to find the one we're in now at a price we could afford.

The day we settled on Stewart Grove is the day Dustin found the building for my bakery. It wasn't in the plan to start my own business. After searching help wanted ads and not really finding anything in my preferred field, I was preparing to settle for a job at the local furniture store, just to ensure we'd have enough income to pay the bills.

But Dustin wouldn't hear of it.

He made a presentation. One night after work, I came home to find his laptop open and the listing for the small available storefront building front and center. He had researched leasing and buying options, equipment purchases, insurance rates, and even demographics for the town we were getting ready to move to. Using the money we'd make from selling the house, we had more than enough for the down payment, as well as what we needed for collateral. We also had a little money left in my savings account from Mom's life insurance, which, coupled with Dustin's state money for his disability, would be plenty to cover moving and living expenses until we got the bakery operational and profitable.

It wasn't an easy sell.

No way did I want to risk all of our savings for something that may not be successful. What if it failed to take off? What if there was a reason for no other bakery in Stewart Grove? I'd invest all of our savings, time, and energy for what? To still have to find a job flipping burgers at a fast food restaurant or selling couches and dining room sets at the furniture store?

I was terrified.

But Dustin wouldn't let me say no. He wouldn't let me fail, even though the risk was high. He was just as invested in this project as I was, and it wasn't even his dream. He had my back one hundred percent, just like I have his. He's my brother. The same blood runs through our veins. He was one of the only living relatives I had, and I've never been closer to anyone else. Not even my girlfriends back in high school. They never understood why I'd rather sit at home on a Friday night, watching television with Dustin, than out sitting in the bleachers at a football game. Because ever since Dustin was born and we discovered he had a disability, I felt some sort of responsibility for him. He was my flesh and blood, the one who relied on Mom and me to help take care of him. He has the biggest heart of anyone I know, and I'd rather spend time with him, soaking up his goodness and his generosity, than doing anything else in this world.

"I'm getting hungry," Dustin announces, putting the last of the clean dishes away on the shelves.

"Me too," I reply, realizing my stomach has been growling for a while, but my nerves got the best of me today.

We wrapped up training with Daisy, who is eager to start Monday morning when Sugar Rush opens its doors for the first time. We kept our focus on the front end of the business, which, fortunately, she picked up quickly. She'll be in charge of the cash register and filling orders, with the help of Dustin. Together, they'll serve coffee, tea, or any of the other bottled drinks we'll carry. Eventually, I'd love to add more specialty drinks like lattes and espressos, but it's just not in the budget right now.

Also today, the front door and windows were done, complete with a new Sugar Rush logo front and center. I opted to include our hours on a sign positioned by the front door instead of having them added beneath the logo on the door, mostly because they may change once we get going. It all depends on how busy we are.

Or aren't.

But I won't think of that right now. My anxiety is already through the roof, and the last thing I need to focus on is the what-ifs.

The health inspector also made his final inspection, giving us full approval to open our doors. Holding that piece of paper was probably the proudest moment I've had since beginning this venture. It means we've met all of the criteria for health and safety to serve food to the public. The moment he left, Dustin helped me frame the certificate and position it on one of the shelves near the front door.

Now, as we finish cleaning the kitchen for the night, I'm finally able to let go of the stresses of the day and focus on putting some food in my stomach.

"Can we still order burgers from across the street?" he asks, his face lighting up with excitement.

"Sure," I mumble, tossing my washcloth in the bin I'll take home tonight with dirty towels and rags.

At the mention of burgers, my mind instantly goes to Jasper. I haven't seen him since he stormed out of here Tuesday morning, which suits me just fine. He has this uncanny ability to easily get under my skin, and the last thing I want or need this week is added anxiety. Plus, though I'd never admit to this out loud, I've thought of him plenty throughout the last several days and have been struggling to evict him from my daydreams. His handsome face. Those dark, alluring eyes. Big hands that promise amazing skills in the kitchen and dirtier ones in the bedroom.

Seeing him would only make those images worse.

I walk up front, double-check the lock on the front door, and flip out the lights, leaving only one strip on, over the counter. Isaac's the one who actually suggested it when he stopped by yesterday to see the progress. They're directly over the cash register, plus shine just a touch in the kitchen. If someone was inside, they would be easy to spot from the road. Makes complete sense, and I'm incredibly grateful for the suggestion.

Before I head back to the kitchen, I can't help but stop and stare at the name on the window. I can't believe it's finally here. All the planning, the tears, the apprehension. The late evenings, early mornings, and sleepless nights. Worrying and wondering if it would ever come together, and now it's time. In just three short days, the doors will be open, and I'll be selling my own baked goods to the residents of Stewart Grove.

I catch movement across the street and turn my focus to the couple walking into Burgers and Brew. There's a group of people standing by the door, clearly waiting on a table. I can't help but wonder if I'll eventually have the same kind of success. Customers lining up, waiting for their chance to have a table. Only my customers will be vying for one of my gooey cinnamon rolls or a slice of my famous pecan pie. They'll be lined up to the door, spilling onto the sidewalk out front.

Hey, a girl can dream, right?

"I check their social media page, and tonight's hamburger special is called the Panty Melter. It's loaded with four kinds of cheeses. Can we eat there?" Dustin asks, his brown eyes full of anticipation.

"They look pretty busy, Dust. It may be easier to take it to-go," I suggest, but the moment I see disappointment in his eyes, I wish I could recant my statement.

"Oh, yeah, you're probably right. It's seven on a Friday," he concedes, turning to grab his coat off the hook by the back door. I can tell by the way he's walking he overdid it today. Dustin worked hard and only took breaks when I forced him to sit. Now, he's relying on his walker more and could probably use his wheelchair.

"Well," I start, glancing across the street through the front window. "We could see how busy they are. If there's only a short wait, we can stay."

He offers me a big smile. "Deal."

"But I think you should take the chair, Dust. You busted ass today."

He opens his mouth to argue, but I can tell he sees merit in my suggestion. "Yeah, all right," he replies, reaching for his chair and getting himself settled. He wheels himself to the door and waits for me.

I button up my peacoat and wrap a scarf around my neck, grateful for the touch of warmth it provides. After slipping my gloves on my hands, I open the door so Dustin can exit and make sure it's locked behind me.

We head down the alley to the sidewalk. Fortunately, there's no snow or slush left, just bitter cold temperatures. There's little traffic, so we're able to cut across the street quickly. I pull open the heavy wooden door and am greeted with warmth, laughter, and an amazing aroma.

I step aside, making sure Dustin gets in with his chair. The couple I watched walk in earlier moves a little, allowing my brother to easily maneuver the entry.

"May I help you?" the hostess asks with a friendly smile.

"How long for a table for two?" I ask, glancing around the room.

"Not long at all," she replies, glancing at her computer screen. "I have a handicap accessible table being cleaned now. Five minutes?" she offers, earning me a nod in reply.

The couple waiting is taken to a booth, leaving just my brother and I at the front. "Only a few minutes," I tell Dustin, earning me a smile in return.

I take in the ambiance and the fast pace of the restaurant. Dark woodwork, with a combination of booths and tables. There are three or four servers taking care of them, most of which are filled with happy customers. The food, from what I can see from here, looks amazing and smells even better, causing my stomach to growl loudly.

This burger joint is like nothing I've ever seen before.

"If you'll follow me," the hostess suggests, grabbing two menus and making her way down the wide main aisle. She leads us to a small table for two along the wall, one of the chairs already removed. It's near the wide doorway that leads to the bar, so there's plenty of room for my brother's wheelchair at the table, and we don't have to worry about anyone sitting behind him. "Tonight's special is the Panty Melter burger, hand pressed and grilled to order, topped with cheddar, Monterey Jack, colby, and smoked Gouda, served with freshly cut steak fries. Your server will be with you shortly."

The moment she leaves us, I moan in pure pleasure. "That sounds amazing," I mumble, praying no one else heard my excited little noise.

"That's what I'm getting," Dustin informs, but peruses the menu to be sure. After only a few seconds, he busts out laughing. "Lyn, check out the names of the burgers."

I open my menu and gasp. They're so...sexy. Strip and Go Naked, Ride A Cowboy, and "Up All Night" are the first three on the list, and I find them fascinating. "Holy shit," I whisper, scanning the rest of the selections and taking in their ridiculous names.

"Right? What a brilliant marketing plan," Dustin boasts.

"Thank you."

Startled, I look up into Jameson's hard, dark eyes. Though, once I give him a slow smile, he seems to relax those stress lines. There's something different about this man. You can tell he's gruffer, and quite possibly had a rougher life than most. He wears his no-bullshit demeaner like a protective shield, one that tells people to stay back and leave him alone, but I don't think that's who he really is, what he's really about. Of course, I have only two small encounters to base my opinion off of, but I really don't think he's as bad as he leads people to believe.

"Though, I can't take credit for the names. It was actually Jasper's demented mind that came up with them. Numbers was afraid they were too risqué, but turns out, we live in a town with a bunch of dirty bastards," he adds with a crooked smile.

Dustin and I both chuckle. I also notice the use of the nickname they gave Isaac years ago. Jameson told me about it after they helped us move the furniture at the bakery. Over a chocolate scone, he informed us about Isaac's passion for numbers, which ultimately led them to giving him the nicknames Numbers or Newton, for Isaac Newton.

"They're definitely clever and unforgettable," I agree, closing my menu and setting it aside.

Just then, our server arrives at the table. "Hey, guys. Welcome to Burgers and Brew. Can I get you a drink?" she asks politely, giving Jameson a quick nervous grin.

"I'll have an ice water, no lemon," I tell her.

"And for you?" she asks my brother.

"Bud Light, please." He glances up at me. "You sure you don't want a drink? One won't hurt, especially this early." I know he means well, but his suggestion slices at my heart.

Dustin and I have gone round and round about this in the past. When we go out somewhere, I don't drink. I refuse to get behind the wheel, even after having just one sip. I won't risk him or anyone else on the road for a beer or a glass of wine. Not when my whole world was shattered by someone who thought it was okay to drink and drive. That will never be me.

"I'm okay, thank you," I reply politely, hating the way my heart thunders in my chest.

"Okay, I'll be back with your drinks," she states, turning to head away.

"Bring them some of the curds, will ya, Jani?" Jameson suggests to the server.

"I'll put in the order, Tank." Then she disappears toward the back of the restaurant.

"Tank?" I ask, a hint of a smile on my lips.

He shakes his head. "Nickname. My last name is Tankersley. Everyone calls me Tank but the guys. Oh, and don't worry about the curds. Those are my treat."

"You don't have to do that," I argue, but am cut off.

"My treat," he replies with a little more authority. "They're my favorite, and I don't just buy curds for anyone, you know. They're Wisconsin cheese curds with a zesty ranch dipping sauce. Way better than that wing franchise has," he states with a grin. "You don't drink?" he asks casually, leaning against the doorway behind my brother.

"Oh, uh, I do," I reply softly. "Our mom, she, well, she died four years ago from a drunk driver. I only drink at home."

He nods in understanding. "I get that and totally respect it. Sorry for your loss."

"Thank you," I whisper, my eyes locked on Dustin's. Neither of us are big drinkers, but my brother does enjoy a beer every now and again. Since he can't drive, he has a little more liberty to do so than I do, which suits me just fine.

"Hey, have you met Walker yet?" Jameson asks, standing up straight and turning toward the bar. "Yo, Walk, come here a second."

I glance around his big frame to see another man get up from a pub table and head our way. He's tall, dark, and quite handsome, really, but what catches my attention is the woman and small girl still sitting at the table.

"Walk, this is Lyndee and Dustin from the bakery across the street," Jameson says. "This is Walker Meyer, the fourth owner we told you about. He runs the bar side of the business."

Walker steps forward and holds out a hand. "You made that basket of goodies? I had to tackle this guy just to get my hands on an éclair," he says with a laugh.

I shake his big, warm hand and return his chuckle. "Well, thank you. I'll take that as a compliment."

"Definitely. Jameson and Numbers raved about them when they returned. Sorry I couldn't help that morning. Lizzie had a dentist appointment and was nervous, so I went along," he says, pointing over his shoulder to the little blonde with curly pigtails. She's dipping fries in ketchup and offers a wave. "I'll introduce you to Mal and Lou before they leave. Mal has been dying for you to open since I told her about your bakery."

Before I can respond, inviting them all over for free pastries whenever they want, as a thank you, another shadow falls on our table. "Hey, I thought that was you two. Welcome to Burgers and Brew," Isaac says, squeezing my brother on the shoulder.

"Thanks!" Dustin replies eagerly. "We're excited to be here."

Our server returns with our drinks, but it's a tight fit. She has to carefully maneuver her way through the growing crowd around our small table of two. But even though there are people standing around us, it's not overly crowded. They're not overshadowing the tables around us, making anyone uncomfortable with their presence. "Are you ready to order?" she asks.

"We are," I state. "I'll have the Panty Melter." My cheeks blush under the watchful eyes of the owners.

"Me too," Dustin adds, handing off our menus.

"I'll get those right in. And your appetizer will be out any moment."

We chat for a few minutes, the guys falling into an easy teasing as they tell my brother and me more about opening the business. Jameson even elaborates with greater details about the brewery next door. Their excitement and energy are contagious, and as someone who's been embarking on the exact same journey, I feel a kinship to these men. They understand.

Just as they start to tell a horribly embarrassing Jasper story from college, a fourth shadow falls over the table. "Well, I should have known I'd find you all standing around, not working."

My wide eyes fly upward and slam into dark, mesmerizing ones. They're narrowed into slits and radiating enough annoyance to power a submarine. Yet, when my heartbeat kicks up, it's in elation, not displeasure. Plus, my breathing does that weird little hitch it only does when he's near. Everyone around the table says something, but I don't hear their words. All I can do is focus on the imposing, gorgeous man standing beside me.

Jasper's here.

Jasper

When Jani came back to retrieve the cheese curds, I overheard her mention to my dinner shift assistant chef, Doug, that she had to deliver them to a table where all the other owners are standing, talking to a young couple. She wondered if it was a sibling to one of them, but something told me it wasn't. Call it my Spidey-sense, or my Lyndee-sense.

Everything started tingling.

I told her I'd deliver the order, barely gave Doug a backward glance when I said, "Watch the grill for a minute," and bolted for the door, despite the fact we were stacked up with tons of dinner orders and he has his own job to do.

I press through the doorway, dodge a surprised server, and head for my friends. The first thing I spot is the wheelchair, confirming my suspicions of who's here. As I approach, I hear laughter, particularly Lyndee's. It's like an angel's call, beckoning me to the Promised Land.

"I swear to God, I've never seen his bare ass move that quickly from a bedroom window before in my life," Walker says, causing a ruckus from the entire group and me to stop in my tracks.

I know that story.

Bastards!

"Hey, man. Whatcha doing out here?" Jameson asks, pulling everyone's attention my way.

"Delivering appetizers," I reply, grinding my teeth so hard I swear I crack a molar.

I step forward and set the curds down on the table, taking in everyone's positions. Walker is standing beside Isaac, behind where Dustin sits, and Jameson stands directly beside Lyndee. His arm dangles mere centimeters away from her arm.

I almost growl.

Her stunning brown eyes widen, and Jameson snorts a laugh, letting me know I may not have actually contained the possessive noise.

I give Lyndee a quick smile and turn to her brother. "Good to see you."

"You too. We're excited to be here," Dustin replies, a glimmer of excitement in his eyes.

"What did you order?" I ask, giving him my complete attention.

"Lyn and I both got the Panty Melter," he states, reaching for his beer.

"Excellent choice. I'll make sure they're extra gooey," I retort, turning a cocky grin Lyndee's way.

"And Jameson ordered us these cheese curds. He said they were his favorite," she replies innocently, taking one of the pieces of breaded cheese and popping it in her mouth.

My eyes instantly narrow and zero in on my friend. "Did he?" I comment, staring down Jameson.

He only laughs, clearly not fazed by my annoyed glare. "They are my favorite," he declares with a shrug and a wicked grin.

"Well, as fun as this is, I'm going back over to Mal and Lizzie to finish our dinner. Lyndee, we'll stop by on their way out and I'll introduce you," Walker states, turning and making his way back to where his girls are waiting.

"I'm going to check on the reservation list. Lyndee, Dustin, enjoy your meal. It's on the house tonight," Isaac announces.

"Oh, no, you don't have to do that. We're happy to support another local business," Lyndee insists.

"No way, not after those goodies you sent us. Tonight, it's on the house," he states before giving them a wave and walking off.

Jameson, the asshole he is, seems to just get comfortable. The fucker just smirks, overlaps his left foot over his right, and relaxes into his stance, arms crossed over his chest.

"Well, I should get back to the kitchen." Before I turn, my gaze catches hers and I swear the entire room can hear the thunder of my heart trying to beat out of my chest. I'm certain Lyndee can, maybe even feel the heavy thump from three feet away. "Enjoy your dinner."

"Thank you," she replies quickly, offering me a small grin.

With a nod, I turn to Dustin, pat him on the shoulder, and return to my domain, my gut heavier than it was when I came out here. I push through the door and find chaos erupting around me. Doug is trying to keep up on the grill, but he just doesn't have the expertise to systematically move that many burgers in a short amount of time.

He's not me.

I jump right back in, barking orders and doing everything I can to get caught back up. I was only out in the dining room for five minutes, but all hell broke loose in that short amount of time. This is why I hate leaving anyone else in charge in my absence. Yes, they manage, but no one runs this kitchen like I do.

Time to put Lyndee out of my head and do my thing.

Ha! Fat chance of that, buster.

Once the kitchen has been completely closed down, the restaurant long empty, and the bar hopping, I finally make my way over to where the action is. The moment I saddle up to the end of the bar, Walker has a bottle in his hand and the top off. "Busy night," I say, taking my first long pull of beer of the night.

"Yep. He draws more and more of a crowd," my friend replies, nodding to where Jameson plays guitar on the small one-step stage in the corner of the room.

This is the time where the bar is somewhat quiet, patrons enjoying his weekend acoustic sessions. Friday and Saturday nights, our friend plays. Crazy to think it started as just a way for him to practice whatever song he was working on, but now, he's a big part of the draw. Burgers, beer, and damn good music.

I glance around and find every seat filled, including some with familiar faces. As in, ones I've met up with well after the bar closed. Shit, I think there's even a small group sitting together that all looks very familiar. When I get a few waves and red-stained grins promising dirty favors later, I look away. Any other night, I'd eagerly anticipate one of them coming over with a proposition, but tonight, well, I'm just not feeling it and kinda hoping no one approaches me.

"This is exactly why I refused to dip my quill in company ink, man."

I look up and smack directly into Walker's laughing gaze. "Shut the fuck up."

That only makes him laugh even harder. He dries a few glasses and sets them on the shelf behind him. When he turns back around, he tosses the towel over his shoulder and leans in. "There comes a point in every man's life where the endless supply of willing women gets old."

"What the hell are you talking about?" I ask, chugging half my beer because I, in fact, know exactly what he's talking about, or alluding to, at least. Maybe I should say *who*.

He's way off base, though.

No way am I ready to commit my cock to one woman for the rest of my life.

Ain't happening.

Just because he cut off his balls when he met Mallory and willingly handed them over to her doesn't mean I'm going to do the same. He thinks just because he's happy, everyone else should be too. Well, forget that. I'm more than happy living the single life, hooking up like always.

Keep telling yourself that.

Walker just grins. "Jameson and Isaac told me you knew the woman across the street from college. She's the one who had your panties in a bunch back then, right?"

I gape at my friend. "What? That didn't happen," I argue, but my too-observant friend just shakes his head. The bastard makes a damn good bartender, or therapist as they're often referred to. "You guys never even met Lyndee."

"True, we didn't, but we witnessed how agitated you'd get after those classes and how competitive you were with her. We may not have met her, but she made an impression on us, only because she made one on you."

Bastard. He's just standing there, all smug and righteous, like he knows everything about me. "Whatever," I mumble, finishing off my beer in one more swallow.

Walker just laughs again as he reaches down and grabs a fresh bottle, pops the top, and slides it in front of me. "You want to hear what I think?"

"Don't you have a job to do?" I practically growl.

"Yeah."

"Then go do it and forget about analyzing something that doesn't deserve a second thought. I'm not into her, if that's what you're thinking. I've barely even thought of her," I insist, the lie rolling off my tongue like turpentine.

Now, he's practically doubling over with laughter. "If you say so." He sobers, clears his throat and leans in. "Good to know you're not interested, because there's a lady at the table over there that hasn't taken her eyes off you since you walked in and sat down. I guess since you're not hung up on anyone else, you might as well go over there and buy her a drink." He turns and heads down the bar to start making drinks, leaving his words hanging over me like a horrible headache.

I glance over my shoulder and spy a brunette with smoky makeup in a booth along the wall. Her friends' attention is pointed at Jameson, but hers is directed at me. She sips a martini and gives me a grin. I know that smile. It's one a woman gives a man when she's interested in a shag.

Keeping my eyes on her, I turn a little and bring my drink to my lips. I watch her observe me, knowing this is exactly what I need to do to push Lyndee out of my mind. I've been all over the damn place since Monday when I discovered she was opening across the street. She invades my thoughts, day and night, and I'm tired of her fucking with my head. I thought maybe sleeping with her was the perfect solution, but by Wednesday morning, I had talked myself out of that. It was a horrible idea.

The brunette nibbles on her plump bottom lip. Normally, I'd find it sexy, but tonight, it feels forced and overdone. Why do all women bite their lip? I mean, Lyndee did it Monday afternoon when I was there, but not like this. She wasn't trying to draw attention in that seductive way.

Forget about Lyndee.

I scan what I can see of her appearance, which is from the chest up. Tight red shirt with ample amounts of cleavage pouring out of the V-neck shirt. Lyndee wore a V-neck the other day too, but hers was a bit more tasteful. Not nearly as tight, nor were her tits popping out of the top like her shirt was two sizes too small.

Goddammit.

Just as Jameson finishes his set, the energy in the room starts to pick up. Everyone knows what's about to happen, and to be honest, I'm still shocked it does. It's a tradition on Friday and Saturday nights that dates back to the very first weekend we were open.

At eleven on the dot, Jameson sets his guitar down and everyone watches as Walker heads for the jukebox. With bated breath, we wait for tonight's song selection. I slip behind the bar and pour a shot, like one of us does every time this happens. Tonight, I choose tequila, something he's not a huge fan of. Serves him right for meddling in my business like a fucking girl.

Finally, the song starts, and the crowd goes wild. The familiar opening melody of "Looks That Kill" blares through the speakers, and the brunette catches my attention. She's grinning like I chose that song just for her.

The entire bar starts to belt out the Mötley Crüe song as my friend makes his way back to the bar. He heads for the center, places his hands on the top, and hoists himself up. And yes, every patron is egging him on. Walker starts to dance, shaking his hips and ass like it's his fucking job, and I guess, it is. That first night, we all had way too much to drink, celebrating our opening and praying for success, and I have no idea why he ended up on the bar at eleven o'clock, but he did.

And it was epic.

So ever since, we salute our favorite band with one of their songs at the stroke of eleven. Word spread so fast about the dance that it was expected, patrons coming from all over to observe the craziness by my friend.

I'll never forget the night his girlfriend witnessed his bar top dance for the first time. I thought for sure he was toast, their relationship over, but do you know what? She laughed and egged him on. Didn't complain about the panties thrown behind the bar or the numbers slipped into his palm. It takes a strong woman to not get jealous and pissed, but she saw instantly what we all knew.

Walker was pussy-whipped.

No way was he going to step out on Mallory, not then or now. He's so deliriously in love with her you get a toothache from watching them.

So even though he's on the bar, dancing and thrusting his hips like he starred in *Magic Mike*, we all know he's only going home with one woman, and she isn't in this room. She's at their shared home with her daughter, waiting up with a glass of wine for her man to get home. I've never understood the appeal, but I guess I can see how less drama and headaches can be appealing.

"Hey, you." I turn to see the brunette from the booth sliding between my stool and the one next to me, her tits pressed firmly against my arm.

"Hi," I reply, giving her one of my trademark panty-dropping smiles.

She moves her martini glass to her lips with her right hand and practically purrs, "Mona." She reaches out her left hand for me to take, her long, fake nails painted a deep red color, but that's not what catches my attention. No, my eyes are riveted on the huge sparkly diamond ring on her left finger.

"Jasper," I croak, staring at what looks like an engagement ring and its accompanying thin platinum band.

Fuck.

When my eyebrows draw together in question, she just shrugs her shoulders. "I'm in town for the weekend with some friends." She glances at her own ring. "He knows I like to have fun," she says, leaning into my personal space, her red lips dangerously close to my ear. "And you look like someone I can have fun with."

I can't help but smirk. Oh, I'm definitely the *fun* kinda guy, but my eyes just keep going back to that damn ring. I don't make a habit of sleeping with married women. Oh, it's happened before, but both times were accidents. Neither was wearing a ring, and they both conveniently left that part out of our introductions.

But now, even though she's gorgeous and giving me those fuck-me eyes, seeing that damn ring is like being doused with a bucket of ice water. Well, that and the fact I can't help but picture Lyndee. Her light makeup is such a stark contrast to the woman beside me. She has a natural beauty she doesn't have to accentuate with smoky eye shadow and layers of mascara.

Dammit. Stop. Thinking. About. Lyndee.

Mona drains the rest of her drink and sets her empty glass down beside me. A shadow falls over us, and when I look up, I find one of my best friends still on the bar. His gaze is curious and holds a hint of irritation as he crouches down and grabs the shot glass, throwing it back and draining the contents. I can't help a smug smile as he pulls a face and sets the glass back down, daggers aimed directly at me like bullets from a gun.

Serves him right.

Mona smashes her tits against my arm and leans into my side. "So, are you going to buy me a drink before we head back to my hotel room, or should we just leave now?" I can smell the gin on her breath.

Normally, a forward woman is hot as fuck, but I just can't seem to get into her advances. Everything about this is...wrong. And I don't mean to sound like a dick. She's stunning and that wicked gleam in her eyes is no doubt promising a night of naughty bedroom fun, but I'm just not feeling it tonight.

"Sorry, love, but I'm not available this evening."

Lies. I'm available.

Mona pouts. Like actually juts out her bottom lip and whines. "No." She draws out that single reply as if it has fourteen syllables, grating on my nerves instantly. I've never understood why people do that whiny shit. I mean, even Lizzie doesn't whine like that, and she's three.

"'Fraid so, darling, but enjoy your night," I reply, sliding off my stool and heading for the back hallway, beer bottle in hand.

If I'm choosing to not get laid, there's only one other escape for me. I make my way back to my kitchen and prepare to dirty everything I just cleaned. As I flip on the lights, an idea pops in my head. I'll bake a pie. Walker can take it to his great aunt's house tomorrow. Aunt Edna will hate it, only because she knows my pecan pie is better than hers, which makes me grin. I've gone round and round with the older black woman on many occasions, only because it's so much fun to get her going.

Pecan pie.

Of course you're making one. It's the only thing you haven't been able to best Lyndee at.

Well, stand back, Lyndee Gibson. I'm about to blow your socks off with the best damn pecan pie recipe out there. Your reign at the top is officially over.

Lyndee

I'm a mess. A stressed, freaked out mess.

I've been at the bakery since before the sun rose, anxious to get a jump on the product I'll feature during tomorrow's grand opening. I've baked breads, pies, cookies, and cakes. I have the dough ready to go in the fridge for tomorrow morning's pastries. I recleaned the coffee pot and made sure napkin holders and other necessities are filled to the brim. Hell, I've even triple-checked to make sure the oven was properly hooked up and the refrigerator was operational. As tired as I am, and knowing I have to get up super early tomorrow, I just can't seem to make myself go home.

I took Dustin home two hours ago. He was exhausted and ready to relax, though it was a hard sell to get him to leave. He wanted to stay if I was staying, but I knew he had reached his limit. He was willingly using the wheelchair, his motions more stiff than usual. He had been here early with me both yesterday and today, and it was taxing on him. Now, he's watching television in his room and probably on his second frozen pizza.

When I glance at the clock, I see it's after nine. I *need* to go home. Three in the morning is going to be here before I know it, and the last thing I want is to fall asleep while rolling the dough. Though, I don't foresee that happening. I imagine I'll be too amped up on adrenaline and caffeine. I probably won't even realize I'm tired.

A knock on the front door grabs my attention.

Holy shit, someone's at the door. Should I go out there? What if they're here to kill me?

Seriously, Lyndee? You think most murderers knock on the front door to grab your attention? Why not just use the back door where they're not standing directly beneath a streetlight?

Setting my towel down on the island, I slowly head to the front and peek around the doorway. My breathing hitches and surprise sweeps through my exhausted extremities. What is he doing here?

Jasper gives me a tentative wave. "Hey," he says through the glass.

My feet carry me to the entrance, and I unlock the door. "Hi."

He runs a hand through his messy hair. "I was just...well, I was leaving work and saw your lights on in the kitchen."

I'm only slightly hesitant as I step back and grant him access. "Oh, yeah," I respond, locking the door behind him. "I really need to go home and get some sleep, but..."

He turns around, his hands shoved in the pockets of his dark blue jeans, and gives me a grin. "But...you're too amped up to sleep. I get it."

I sigh and sag into the first chair I can find. "Yeah. I'm exhausted, but I can't seem to shut my mind off."

He nods in understanding. "Right before we opened Burgers and Brew, I swore anything that could go wrong *was* going to happen. I even called an electrician to double-check all the appliances, which was crazy since all of them were brand new and I'd been using them for two weeks to train the staff."

I give him a tired smile. "I completely understand that."

"Well, I'm sure everything is going to be fine tomorrow."

"I hope," I whisper, glancing down at his shoes. He's incredibly casual this time. Instead of the pressed slacks and polo shirt, he's wearing a pair of worn boots, jeans, and a hoodie sweatshirt beneath an old brown leather coat.

The room is filled with silence, but it's surprisingly not awkward. I find myself just taking him in, noticing how he's starting to relax against the counter, and realize I'm relaxing too. Back in school, our exchanges were always tense and full of electricity. I always thought it was because of some unspoken competition we seemed to constantly be engaged in, but now I'm not so sure. Looking back, it feels...sexual.

Yeah, I'm definitely exhausted.

"Did I ever tell you how I met my friends?" he asks, the softest smile playing on his full lips.

I shake my head. I know they met in college, Isaac mentioned it to me in conversation, but don't know the story. I mean, it's not like we were friends back then and actually told each other those kinds of things. No, we were competitors, and competitors didn't exactly share personal information that could potentially be used against us.

"Well, Walker and Jameson were friends from high school. Jameson didn't actually go to college, but he was always visiting Walker on the weekends. We met at a frat party at the beginning of our senior year and hit it off. We were all standing around bitching about the horrible rap music pumping through the house. Turns out, we were all fans of Mötley Crüe, so we'd get together and drink a few beers, play cards, and listen to them.

"A year later, we ended up at this dive bar across town. You know the kind they feature in murder mystery shows where catching the killer is going to be a bitch because of all the DNA covering everything?"

I can feel myself making a horrified face, and his laughter only confirms it.

"Yeah, I know. For someone who cleaned his kitchen at least two times a day, being there was not a picnic for me. But Jameson and Walker got pulled into a billiards game, so we hung out for a while.

"Anyway, Jameson ended up with a baggie of weed. I had smoked it a few times, but never really saw the appeal. We ended up in the dingy bathroom, passing a joint like a couple of cool twenty-two-year-olds," he says, shaking his head at the memory. "It was just the three of us in that nasty bathroom with a half-smoked joint when Numbers walked in to use the john."

My eyes widen in shock.

"Yeah, I know what you're thinking. Isaac at a seedy bar? I think he was in pressed khakis or some shit like that, but he was there, looking all sorts of uncomfortable. I could tell he didn't even want to whip it out to pee, but I think he realized he was about out of options. Just as he starts to go, the alarm and damn sprinkler system went off, soaking all of us to the bones. We took off out the door, Numbers hot on our heels as he was trying to zip back up."

A bubble of laughter spills from my lips. "Oh my gosh, are you serious?"

"As a heart attack," he confirms. "We ran out the door and kept going until we were in an alley down the street. That's when we really noticed we'd picked up a fourth. He was standing there, looking like he was gonna piss himself, and yelled at us for smokin' in the boys room. The three of us just bust out laughing. It was like it was fate, considering who our favorite band was. So from that day on, Numbers was our fourth, and we haven't looked back since."

Shaking my head, I reply with a giggle, "That's some story. I can't believe you all met that way."

He shrugs his broad, muscular shoulders. "We aren't proud of that night, but it's what brought us together as a group. And none of us have touched that shit since. No way were we risking anything just to get stoned."

I continue to watch him, his entire demeanor completely relaxed, as if he were speaking to a buddy. Though, I know that's not true. Jasper and I have never been considered friends. His smile is easy and slightly lopsided in a way I haven't noticed before. Maybe because he's truly comfortable for the first time.

A yawn startles me, my hand covering my mouth quickly.

"Well, I'll let you get home. You have a big day tomorrow," he says, pushing off the counter and standing up to his full height. Even when I rise too, he's towering over me.

"I do. Thank you for checking on me," I reply, another yawn catching me by surprise. I can't believe how suddenly exhausted I am. It's like chatting with Jasper helped me to relax for the first time all weekend.

"No problem," he says, heading for the front door. He releases the lock and pulls the handle, letting the nippy December air blow through the entry. Jasper glances around before he meets my gaze. "Hey, this place looks great, Lyn. You've done a great job."

My heart blasts into my throat like a rocket leaving the ground. Was that praise? Jasper was never one to pay compliments. "Oh, uh, thank you."

He nods once and steps through the door. "Good luck tomorrow."

"Thanks," I whisper, my throat burning with emotion. I can feel the sting of tears behind my eyelids, and I just pray they don't make their appearance until after he's gone. Back in school, Jasper used to feed on emotion like algae, slowly exposing and sucking the life out of you.

"Lock up," he instructs before heading for a fancy vehicle parked in front of my business. Of course he would drive a Mercedes sports car.

I turn the lock and give the door a tug, ensuring it's secure. I stand there and watch as he starts his car, headlights flooding the street. He doesn't move right away, probably warming up the interior or checking his phone for messages.

When I realize I'm still standing there, watching like a stalker, I head for the kitchen and start turning off the lights. I double- and triple-check to make sure everything is in order—and yes, I ensure the fridge is still working right—before I grab my coat and make my way to the back door.

After confirming the door is locked, I cross the alley to my car. It starts easily, even though it's cold outside, and I wait a few minutes for it to warm. As soon as it's pumping warmth through the vents, I pull out of the small parking area and head for home. I opt to use the main street, wanting to catch one more glimpse of Sugar Rush before it's officially opened, and am shocked when I find the car still parked in front. As I slowly drive by, Jasper pulls out onto the roadway, giving me a friendly honk as we pass.

What was he still doing there? It had been nearly ten minutes from the time he exited my business and I passed him on the street. Was he waiting that long for his car to warm up?

I'm sure that's it.

It's not like he'd be waiting to make sure I got going safely. That's not like the Jasper I once knew.

Only, I'm not sure I ever really knew him at all. I saw what he wanted me to. Maybe there's more to Jasper Kohlmann than meets the eye. Not that I'll be getting to know him any better than I do right now. Oh, no. He was only being polite, making sure everything was all right when he saw lights on. Nothing more than a businessman checking on a neighbor.

That's all it was.

I'm sure of it.

From the moment I flipped the sign to open, I've been hopping busy. Believe it or not, there was a small three-person line waiting on the sidewalk at six to be the first to try the newest bakery in town. I wasn't sure whether to hug those individuals or maybe give them an unlimited supply of free pastries as a thank-you, but, fortunately for my bottom line, I did neither. I did, however, offer them a free cup of coffee with their orders and chatted with them while Daisy completed their orders.

As six rolled into seven, the customers kept coming in a steady stream, but it was the seven o'clock hour that really got us moving. I found patrons lined up to the front door as they waited patiently to place their orders. Dustin helped pull items from the case and wrap them up, while Daisy focused on the register. I was constantly running from the back to the front to refill what I could.

It was organized chaos, and I loved it.

At ten thirty, I'm elbow-deep in dough when the bell chimes over the door. There was a brief lull in customers, one we all took advantage of. Daisy was cleaning tables out front, while Dustin was taking a short break and sitting in his chair, watching me roll dough for more cookies.

I glance up and see familiar faces checking out the case. Smiling, I quickly wash my hands and head up front, meeting Daisy at the edge of the counter. "I'll take care of them," I tell her as I move to our newest arrivals. "Good morning."

"Hey, Lyndee," Mallory replies, her eyes as wide as the donuts on display. "This all looks so amazing. Congratulations."

I beam instantly at Mallory's compliment. Even though I've only met her one time, last Friday night at the restaurant, I instantly felt a kinship with her. She was friendly, smiled easily, and teased Walker and his friends good-heartedly. And Lizzie? Don't get me started on her. The cutest little three-year-old I've ever met.

"Yeah, congrats on your big day. How has it gone so far?" Walker asks.

"Busy," I reply proudly. "I've already gone through all the fresh bread I baked this morning, and the donuts are almost gone. Good thing it's after typical breakfast time."

"I want a sprinkle donut!" Lizzie cries, searching the case desperately for her selection.

When I give it a look, I see no sprinkle donuts. "Oh, no, I don't see any." The second the words are out of my mouth, her face falls.

"But…I might have something special in back for you. Wait here, okay?"

I turn around and hightail it back to the kitchen. I know we brought out most of the donuts, but I thought we kept a few in back…just in case. I'm happy to find a half dozen cake donuts on a tray in the cooling rack. I wash my hands quickly, slip on my gloves, and grab the plain donut.

"Hey, Lizzie?" I holler, through the doorway. When she looks up with eager eyes, I ask, "Chocolate or vanilla frosting?"

"Tocklet!"

Nodding and smiling, I move back to my counter and get to work. It only takes a few seconds to decorate her special donut. I smother on the frosting and grab my pipping bag. It already has white icing in it from the name I added to a small birthday cake, so I use it to write her name around the top of the donut. Then, I add multicolored sprinkles.

Lots of them.

When it's finished, I slip it on a plate and head up front. "One special chocolate sprinkle donut," I announce as I slide it onto the counter.

Lizzie's eyes widen with delight. "It says my name! My teacher taughted me my name."

"It is your name," I reply with a grin.

"Tank you!" she beams, reaching for the treat with two hands.

"And Walker and I will split an apple fritter," Mallory says, reaching into her purse for her wallet.

When I glance his way, he holds up two fingers and mouths the number. Chuckling, I grab two fritters with wax paper and set them on the counter.

"An orange juice and two coffees, also," Mallory adds, pulling a ten out and setting it on the counter.

I ring up their order, giving them two cups of coffee for free. "Six fifty-seven."

"Keep it," Mallory instructs, waving off her change, just as I see Walker slip a few more bills into the tip jar.

"That's not necessary," I reply, though I'm not sure which one I'm really talking to.

"Of course it is," Walker argues. "We want you to succeed."

"Stop by every once in a while and grab something for breakfast or dessert, and I'll be sure to succeed," I reply, my heart filled with hope. "Oh, and maybe tell your friends about us?" I add with a laugh.

"Done, but you already know all my friends," Walker insists with a chuckle.

Just as they move to a table to enjoy their breakfast, the door opens and in walks a smiling Isaac. "Morning."

"Good morning," I reply with a warm smile. "What brings you in this morning?"

"One of those chocolate scones and a cup of coffee, please. Walker said he was bringing the girls over for breakfast, so I thought I'd join them," he says, pulling a twenty from his wallet.

After I total his purchase and return his change, he drops it all in the tip jar. My eyes are ridiculously wide, which makes him chuckle. "We take care of our own," he whispers with a wink, before turning and heading to an open seat with Walker, Mallory, and Lizzie.

Daisy takes over the front counter, waiting on the customers who come in after Isaac, when Dustin comes back up to the front. "Hey, guys," he says the moment he spots the ones from across the street.

"Dustin," Isaac greets, standing up and making sure my brother has enough room to get by with his walker.

"Oh, the scones are my favorite too," my brother says as he takes one of the empty seats at the table beside them. "How's your donut?" he asks Lizzie.

"It's dood! How's come you gots to walk with dat?" she asks, pointing her gooey finger toward the walker.

"Well, this is my walker," my brother starts, but is cut off.

"Hey! Dat's your name, Walk!" the little blonde coos across the table at the big guy.

"It is my name, yes. It's also the name of the device that helps him walk."

"When I was born, I didn't get enough oxygen, so I have a disability. It means I have trouble walking and get really tired easily," Dustin replies to the little girl.

She seems to think hard about his explanation, her eyes bouncing between my brother and his walker. "I det tired too when I wunded a wot at wecess. Will you come pway wiff me? I wike Barbies and dollies."

"I'd love to, if your mommy and daddy say it's okay sometime," he replies.

"Pweeese, Daddy Walk? Can he come pway?" Little Lizzie begs the man across from her. I can see the softness in his eyes, the adoration on her sweet face.

"Sure, Lou. Maybe someday after preschool," Walker replies, glancing over at Mallory, who just grins back.

"Daddy Walk says it's otay," Lizzie informs my brother. Dustin just smiles at her, which she returns, chocolate smeared across her cheeks. My heart trips over itself in my chest at the pure beauty of friendship.

The door opens again, catching our attention. Jameson walks in looking a little rough. "I'll pay you double for the biggest coffee you have," he mumbles to Daisy, who hurries to grab him a large cup and fills it with caffeine.

"You okay?" I ask, walking up beside him.

"Uhhh," he groans. "Yeah, I'm fine. Late night."

I take in his bedhead and the wrinkled shirt beneath his beat-up leather jacket and a smile breaks out across my face. "Someone's doing the walk of shame," I whisper-yell, barely able to keep my laughter in check.

"Zip it, Pixie," he teases, keeping his voice low. "I don't need them finding out."

I roll my eyes and shake my head. "I had you pegged in the first two seconds of walking in here. You don't think your friends, who have known you your entire adult life, are going to pick up on the fact you're still wearing yesterday's clothes and reeking of cigarettes and Ralph Lauren's Romance?"

His eyes widen comically. "How do you know that?"

"I have a bottle at home," I reply with a shrug. "It's nice."

"Tank!"

Jameson throws a wad of bills on the counter, pastes the biggest, brightest smile on his face, and turns around. "Lizard!" He heads over and takes a seat across from Dustin.

I can't help but just stand and watch this small group interact with one another. They're like a little family, one, it seems, they've gladly pulled my brother into the fold. Yet, as I sit here and watch them interact, I can't help but wonder where Jasper is. Across the street in his kitchen, I'm sure. It's where he spent every free second he had in school.

I know.

I was there with him.

Jasper

"I brought you something, sweetheart," Isaac sings, dropping a small white bag onto the counter in front of me.

"What's that?" I ask, keeping my eyes focused on preparing a burger. I already know what it is. I could smell the sugar the moment he stepped into my space.

"A surprise. Maybe the sugar will help get you out of your pissy mood," he teases.

"I'm not pissy. I just don't like being bothered when I'm working."

He snorts a laugh. "See? Pissy. I'd suggest maybe getting laid, but Walker says you had a little trouble with that Friday night."

That makes me pause. "I wasn't having any trouble," I insist, my eyes dancing with annoyance, while his are laced with humor.

"No? Huh, it must have been someone else who went home alone, even though a perfectly good woman propositioned him," Isaac replies with a shrug, leaning against the sink and looking a little too comfortable.

"Just because I wasn't interested doesn't mean I was having trouble," I retort, returning my attention back to the burger. We're not open yet, and I'm trying to perfect a fire-melted technique that leaves a layer of crispy cheese on top. I think it'll be a great change-up to the Panty Melter burger we feature.

When he doesn't reply, I turn his way, finding him grinning from ear to ear. "Keep telling yourself that, buddy." Isaac straightens up and adds, "We get to do a walk-through of the brewery today. I thought we'd move our meeting over there."

"Sounds good," I reply, actually very excited to see how it's coming along. Jameson has been working his ass off to get it opened in the first quarter. As of his last report, we're on track to potentially open mid-February. The construction is almost done, and then comes the fun part.

Making beer.

While it's not my area of expertise, I'm very excited about this new venture. I could see the subtle change in Jameson since we agreed to open the brewery next door. He felt like a drifter, even though he's a vital part of our success. He wanted more, needed to feel like he was helping in a bigger capacity. I totally get and respect that. He's overseeing the construction and setup of our new business, and will manage it, with the help of Isaac. Then Jameson will run the day-to-day operations. We're still ironing out all the details, but we're getting there.

"I'll leave you to your creating," Isaac replies, walking out the door. It's at that moment I realize he left the white bag sitting there. I push it aside with a little too much force, causing it to tip over. A cinnamon roll falls out and my mouth starts to water.

Dammit.

I set the blowtorch down—yes, I'm using a blowtorch to melt cheese—and stare at the sweet treat. My stomach growls angrily, as if I hadn't consumed a protein bar on my way to work just a little bit ago. Traitorous stomach is all excited at the sight of something Lyndee whipped up this morning.

And my cock is quick to follow at the vision of her making it, flour streaked down her cheek and icing on her nimble fingers.

Before I can think better of it, I reach for the pastry, ready to have my first real taste of something she offers in her bakery, not including what my asshole friends smeared across my lips last week. When I take my first bite, my tastebuds erupt. It's still fucking warm, and I groan. The icing is sweet and firm, and the roll is fluffy and rich. I take a second bite, followed by a third, and before I know it, the damn thing is gone.

I'm a little disgusted at myself, at apparently having absolutely no self-control when it comes to Lyndee's pastries. What's worse, I'm damn proud of her for making such a perfect sweet roll. I want to run across the street and tell her, though I know that's a horrible idea. She's in the middle of her very first day of being open and probably busier than hell. But that's not what really keeps my feet planted where they stand. I'm liable to pull her into my arms and kiss the hell out of her, and that's a very bad idea.

One kiss is harmless, but I know I won't be able to stop at one. I'll crave more.

I push her out of my head like I've been doing for days and focus on my work. Grabbing my blowtorch, I set out to find the perfect melting technique for my cheese. It only takes me two more tries to figure out the best way, and once it's scorched to perfection, I scrape it onto the burger and watch it slowly melt down the side. Now *this* is a cheeseburger.

An idea pops into my head, but I quickly push it aside.

I'm not going over there.

Not now.

Not later.

Keep telling yourself that.

The walk-through is great. I can see every emotion on Jameson's face as he shows us around. For a man who hides behind attitude and a pissed-off demeanor, it's pretty fucking cool to witness. After a brief tour and a chat with the construction manager, Derek, we head back over to the bar to finish our owners' meeting.

"So, now that we don't have little ears around us, are you going to tell us why you reeked of too much perfume and sex this morning?" Isaac asks, catching my attention.

"What?" I ask, glancing at Walker, who just grins.

"Our boy stumbled into Sugar Rush this morning in yesterday's clothes, like he hadn't slept a wink last night," Walker confirms.

"Are we fucking gossiping now?" Jameson grumbles, taking a seat at the table.

"You thought because Lizard was there, we would forget all about that?" Isaac asks with a hearty laugh.

"Hoped," Jameson mumbles, reaching for a glass of water already on the table.

I hold up my hand. "Wait, I have to go grab the food. Don't say another word until I get back," I add, practically running back to the kitchen to get the four burgers I prepared and left under the heat lamp before our tour. As soon as I'm back, I say, "Go."

"What's to talk about? Is that what we do now? Sit around and gossip about who's getting laid and who's not?" Jameson gripes, taking the plate I offer. "No, this one has pickles," he adds with a gag.

I hand the plate with pickles to Walker as he replies, "I'm getting laid, just so we're clear." He gives us all a big cheeky grin, and as if he conjured her up from his imagination, Mallory walks into the room and heads for the bar. She glances over her shoulder and finds my friend's eyes firmly locked on her ass. I'd be jealous if I wasn't so damn happy for my friend. He deserves someone like Mallory and Lizzie in his life.

"Me too," Isaac mumbles, clearing his throat and shifting in his seat.

"You're what?" I ask, pulled back to our conversation.

Again, he moves in his chair. "I'm, uh, getting laid."

My eyebrows arch sky-high.

"Seriously? Since when?" Jameson asks right before taking a huge bite of his burger.

"Well, since Savannah and I ran into each other a few weeks ago." Isaac doesn't meet our eyes, and I have to swallow my groan.

"Savannah? Really?" Jameson asks, apparently unable to filter his own comment.

"Yes, Savannah. What do you all have against her anyway?" he demands, glancing around the table. It's not that we have something against her, per se, it's that their happiness is always short-lived. They've dated off and on for a few years, and each time it ends the same. Isaac jumping in with both feet and Savannah stomping all over his heart.

"Nothing," Walk insists, trying to smooth everything over. "Maybe it'll stick this time," he adds lamely, mostly because we all know it won't.

Isaac nods once and turns his attention back to Jameson. "You okay with that?"

Jameson, not one to pull punches, replies, "Whatever, dude. It's your life."

"Yes, it is." Isaac takes a bite and glances over at our tattooed friend. "So, are you going to tell us what happened with you last night?"

Jameson groans. "Why? You need the juicy details, Numbers?"

"No, definitely not, but we're all curious. You haven't seen anyone since Amie," Isaac replies.

We all catch the way Jameson averts his eyes, a flush of guilt crossing his features.

Shit.

"Amie?" Walker asks. "Where'd you run into her?" he asks without judgment.

"Her front door," Jameson answers with a laugh.

Jameson and Amie have been...*friends* for years. Hell, who am I kidding? They're fuck buddies, and it seems to work for them. She's got a reputation of getting around, which doesn't seem to bother my friend. When either of them has a particular itch to scratch, they hook up. It's been going on for years, though we can't seem to understand why. She's whiny and annoying when she's in here, hanging all over any guy she can. Probably to get Jameson's attention, but he never seems to mind.

"So, let me get this straight. You can screw Amie, who has been seeing you and half the town for years, but I can't date Savannah?" Isaac asks, unable to mask his annoyance.

"Yes, and do you know why?" Jameson replies, giving Isaac his full attention. "Because what Amie and I do is just that. Sex. We fuck and go about our lives. But you and Savannah are like gasoline and water. You don't mix. Every time she comes back, you jump in with both feet, only to find out she's not really in the same fucking pool as you. She uses you, but you refuse to see it."

Walker and I stare at each other from across the table, both of us afraid to take a breath. Jameson's not wrong. At all. The problem is Isaac is too obsessed with Savannah to see how she treats him. The last time they dated was for about four months, and she broke it off with him when something newer and shinier came along. We hate it. We hate seeing the sadness in his eyes, because Isaac is a good man and doesn't deserve to be treated like that. All he wants in life is to belong, to have someone to love. Has since his dad walked out on them when he was a kid. This thing with Savannah is like a merry-go-round ride that you can't get off. Round and round they go, until the ride breaks down again.

"Well, I guess you're entitled to your opinion," Isaac finally replies curtly.

"So, basically, what I'm getting out of this," Walker starts, looking for a redirect, "is Jasper is the only one not getting laid."

"Leave me alone. I'm not a project."

"All I'm saying is you *could* be, you know," Walker states, shoveling fries into his mouth.

"Ahhh, yes, the woman across the street," Isaac teases, smirking at me.

"Shut up, assholes," I grumble. "That shit isn't happening. I'm not into her. Period."

"She asked about you earlier," Walker adds.

My ears perk up and my eyes automatically move to the windows at the front of the bar. "She did?"

All three of my friends—or should I say *former* friends after this little stunt—are sitting there smiling at me.

Assholes.

I walked right into that one.

I've been done with work for an hour, but I can't seem to make myself leave. Not because I don't trust Ross, the dinner shift chef, who works three nights a week for me. Because when I was near the windows earlier, I noticed lights still on in the bakery, even though she was long closed.

I need to stay away.

So, I busied myself in my office and tried not to be a shadow on the wall in the kitchen. I really do trust Ross. In fact, he's the only one I feel comfortable enough to turn over my grill to a few nights a week. In the beginning, I didn't trust anyone. I worked them all, seven days a week, lunch and dinner. I thrived on it, really, but the guys wouldn't let me burn myself out. We hired Ross after the first year to work three nights a week, giving me the small reprieve they insisted I needed. It does hold merit, though I'll never tell them that.

Twice since he arrived, I casually strolled up to the front of the restaurant under the guise of checking things out. You know, making sure the servers were doing their jobs and the hostess was ready. Things I did *not* need to check on. Our staff is top-notch. Yet, while I was up there, I was able to see the small bakery across the street.

The lights had been on in her kitchen.

For the third time, I move from my office, this time heading for the bar. At least over there, the hostess won't wonder why the hell I'm up front again, and since Walker doesn't work on Monday nights, I won't have to worry about him giving me shit for spying on our neighbor. As I approach the window, I peer through the gap of a beer sign and find the business across the street the same as I left it thirty minutes ago. Lights are on in the kitchen.

I make a rash decision and return to the kitchen. "Hey, you mind if I use a corner of that grill?" I ask Ross as I wash my hands.

"Not at all, boss," he replies, making sure I have enough room to work.

I press two fresh patties and drop them on the grill top, seasoning them with my own special blend. I drop two big handfuls of cut fries into the grease and grab my spatula. As the hamburgers cook, I add four strips of applewood bacon to the grill and grab an avocado. I cut it easily, securing the unused strips in a container and toss it in the fridge.

Once I flip the patties, I prepare the bun. First, it's toasted, then the top half smothered in mayo. Grabbing two slices of aged cheddar, I lay them on the meat to melt, while placing the slivers of avocado on the top bun with the mayo. When the patties are cooked, I place two slices of bacon on top of each and place them on a bun, before adding the top. I have two perfect Strip and Go Naked Burgers.

Don't think about how much you'd like to strip and go naked with a certain woman...

I secure each hamburger with a healthy amount of fries into a Styrofoam container, clean up my mess, and grab my keys. Once my office light is off, I holler, "See you later," to Ross and head out the back door.

The temperature is brisk and bites my cheeks as I make my way to my car and fire it up. Of course she starts right away, growling with horsepower and ready to run. Unfortunately, she's not going to stretch her legs yet. Instead, I drive from the lot and to the street out front, pulling to a stop in front of Sugar Rush.

"What are you doing?" I whisper to no one.

I should pull away and head home, but that's not what I do. Pulling my keys from the ignition, I hop out of my car, two burgers in hand. I consider knocking on the back door, but I noticed it's not lit the best back there and don't want to scare her. With that in mind, I raise my hand and tap my fist on the glass entrance loud enough to catch her attention.

It only takes a second for her to peek around the doorway between the kitchen and front room, a look of question on her beautiful face. I hold up my hand in greeting, and a smile quickly follows. Lyndee is hesitant but makes her way to the front door and releases the lock. "We have to stop meeting like this," she greets, offering me a small grin, her delicate hand holding the handle.

"Yeah, sorry about stopping by unannounced, but I saw the lights and I..." My words trail off, whatever thought I was about to say getting jumbled in my brain. All I see is the way the light reflects off her hair like a halo. Her brown eyes are bright, almost like chocolate embers of fire. And her face, there's a smudge of flour across her cheek and nose I want to wipe off.

With my tongue.

She looks at me expectantly, waiting on me to pull my head out of my ass and finish my sentence. This is when I should definitely walk away. My mind is all over the damn place, just like it's been since I found out who was opening this place one week ago today. Hand her the food and go. It's the only way to save my sanity.

But that's not what happens. Words I shouldn't say come out of my mouth.

"I brought dinner. May I come in?"

Lyndee

I step aside, allowing Jasper to slip by me. I catch a hint of his sandalwood scent mixed with grease and cheese, which surprisingly, I seem to like. Of course, the smell could also be coming from the Styrofoam containers in his hand, and considering the way my stomach responds noisily, I'd say it likes the aroma too.

Jasper doesn't call me on my blatant hunger, fortunately, just moves to the kitchen. "Where's Dustin?"

"He went home. Today was a long day for him, and he was tired."

"I made him a burger," he adds, setting the two containers down on the end of the large island and pushing one in my direction.

"He was cooking a frozen pizza when I left to come back here," I tell him, not reaching for the food, even though it smells like absolute heaven.

Jasper's wide eyes meet mine. "Frozen pizza?" he shudders, making a big display of his disgust.

I roll my eyes and pop open the lid of the container in front of me. "We can't all be world-class chefs," I tease, my mouth watering as I gaze at the fresh fries and gooey cheeseburger.

Jasper snorts. "Uhh, we graduated from the same school, Lyn."

I wave him off, taking a fry and popping it into my mouth. "Yes, but we had our eyes set out on two different types of cooking. I'm a baker, and all that other stuff was just fluff. Your fries are amazing," I state, sliding a second between my lips.

"We cut them ourselves and it's my own blend of seasonings," he confirms, leaning a hip against the island, the smallest smile playing on his lips as he watches me eat. Usually, I'd be embarrassed to be the focus of someone's scrutiny like this, but I know Jasper. He likes to watch you eat. He wants to witness every expression, every moment someone enjoys his food. And he's just cocky enough to know they'll enjoy it. Always has been, always will be.

"You don't make your own pizzas?" he asks, clearly unable to get past the quick Tombstone meal.

I shrug. "I've made homemade before, but frozen wins hands down when you're under a time crunch."

Jasper stares at me as I eat another fry. "I suppose I can understand that, but nothing beats homemade anything."

"You're right," I agree, picking up the burger and examining the toppings. "Is that avocado?"

"It is. Try it before you knock it," he instructs, watching me intently as I bring the burger to my mouth.

"I've had avocado before," I retort with a clip to my tongue. "I was just looking at what was on here."

He just smirks, as if he's enjoying getting me all riled up. "Avocado, bacon, and mayo. Oh, and cheddar cheese."

My mouth waters, but to be honest, it would probably do that without knowing what was on the burger. I'm so darn hungry, chastising myself for not hanging around and stealing a slice or two of Dustin's pizza. I take a tentative bite, enjoying the hell out of the savory explosion of bacon mixed with mayonnaise. "Wow, this is delicious," I mumble with a mouth full.

The smile he gives me spreads slow across his lips, my body reacting immediately. Heat floods my core, a sharp tingle between my legs, like I was shot with Cupid's lust-tipped arrow. "Isn't it?"

I point to the other container, and as soon as I can get words out past the mangled meat and bun in my mouth, ask, "Aren't you going to eat?"

Jasper snorts, shoving his hands in the pockets of his pants. "Classy lady," he mocks, causing me to roll my eyes. "And I brought this for Dustin."

Once I swallow, I reply, "He's already eaten. You might as well have it, so it doesn't go to waste."

He seems a little uncertain, and maybe even a touch uncomfortable. "Oh, I wasn't going to stay. Just dropping off food."

"Well, you don't have to stay, I guess. You can take it with you, but something this good shouldn't be wasted," I state, wishing my heart wouldn't beat a little harder at the thought of him leaving.

"I don't have to go," he replies quickly, reaching for the food container and opening the lid. His mouth opens but doesn't say anything. Instead, Jasper shovels a handful of fries into his mouth, as if they could keep him from saying whatever was on the tip of his tongue.

We stand in silence, both eating our food and stealing glances of the other without getting caught. Of course, every time I look his way out of the corner of my eye, he busts me, and I can feel his occasional gaze on me like a caress.

"So, tell me what you've been up to since college," I finally say when my burger is almost halfway done.

Jasper clears his throat. "Well, after graduation, I went to Cleveland and worked at a restaurant there. I started as a sous-chef for an abysmal man who barely knew the difference between braising and broiling. On top of that, he smelled like meat, but not the kind he was preparing. It was like he rubbed it in his armpits every morning and forgot to shower."

My face must show how incredibly horrifying his words are, because he laughs when his eyes meet mine.

"True story. I dealt with his incompetence and lack of personal hygiene for a couple of months before I had to do something. Renaldo's had a ton of potential, but the customers just weren't returning the way they should have been. The food was subpar and overpriced. I went to Renaldo one night and told him if he made me head chef, I'd double his profits by the end of the year, or he could fire me. He gave me six months to help turn around his restaurant, and if I did it, he'd rewrite my contract and include profit sharing. It was really a no-brainer for him."

"Cocky," I blurt out, wiping a smear of mayo off my lip.

He just gives me that arrogant grin. The one I know and expect to slide so effortlessly across his face. "You know it."

"And did it work?"

"Three months. He doubled his profits in three months and had reservations booked up almost two months in advance."

"Wow, that's amazing," I reply, proud of a young Jasper to be able to walk into a kitchen and turn it around within such a short amount of time.

He lifts a shoulder. "It was. I only stayed through the end of that year, though."

"You did?" I was surprised by this revelation. If Jasper was offered a new contract, including profit sharing, why on earth would he leave before he was able to take advantage of it?

He nods. "Sure did. Believe it or not, some of the staff didn't like me much. Several tried to overthrow me," he replies with a chuckle.

I try to cover my laugh with a cough, but he doesn't buy it.

"It's okay, you can laugh. Their coup didn't work. I would have stayed, making their lives miserable as long as possible, but I was offered another job just down the street. I helped Renaldo's, and then turned around and worked for his biggest competitor," he states matter-of-factly.

"Really?" I ask, the food I'm chewing suddenly stuck in my throat.

Jasper shrugs. "Sure, why not? Isn't the name of the game to make money, while doing what you love? Otherwise, why else do it? Lamonte's had a great reputation and excellent cuisine. Their head chef was retiring after almost thirty years, and they were willing to pay me what I was worth."

"Wow, good for you," I reply, only finishing about three quarters of my food before my stomach feels like it could explode.

"I'd probably still be there, if not for beers and burgers with my friends one night several years ago. We had always said in college there was no place to eat good burgers, even went as far as considering what we'd do if we ever had our own place. Well, one night, we were sitting around at Walker's house. He was bitching about the bar he was working at, when Numbers mentioned we should just open our own place. It was the first time we actually considered it, not just friends bullshitting, you know? We ended up deciding to check into it, which was the start of our partnership. That was about six years ago," he says, taking another healthy bite of his food. "Are you done?"

"If I eat another bite, I'm going to have to unbutton my pants." The moment the words are out of my mouth, I wish I could pull them back in.

Jasper's eyes flare with desire, the brown of his eyes turning black as they slowly drop down to my waist. He can't see behind my apron, but I can feel his imagination running wild, as if he can physically see my pants unfastening.

When his eyes meet mine, humor mixes with lust. "I could help," he offers easily, his voice low and gravelly. It reminds me of that one time...the time we almost kissed.

Rolling my eyes, I opt to keep this friendly. Mostly because it would be too easy to get sucked into naughty banter with Jasper. With that wicked gleam and devilish smirk, he's what daydreams are made of. The problem is he knows it too.

"No thank you. I don't need assistance."

He tsks. "Too bad. Next time, maybe?" He waggles his eyebrows suggestively to punctuate his offer.

I can't stop the giggle that spills from my throat as I shake my head at his antics.

"So, how about you? What have you been up to for the last ten years?" he asks, finishing off his food in just a few bites.

"Oh, nothing exciting," I reply, referring to the fact he worked at fancy restaurants, probably making more money in a year than I've made in the last five combined.

"I doubt that. We always had different food paths on the horizon, so where did yours lead you?" He's referring to the known fact he was going places after graduation and I was headed home to bake.

"Home, mostly. I worked at a bakery there until it was sold, and the new owner didn't share the same vision for the future. My mom had been gone a little while by then, and Dustin and I were looking for a change."

"Why Stewart Grove?"

"My brother found our condo online. It's handicap accessible and perfect for his needs. Then, during his search of the town, he discovered this place for sale. Dustin's stubborn and like a dog with a bone once he sets his mind to something. He knew I wanted to work in a bakery and convinced me to open my own."

"And how do you feel after your first official day open?" he asks, seeming to be genuinely interested.

"I'm exhausted," I reply with a chuckle. "We did really well today, which surprised me, considering my only advertising is word of mouth and social media. I sold out of a few things early on, letting me know how I need to make adjustments moving forward. Plus, I took three cake orders for this weekend."

He awards me with a sincere smile. When he does that, it makes me weak in the knees and a little breathy. "You're going to be needing to hire more staff before you know it. Maybe even someone who specializes in a certain area, like cake decorating or breads and pastries, so you can focus on what you want. I could put some feelers out for you. I know a lot of people in this town now, a few which are in the industry. I'll make a few calls and—What?"

I shake my head. "You're just as bossy now as you were in school," I reply, hoping he doesn't take it as an insult.

When he barks out a laugh and shrugs, I realize he knows exactly how pushy he can be. "Guilty. I was just offering to help, but if you don't want it," he starts.

"No, I do appreciate it, but I've only been open a day. I don't really know what I'll need yet. It takes time."

He watches me, those dark eyes assessing. "True."

"Besides, I'm not taking too many custom orders right now. I want to focus on selling stock in my case, like pies."

"Ahhh, yes. *Pies.*" There's something in his tone that heckles my nerves.

"Do you have a problem with me selling pies?" I ask, slightly confused on why he'd have an issue. I mean, I own a bakery.

"Oh, no. Not at all," he sings. "I recall your *pies* well."

Then it hits me. "You're still mad about the pecan pie thing?"

"*Thing?* You mean you barely edging by my top class grade with your rendition of a pecan pie?" His eyes flare to life with passion and maybe even a touch of anger.

"My pie won me that grade fair and square, buddy. In fact, I've won awards for that pecan pie," I argue, crossing my arms over my chest and narrowing my eyes.

"Fairs and festivals don't count as winning awards," he argues, stepping forward and slowly making his way to stand before me. When he does that, I have to look way up, reminding me of how tall he is in comparison to my short five-foot-two-inch stance.

I stand tall, refusing to let him affect me in any way. "I'll have you know; my pie was featured in *Foodie News!*"

He snorts. "Like that's a big deal," he replies, even though we both know it is. *Foodie News* is a leader in both print and online food-related news all over the world. That feature was the highlight of my career, thus far.

"You're just jealous because you lost to a little ol' girl and didn't get the top grade. I bet that's been a thorn in your side ever since," I retort, realizing I'm poking the bear with a very big stick.

Fire blazes in his eyes as he glares down at me. Though, it's not a fear-inducing look. In fact, the way my body burns, I'd say it has the exact opposite response. Jasper takes one more step forward until we're practically chest to chest. He leans down just a touch and whispers, "I haven't thought about it since."

I can't stop the snort that erupts from my body like Mount St. Helens. "Clearly," I reply sarcastically, rolling my eyes so dramatically, there's no missing the fact I don't believe him.

His eyes narrow into little slits as he focuses on my...lips.

My lips?

"Do you ever thing about that almost kiss?" he whispers, his words coming out in little pants.

All the time.

"What kiss?" I ask, barely breathing as he inches ever so slowly toward my face, his lips drawing closer and closer with each passing second.

Jasper smirks, clearly not believing my reply for a second. "No? Not at all, like when it's late at night and you're in bed? Or maybe in the shower and all alone?" He lifts his hand and brushes hair off my forehead, his warm touch lingering against my flushed skin.

"No," I croak out, my throat parched and gravelly.

He tsks, the smirk turning into a full-watt smile. It's breathtaking, really. I've never known a smile to be that beautiful, that mesmerizing. He leans down, his full lips dangerously close to my own, and I suck in a deep breath of oxygen.

Is he going to kiss me?

He moves slightly to the right, tucking loose hair from my ponytail behind my ear. His lips barely brush against my cheek, igniting a deep-burning inferno in my gut. Jasper holds my hair, his thumb making contact with my neck and sending shivers of lust bolting through my body. His hot breath tickles the shell of my ear as he whispers, "Liar."

It takes a few seconds before I can clear the sex-infused fog from my brain and consider his word. When it hits me, I jump back, inhaling a greedy breath of air and narrowing my eyes even more. "Am not," I argue lamely, wishing my nipples weren't hard and poking through my top.

Jasper stands up to his full height and gives me a self-satisfying grin. "Whatever you have to tell yourself to sleep at night, sweetheart."

I clear my throat, but before I can form words, Jasper speaks. "Well, it's been great catching up with you, Lyndee," he says, tossing his container in the trash can beside my industrial kitchen island and giving me another smile.

"Whatever," I mumble, tossing my own trash in the bin and following behind as he heads for the front door. I try to catch my bearings as I reach for the lock, hoping he can't see the slight tremble in my hand as I give it a turn. "Thank you for dinner."

He turns around, standing directly in front of me. "You're welcome."

"I'll see you around," I reply quickly, my voice a higher pitch than normal.

He grins. "You definitely will, sweetheart. You definitely will."

And then he's leaving, sliding into his incredibly expensive car and pulling away from the curb.

What the hell was that?

How can I let him affect me like that? After all this time? He still has a way of getting under my skin and making me want to rip off my clothes at the same time. Stupid girl. The last thing you need is to get all doe-eyed over Jasper Kohlmann. He's hot but definitely not my type. I think it's best to remember that. There's no future with a man like that.

Besides a few naughty romps in the sheets?

Exactly. That's all it would ever be, and that's not what I'm looking for. I want a partner. A man who respects my desire to work and understands the commitment it takes to own and operate my own business. Jasper seems like the type of man who, if he ever settles down, would require his wife to stay home, taking care of the kids and joining the PTA.

Besides, it would never work out. We butt heads too much.

Good thing I'm not interested in him like that.

Keep telling yourself that.

Eleven

Jasper

When I can't sleep, I cook, and tonight, I'm wide awake. Sure, I could blame it in part to my insomnia, but I know that's not entirely the reason. I can't stop thinking about Lyndee. About the fire that burned in her eyes, right alongside the lust. About the way her breathing hitched when I got close and the fact she stopped breathing altogether when my lips barely brushed against her cheek.

I drove home hard as a rock and remained that way until I took a shower. It was images of her standing beside me or down on her knees that eventually helped take care of the situation with my cock. Only, it was short-lived. The moment I lay down in bed, it was raring to go once again, as I pictured her beside me, my pillows and sheets absorbing her rich, sugary scent.

I've been in the kitchen for an hour, baking a pie. With Christmas around the corner, I'm working on a few desserts to offer at the restaurant. No, we don't sell a lot of them, most patrons filling up on our delicious hamburgers and fries, but we do sell a few of our desserts. I usually make something that'll keep several days. I change our dessert options often, depending on my mood or the season.

Right now, I have a homemade red velvet cake with cream cheese frosting, topped with a warm fudge drizzle, but I'm suddenly feeling like switching it up to pie.

Chocolate candy cane pie, to be exact.

Once my creation is in the oven, I set the timer and start washing the dishes. When I cook or bake at home, I use everything. I remember my mom always complaining about it when I was younger and wanting to help out. She spent most of the night washing all the dishes than enjoying the fact she didn't have to do much to prepare the meal.

With the dishes drying on the rack and having another ten minutes before the timer goes off, I head for the living room. I consider texting one of my friends—they're used to my random late-night messages—but think better of it. I hate disturbing Walker, now that Mallory and Lizzie live with him, and Isaac sleeps like the dead, rarely waking during my midnight barrages.

Jameson is the one I know will answer. The man sleeps probably as little as I do, though for different reasons. My insomnia keeps me from getting the necessary rest, but for Jameson, it has more to do with his own demons that haunt him.

I fire off a text, even though it's almost one in the morning.

Me: You awake?

The bubbles appear within seconds.

Jameson: Yep. You cooking?

Me: Baking.

Jameson: Normally, I'd say Isaac will be happy, but he may actually be a little disappointed not to go to the bakery. Of course, he could still pop in there without really needing to, right?

Fucker. Why'd I text Jameson?

Me: Who said you guys are getting any of this?

Jameson: Who else do you bake for? Unless you're trying to impress a certain woman across the street?

Me: No

Jameson: No? Keep telling yourself that.

Jameson: Is that why your car was there after you got off work?

I sigh, wishing I would have just kept my phone in the other room.

Me: I took her dinner. She was there late, getting ready for tomorrow.

Jameson: You're such a good guy.

No, I'm really not. Most of the time I fantasized about kissing her.

Jameson: So, how was her first day?

Me: Sold out of a lot of product.

Jameson: Good deal. I hope she's successful. It'll be nice having a bakery in downtown. Plus, she's easy on the eyes. *insert smirk emoji*

Jameson: No comment?

Jameson: Fine, I'll keep talking.

Jameson: I think you really went over there because you like her and refuse to admit it.

Jameson: I mean who wouldn't like her? She's pretty and smart and funny and has the cutest button nose...

Jameson: I bet she doesn't stay single for long.

Jameson: Maybe I'll head over there after work. See if she wants to hang out for a bit. You know...*insert smirk emoji* *insert eggplant emoji*

My fingers are already moving before I can even think better of it.

Me: The hell you will! You can't sleep with her, Tank!

The thought has me seeing red.

Jameson: *insert laughing emoji* *insert laughing emoji* *insert laughing emoji*

Me: I hate you.

Jameson: You don't. You love me.

Me: What do I do? I can't stop thinking about her.

Jameson: How should I know? I'm the one in our group NOT in an actual relationship. I have no advice. Unless you want suggestions for positions in the kitchen to keep your ass from freezing on the stainless steel countertop. Otherwise, you need Walker.

I snort out a laugh just as the sixty seconds to go notification sounds on the oven.

Jameson: I guess my only offering would be if you like her, go for it. Life's too short to settle for midnight baking when you could be enjoying midnight nookie.

Me: Speaking of nookie, no Amie?

Jameson: Not the same. That's casual. Nothing more.

Me: I hear ya. Anyway, I gotta take the pie out of the oven.

Jameson: I expect you to save me a slice tomorrow. You made me talk about feelings like a couple of women. I deserve pie.

Me: Fine. It'll be in my office. Help yourself before Isaac finds its.

Jameson: Deal. Later.

Me: Night

I make my way back to my kitchen, depositing my cell on the counter. I retrieve a mitt from the drawer and pull the baked pie from the top oven. The sweet aroma fills the room, making my mouth water instantly. I'm not big on sweets, at least not like Isaac or even Jameson, but I do enjoy the occasional piece of cake or slice of pie.

Or maybe a chocolate iced Bavarian long john donut.

You know, like the one smeared across my lips last week.

I have to admit, it was damn good, even if I only caught a taste.

Speaking of taste, my mind goes right back to Lyndee and the almost-kiss. First, the one we nearly shared a decade ago, but also the one from last night. The one I wanted to happen more than I wanted my next breath, yet knew it was a bad idea all the same. It's the reason I'm suddenly pitching a tent in my sweatpants at two in the morning.

Ignoring my cock, I finish tidying up the kitchen. As soon as the pie is cooled, I add dollops of fresh whipped cream and a crumbled candy cane as the finishing touches. Placing my creation in a sealed container, I slip it into the fridge, flip off the lights, grab my phone, and head for the stairs.

There are a few different things I can try, if sleep doesn't come yet, though none of them are super effective. Besides cooking, working out in my home gym is my next go-to tactic. I've tried the whole music as background noise like Walker, but it doesn't work for me. I mean, he uses it because he just needs sound to fall asleep and not for insomnia, but during desperate times, I'd try anything. Well, anything but medicine. Melatonin does nothing, and the few sleep aids I've used made me feel worse the next day than if I were just short on sleep.

Slipping my phone onto the charger, I slide off my sweatpants and crawl into bed. I prefer sleeping naked, even during winter months. When I do actually sleep, it's always on the hot side. I can get sweaty, and it's not for the reason I'd prefer getting sweaty in bed.

My mind returns to the one woman I can't stop thinking about, and the cock I had finally convinced had no reason to be hard for is now standing like a soldier at attention and raring to go. "Jesus," I mumble, closing my eyes, only that makes my situation worse.

All I see is her.

How in the hell am I going to get past this? Past her?

You know what you have to do.

Except Lyndee doesn't seem like the type of woman to just get naked with someone to blow off steam.

Unless...

With starting her own business running her ragged, I'm sure dating is at the bottom of her to-do list. She might actually be interested in that no-strings idea that keeps popping into my head. Perhaps it would be just what she needs right now.

Like me.

Smiling, I ignore my rock-hard dick and settle against my pillow. My eyes close almost instantly and my body starts to relax as sleep draws near. I may not have figured out how I'm going to pitch this idea, but I'm feeling confident she'll see the benefits of it.

And believe me, I have plenty of hard *benefits* to offer.

"You know, if you weren't such an asshole to your staff, you might actually get them to stick around longer than a few months."

"Not now," I grumble, without a glance up at Walker. I keep my focus on making five perfect burgers for a late order.

"Mal says you made the girl cry."

Sighing deeply, I glance up and meet his gaze. "She mixed up the regular mayo and the chipotle mayo, Walk," I argue, hating how three plates came back on Tuesday with complaints about the wrong condiment. "That's not acceptable in this restaurant."

Walker crosses his arms and leans against the doorway. "So you made Petra cry?"

I shrug, returning my focus to the five grilled buns and the freshly grilled patties I'm adding to them. "Not my fault she can't handle the kitchen."

"Sounds like it's more about not being able to handle your criticism than the kitchen, actually. You have to stop making our employees cry."

"I don't do it on purpose," I claim, adding fresh fries to the plates and hollering, "Order up!" I can sense Walker's smile as I scrape the grill. "Isaac's on it. He'll find me a day shift assistant chef."

Walker sighs. "He was out of applicants, Jasp. He's relying on social media to spread the word now," he replies. "You're probably going to have to work without one for a bit."

"I've been without for two days already," I gripe, recalling how my day took a crap on Tuesday and I have yet to be able to catch up with Lyndee. "Besides, Patrick is doing a killer job helping out," I add, noting our dishwasher has stepped up and fills in where he can.

Patrick glances over from the dishwasher and gives me a smile.

"I'm sure he is," Walker states, smiling at the young man who, besides my three best friends, may be the only other person I can't scare off. "I'll let you get back to it." Then Walker heads out of the kitchen, probably to return to the bar.

I try not to let it bother me, that I can't seem to hold employees. I don't expect perfection, but I do expect minimal mistakes. Little things like mixing up regular mayonnaise and chipotle mayo—especially when they're not even the same color— or forgetting to label the containers of cheese so we know which one is which. Stupid, idiotic errors that send my blood pressure through the roof like a helium balloon floating to the ceiling when you accidentally let go of the string.

See? I can totally handle the little things.

I work hard until Ross arrives, then happily retreat to my office. It's not every day I willingly turn over the grill for some quiet. I've been at it for three days and am actually quite grateful Ross is working this evening. As much as I love being in the kitchen, not having an assistant these last three days is taxing. It actually reminds me of when we first opened and maintained our business with minimal staff.

Spending the next few hours in my office, I'm able to dig myself out of the paperwork and orders that have accumulated throughout the week. It's only Thursday, and shit still piles up if you don't stay on top of it. I sort the invoices and confirmations and put them into the bin for Isaac, ignoring the way my stomach growls with hunger. Sure, I could slip out of my office and make a quick hamburger, but ever since I talked about pizza with Lyndee on Monday, I've had a crazy hankering for a homemade pie.

It's near seven when there's a tentative knock on my office door. "Come in."

I'm sure it's Isaac.

When I glance up, I'm surprised to see Lyndee peeking through the opening. "Am I interrupting?" she asks hesitantly.

I sit up straight. "No, of course not. Come on in."

She slips into my office, a white plastic bag in her hand. "I'm sorry to bother you when you're working, but I took a chance," she states nervously, wiping her hand against her jeans, "that, uh, maybe, you were looking for dessert. I mean, you can take it home with you...or give it away, if you want. You don't have to eat it."

I'm already smiling. Her sputtering is endearing as hell. I like it.

"Lyndee?" She looks up at me with gorgeous wide eyes. "What'd ya make me?"

She clears her throat and steps forward, setting the white bag down on my desk. "I was experimenting with peppermint for the shop. Since it's close to Christmas, I wanted to offer a few items that feel holiday-ee."

"Holiday-ee?" I ask, grinning like a lunatic and feeling lighter than I have in days.

"Of course," she says, pulling the small white box out of the bag. "There are two different baked goods. A cranberry white chocolate muffin and a peppermint twist scone."

My stomach chooses that moment once again to growl. "Those sound great," I admit, examining the muffin with a critical eye before taking a small bite from the top. My tastebuds explode with the sweet, yet tangy treat I'm sure is going to be a hit. "Very good."

"Thanks." She beams, before pointing over her shoulder. "Well, I should go. Dustin is in the car waiting. We're going to head home and make dinner."

I'm up and out of my seat before I can stop myself. "Wait."

She stops moving and meets my gaze. "What?"

"I'm, uh, getting ready to head home now. I was gonna make a pizza. The homemade kind, not the ones you pull from the freezer," I tease. "Why don't you and Dustin join me?"

She opens her mouth, no doubt to decline, but the words seem to stick to her tongue. I use that to my advantage.

"It wouldn't take too long to make. You could probably be home and in bed by nine," I blurt out, taking a few steps around my desk until I'm standing in front of her.

"I, uh, don't want to impose," she maintains, shaking her head.

"You're not. If anything, you're helping me by ensuring I don't have nearly as many leftovers." I throw in a panty-melting grin, just to seal the deal.

"Pizza, you say?" she asks, her eyes dancing with hope and excitement.

"Margherita."

"Really? I haven't had that in years. Dustin won't eat it though."

"Well, good thing I have some pepperoni too. So what do you say? Will you and your brother let me feed you dinner tonight?" I try not to sound hopeful, but I'll admit, it's hard. I really want her to say yes.

"Okay."

"Okay?"

She nods.

"Great. Let me grab my coat and we can head out. Do you guys want to ride with me?" I ask, shutting down my laptop.

"That's silly, Jasper. You'd have to drive me back here then afterward, and that's not reasonable when you're already home."

I give her a small smile. "I wouldn't mind."

"Still, I can just drive."

"All right," I reply, grabbing my coat and the dessert she brought, and flip off my light switch. "Let's go."

Twelve

Lyndee

I've made a terrible mistake. The moment Jasper opens his front door for Dustin and me, I realize my error. Sure, I thought twice—hell, a million times—about my decision to agree to dinner on my way to his place, but Dustin talked a mile a minute the entire trip, ensuring I barely got a word or thought in edgewise. Now, I'm stepping into the foyer of his gorgeous home and recognizing I should have declined his offer. This place is...wow.

"Come in," he says, stepping aside to allow us entrance. "Let me take your coats."

I slip off my puffer coat and unwrap the scarf around my neck. "Wow, this place is gorgeous," I state as he hangs our coats in the entry closet.

"Thank you. It's a touch on the big side, but I've always been a fan of the Tudor-style architecture. How about I start on the pizzas, and we do a tour later?"

"Sounds good! I'm starving," Dustin replies quickly, following behind Jasper as we head to the kitchen.

And what a kitchen it is.

It's a chef's space, for sure. Gorgeous cabinets, a massive island in the middle of the room, and a double oven I'm totally jealous of. Sure I might have plenty of baking space at work, but at home, I have a standard single unit. Then my sights land on the refrigerator. "Jesus," I mumble, stepping up to the gleaming stainless steel and running my hand down the handle.

"It was a requirement when I remodeled the kitchen. A standard refrigerator wasn't going to work for my needs," he says, stepping up beside me and pulling items from within, including bottles of water. I steal a peek inside the space, smiling by how organized it is. The containers all have labels and dates.

Jasper moves to a massive pantry and grabs what he needs, setting it all on the island behind him. When my brother takes a seat on one of the barstools, I ask, "What can I do to help?"

"Do you want to pick a wine from the fridge?" he asks, washing his hands at the sink.

"Sure," I reply, opening the big appliance, but not finding any wine.

"Oh, I have a wine refrigerator over there," he adds, pointing to a cabinet along the side wall.

It's only upon further inspection that I realize the handle is different. When I pull it open, I'm surprised to find a custom space just for wine. There are several bottles of whites and reds with vintage years older than me.

"There's another cabinet next to it with room temperature reds, if you prefer that," he adds.

Opening the cabinet, I find more bottles of expensive wine, as well as glasses and a variety of openers. I choose a chilled red that will pair well with pizza and use the electric opener to remove the cork. Plus, it's a sweeter red, which my brother likes. Pouring two glasses, I set one down in front of Dustin and take the other around to Jasper. They're in a heated conversation about the Reds and how their lackluster season played out this year.

"Thanks," he says, reaching for the glass and taking a drink. "Aren't you having any?"

"No, I'm driving," I reply, reaching for one of the bottles of water.

Jasper nods and reaches into the bowl to start mixing the dough with his hands. I watch for a few minutes, ignoring the conversation they're having, and just focus on his hands. They're large and press the ingredients together so easily, so effortlessly it's hypnotizing. All I can picture is those hands kneading *other* things...

"Lyndee?"

"Huh?" I ask, glancing up into Jasper's chocolate orbs. His dance with delight, as if he knows what I was thinking about.

"I was just asking if you'd cut the tomatoes for me."

I make a noise of confirmation before moving to the sink and washing my hands. I retrieve a large knife from the block on the island and find a bamboo cutting board in the cabinet below it. Carefully, I slice into the tomatoes. "Wow, these knives are amazing," I state when there's a lull in their conversation.

"I custom ordered these knives from Japan. They're designed specifically for my hand. Expensive, but so very worth it. Once you use one of those babies, you'll never buy another Target knife again," he says, holding up his dough-covered hands.

Those big, capable hands...

"You know, if you slice the tomato this way, you'll have minimal spilling of the seeds," he says, reaching over and demonstrating how I should properly cut the tomatoes.

"But won't I still end up with tomato slices by doing it this way?" I ask, my eyebrows arched in confusion. I realize there are different methods for cutting tomatoes, but this is the way we were taught in school for slim, perfect slices. I mean...it's a tomato.

"Yes, but this way is better," he replies boastfully.

"Your way?"

He gives me another of his full-wattage grins. "Exactly."

Sighing, I shake my head and continue cutting the tomatoes my way, ignoring the look of exasperation he throws me. Instead, I cut the vine-ripe tomatoes into thin slices and set them aside, while Jasper rolls the dough out into two perfect circles.

"Will you grab the bowl of marinara?" he asks, nodding toward the glass bowl set between us.

"Is this homemade?" I ask, opening the lid and taking a whiff.

"It is. I've never used canned or jarred. That would be a travesty."

"Lyn used jarred sauce the last time we made homemade pizza," my traitor brother announces.

Jasper's eyes widen comically. "How is this even possible? You went to culinary school."

I shrug, sticking my fingertip into the tomato sauce and tasting. "I don't know. I'm busy, but my preferred field was baking. I don't really care about the cooking side, unless it's making my own jam," I reply, taking a second taste of the tangy sauce. Normally, I wouldn't dare be licking my finger and sticking it back into whatever I'm making, but since this isn't for the public, I decide to hell with it. Plus, there's the prospect of annoying Jasper, which is always a plus. "This is good."

He's watching me, but if it bugs him that I'm swiping bites with my finger, he never complains. Instead, he seems to just observe me, the faintest hint of a smile on his lips. "Thank you," he replies with a quick clearing of his throat. "I made a sweet onion jam for one of my burger creations."

I lean forward, my hip resting against the island. "Really? Tell me more," I inquire as he scoops sauce onto the crust.

Dustin groans. "Are you two gonna talk food now? I'm leaving," he grumbles, spinning on his stool like he's going to leave.

"Fine, we won't geek out on food talk," Jasper says, finishing up his pepperoni pizza with freshly grated mozzarella cheese. "But I will finish by saying, my onion jam would be delicious on some fresh soda bread or something."

My eyes sparkle with possibilities. "Oh, I bet that would be fantastic. Maybe I'll make a few loaves this weekend and you and the guys could try it out."

"Or you could join us Sunday night here and bring it. My friends and I always get together before Christmas and do a dinner, hang out, you know?" He says the words casually, his eyes cast down at the pizza he's prepping.

"Oh," I stammer, unsure of what to say. My eyes glance up to my brother, who's just smiling and watching.

Jasper finally glances up and meets my gaze. "No pressure. We don't do gifts or anything. Well, except for Lizard. We'll get her stuff, but otherwise, we just hang out and eat." He looks across the counter to my brother. "You're welcome to come too."

I look down at the cut tomatoes. "I don't want to impose if you and your friends just do your own thing," I insist.

He sets the pepperoni pizza aside and begins constructing the margherita one. "You're not. The others are bringing their girlfriends," he replies before realizing what he said. "I'm not saying you're my...you know."

"Right, right," I quickly claim. "That would be…yeah. No," I stammer with an awkward chuckle.

"Right," Jasper replies, a little too quickly. I mean, it's not like we're actually dating, and I did just insist that would be bad, but hearing him confirm it deflates that miniscule bubble of excitement that formed in my chest. "Just a few friends hanging out. If you and Dustin aren't doing anything, you're welcome to come by."

I look over at my brother again, the eagerness in his eyes shining brightly. If it weren't an open invitation to the both of us, I'd decline, but I can't dismiss the excitement on my brother's face. I want him to make friends, even if that person is Jasper. Sure, I might think he's part devil, but he's been nothing but cordial and accommodating to my brother. In fact, they seem to get along great when they talk. Even the other guys have been friendly and open with Dustin, which is probably why I find myself replying, "That sounds nice."

Jasper smiles. It's such a pretty smile, and if I'm not careful, I'll end up swooning over that grin in a completely inappropriate way. "Great. I'm making prime rib, creamy ranch potatoes, and roasted asparagus."

"What can we bring?" I ask as he finishes up the second pizza and places it the oven behind us.

"The bread is fine. This Saturday's special is the burger requiring the jam, so I'll make extra to bring home," he says, closing the oven and turning back to me.

"I'll bring some desserts too," I insist, grabbing my bottle of water and taking a drink. If I'm going to subject myself to Jasper on a Sunday night, the occasion calls for some sweets. But then again, he's not too bad tonight.

If you don't count the tomato incident.

Jasper and Dustin dive right into more baseball talk, and before we know it, the oven timer is sounding. The aroma of freshly cooked pizza fills the air, causing my whole mouth to water in anticipation. I will admit—but only to myself—the real deal smells much better than the frozen ones we've been cooking at home.

"I know everyone recommends bamboo or silicone trivets, but I've discovered Enamel-covered cast iron ones actually work better at protecting the pan coating and what's beneath it," Jasper states, pulling two trivets from a drawer and placing them on the counter. "You should check them out."

"I use cooling racks."

"At home?"

Straightening up, I narrow my eyes a little. "No. I use hotpot holders. They're just easier."

He tsks.

Before he can argue why his line of thinking is right and mine is wrong, I grab the pizza cutter on the counter and start slicing. He doesn't say a word, but I can feel his eyes on me, watching and probably grading my performance. I make sure to leave each triangle a different size, something I'd never do at home, but since I enjoy watching the veins in his temple pop out, the ugly inconsistent pieces leave me feeling gleeful.

"You did that on purpose," he mutters, plating two slices of pepperoni and pushing them across the counter to my brother, who dives right in.

I shrug and give him a satisfied smirk. "Maybe."

He blows out an exasperated breath and plates a slice for each of us. "Come on, troublemaker. Let's get you fed so you can get home to sleep. I expect a white chocolate and cranberry muffin just for me in the morning."

I check the clock for the umpteenth time, then chastise myself for doing it. Again.

Why am I constantly looking to see what time it is?

Maybe it's because you really thought Jasper would come by this morning for the muffin.

Then I just get mad at myself all over again, hoping he'll actually come by this morning, but it's not looking too good, considering it's almost ten. Jasper's usually at the restaurant way before now, which means he's probably prepping for lunch and not giving me or the muffin a second thought.

I wish someone would consider my muffin...

Wait.

What?

Where did that thought come from?

Maybe it's the fact I haven't dated in a really long time, not that you have to date to have sex. It's just never been my thing. I've always found value in relationships. Getting to know and eventually trusting someone with your body and your heart. Those butterflies in your belly and the little touches and glances that make your heartbeat kick up with excitement.

I miss dating, but there has been no time for it as of late. Sure, I've considered making time, but that's hard when you're building a business and taking care of your brother.

I'm sure this annoying flutter in my stomach and the anticipation that fills my chest when I think about Jasper is merely because it's been so dang long since I've been on a date. Or had sex for that matter, but we're not going there. And we're definitely not going there with thoughts of Jasper.

Jasper.

And sex.

Jasper and sex.

Sex with Jasper.

I groan out loud just as Daisy pops her head around the doorway. "Hey, Lyn. Someone's here for you," she states with a quick smile before disappearing back up front.

Wiping my hands on my apron, I follow in her wake and stumble to a stop as soon as I push through the swinging doors. Jasper is here. He's standing back, away from the counter, and talking to my brother, and my eyes are drawn to his professional khakis and polo shirt.

"Hey," he says, throwing a wave my way.

Flustered, I start to make my way in his direction, but suddenly stop and turn around. I grab a small white bag and slip one of the white chocolate cranberry muffins I made fresh this morning inside. I'd love to say it was completely on my own, but that would be a lie. I made them specifically with him in mind. Fortunately, I had plenty of cranberries to whip up a few batches of muffins for today.

When I slip back through the doorway, Jasper takes a sip from his coffee cup and catches my gaze. Something softens in those dark chocolate orbs, something that causes a zing to rush through my veins.

"Here," I rush out, practically thrusting the bag into his hand. *Why am I acting so weird?*

"Is this what I think it is?" he asks, sparkling eyes searching the contents of the little bag.

"Maybe," I reply, finding myself grinning.

Jasper takes a sip of his hot coffee. "Well, I don't have much time. I'm still short an assistant chef. Thanks for this," he adds, holding up the bag.

"You're welcome. Anytime."

He doesn't move, but neither do I. We stand there, like two idiots, just staring at each other, grinning. How long we stand there, I have no idea, but the bell over the door snaps us both out of the trance we're lost in.

"Well," I start, clearing my throat.

"Yeah, well," he replies quickly, taking another sip of his drink.

"I should," I stammer, pointing my thumb over my shoulder indicating the kitchen.

"Yeah, I should too," he states, finally taking a step toward the entrance. "I'll talk to you soon."

"Okay."

I don't even realize I'm not breathing until he's out the door and pauses before crossing the street. I watch him go, mesmerized by the way he moves, as I suck in greedy gasps of oxygen. He reaches the big wooden front door of Burgers and Brew and hesitates.

Don't turn around. Don't turn around.

My heart stops beating as he turns around and meets my gaze through the window, holding it for several long seconds. Then, with the slightest smile on his gorgeous lips, he slips inside and disappears. It's only then do I feel myself relax.

"Someone has a crush," my brother sings, causing me to jump.

"Oh, hey, Dust. I didn't realize you were right behind me."

He grins. "Obviously, or you wouldn't have been standing there, gawking and drooling."

I make a face, much like a sister does to her little brother. Except, usually not when she's in her thirties. "Shut up, I was not."

He snorts a laugh. "Okay," he argues sarcastically, clearly not believing me. "I'm going to bring up those pies now."

"I'll help," I say, glancing one last time back to where Jasper disappeared.

"I got it. You go ahead and stay here, spy on the neighbor, and pretend like you're not," he teases before turning around, the squeak of his walker wheels mocking me as he goes.

"Stop being stupid, Lyn," I mumble, steeling my spine and prepared to push Jasper right out of my head. I have things to do. Very important things. I have no time for silly fantasies about rich chocolate eyes and a panty-melting grin.

I glance back across the street, picturing exactly how amazing his ass looked in khaki pants.

Or how his shirt molded oh so snuggly to his chest beneath his coat.

And what about those lips? The ones I can picture so vividly, how soft and firm they'd be sliding down my neck.

"Ugh," I groan, retreating to the confines of my kitchen.

Far, far away from the restaurant across the street...

And the sexy man inside.

Jasper

Holy fuck, we are busy.

I'd expect nothing less on a Friday night, but it's not helping when we're a man down. Doug, the assistant chef for the evening shift, called off sick, and Ross is out of town visiting his daughter and son-in-law, so I can't even call him in to help. We still haven't hired a lunch shift assistant, so I couldn't ask that person to stay. Mark is here doing what he can to man the prep station and the fryers, but it's a struggle. It probably doesn't help I'm barking at him every two seconds, but I can't seem to help it.

I'm flustered.

I'm frustrated.

And dammit, I'm exhausted.

Yet, I won't complain. This is what I signed up for. Busting my ass in this kitchen is what I do, and I'll continue to do so, making sure every order is right before it goes out.

"We're getting backed up out there," Isaac says, blowing through the doorway and annoying everyone like a bad rash.

"We're doing the best we fucking can!" I holler, adding to the tension already fog-thick in the kitchen.

"I know, I know. How can I help?" he asks, approaching, but also not getting too close.

"Grab those fries before they burn and add some salt. Divide the batch between these three plates and get them out to the damn table," I bark without removing my concentration from my grill.

"Got it," he mumbles nervously, stopping only long enough to wash his hands before jumping in to help.

"Gotta move quicker," I mumble, sliding the specialty burgers onto the awaiting toasted buns and pushing the plates closer to him for fries.

"Get off my ass, man. I don't usually do this. Besides, it's not like you allow any of us in here to help anyway. Maybe if you did, we'd be able to jump in and help when needed without getting our asses chewed for not knowing what to do," Isaac retorts, finishing up the plates and yelling, "Order up!"

The shitty part is I know he's right. I've never allowed them to really work in my kitchen. If they can't do it, it's not for lack of asking or trying. It's because I've always insisted they get out and pushed them away. This is *my* kitchen, and I'm damn territorial. Yeah, Isaac may be correct in his angry outburst, but I refuse to admit it.

Not happening.

Just then Jameson slaps through the doors, the familiar scowl on his face. "There's a line to the door," he declares, glancing around at the chaos surrounding me.

"Yes, I know. We're doing the best we can, but it's hard to keep up when you're short-staffed," I argue, throwing six more patties on the grill with aggression.

"Okay, geez, settle down," he replies, throwing both of his hands up in surrender.

"It's a Friday night, Jame, and we're busy as fuck. I'm short an assistant, which is why I'm relying on Numbers and trying not to yell at him for not knowing the salt to fries ratio. Shit, we're producing food, man. That's all I can say."

He scratches his scruffy jaw and glances between Numbers and me. "Don't say shit and food in the same sentence. Okay, I have an idea. Be right back." Then, he's gone.

I huff a deep breath and return my focus to the task at hand, trying to ignore the way Isaac whistles a little tune. Is he doing that just to annoy the hell out of me? Well, it's working, especially since he's whistling "Don't Go Away Mad," and no doubt, it's meaning is directed at me.

Fucker.

Just as I'm about to lay into him for ruining Mötley Crüe for me for the rest of my life, the kitchen door flies open once again. I assume it's one of the servers coming in to collect completed plates or submit more orders, but I realize quickly that's not the case. The hairs on the back of my neck stand up, and I swear I can feel her presence without even glancing up from the grill.

"What are you doing here?" Numbers asks, the happiness evident in his voice.

The water turns on as she replies, "Jameson just said you guys needed help, so I'm helping."

I turn, my eyes drawn to the curve of her ass in a pair of flour-speckled leggings. I'm pretty sure I can actually see a white handprint on the side of her thigh. My cock gives an appreciative little twitch in my pants.

I strain to hear as Isaac goes over and gives her a rundown. Something he says makes her laugh, a sound that both settles the storm raging inside of me, but also burns my gut with jealousy.

Jealousy.

When did I become this man?

The day Lyndee Gibson walked back into my life.

She steps up beside me and gives me a hesitant smile. "Hi."

"What are you doing?" It comes out much gruffer than I mean.

Reaching for a fresh bowl of cut potatoes, she dumps them into the basket and drops it into the grease. "Jameson said you guys needed help. So I'm helping."

"I don't need your help." I cringe at my automatic response.

She shrugs and glances around. "I'm sure you'd manage fine, but it's busy out there and he said you're short an assistant chef. It's been a while since I've worked in this type of kitchen, but I can handle it," she replies, lifting her chin ever so slightly and meeting my intense gaze.

I flip my patties and spread more seasoning before moving on to the ones ready to come off. I don't ignore her—there's no way in hell I can, especially when she smells all sweet and delicious—and it takes all my focus to keep my eyes where they belong.

On my grill.

"You're also in charge of grilling the buns there," I state, pointing my spatula toward the device that toasts the buns. "Put them in the top and press down the lever, like a toaster you'd have at home. The buns will come out the bottom on the tray."

She doesn't reply, just does as she's told. Lyndee moves around easily.

"Do you have a ratio?"

I stop. My wide eyes turn to look at her as she dumps the basket of fries and reaches for the seasoning bottle. "What?"

Lyndee shrugs. "Well, I remember how crazy you were in school about making sure there was the right amount of seasoning on whatever you were making, so I figured you had some weird system for seasoning your fries."

I swear, I just fell in love with her.

"Uh, yeah," I answer, wiping my hands on my apron and reaching for the bottle. "Like this." I demonstrate my perfected technique for spreading seasoning across the hot fries. It requires you to move and shake in two long passes, instead of just haphazardly throwing the flavoring and leaving big globs.

I see the corner of her lip curl upward. "I can handle that," she replies, reaching for the shaker in my hand. Our fingers touch and electricity shoots up my arm.

"No doubt you can," I mumble, stepping back and severing contact.

"You just stay on your side of the kitchen, you hear me, chef?" she asks, a hint of laughter in her voice. "I don't need you coming over here and messing up my system. I got this," she declares, holding up her hand dramatically in my direction in the universal stop sign gesture.

As a grin spreads across my mouth, I turn to face my grill, the tightness in my chest finally starting to ebb. Even though we're busier than hell, I relax and let Lyndee help. It may look like nothing to everyone else, but to me, this is everything. An olive branch has been extended; one I've grabbed on to with both hands.

I've never been so grateful.

I keep stealing glances. She's leaning against the counter and chatting with Katelyn, the high schooler who works a few evenings a week as a dishwasher on the nights she doesn't have cheerleading. I have no idea what they've been talking about for the last twenty minutes or so, but there's been a few giggles and a lot of smiles. Considering Katelyn already put away the final dishes, it's not like I can get mad at her for talking on the job. Technically, she's done.

A few minutes later, I head for the lights, ready to shut down the kitchen. "You ready, Katelyn?"

"Yep! All done." Her reply is upbeat, as is her bouncy walk as she moves to the doorway. "It was nice to meet you, Lyndee. I'll stop by the bakery soon."

"Good night, Katelyn. Drive safely," Lyndee responds with a warm smile.

I glance her way and hold up a finger. "I'm going to walk her to her car. Stay here." If she's upset by my gruff demand, she doesn't show it, just gives me a small grin and nod.

It only takes me a few minutes to make sure Katelyn gets off okay before I'm returning to the kitchen. The sounds of Jameson playing guitar filters down the hallway, making me smile. That man is crazy-talented, and I love to listen to him play.

When I reach the kitchen, I find Lyndee slowly walking along the back wall, taking in the storage shelving system. She stands in the shadows, the one remaining strip of light barely reaching her slender frame. "These are impressive," she says without turning around, clearly hearing me enter the room.

With my hands stuffed in my pockets, I make my way to where she stands. "We spared no expense when it came to the kitchen but had to cut costs elsewhere. The original storage units were cheaply made, even though they still cost a pretty penny. After we had our first profitable year, I asked for replacements. I knew these would be expensive, but they are so worth it. We've not had one issue with sagging under the weight, and they're made of steel. Best upgrade we've made so far," I tell her, watching her profile as she takes it all in.

"Someday, maybe I'll have shelves like these too," she replies longingly.

I take a step closer, eager to catch her sweet scent, but all I smell is grease and meat. It actually makes me smile, because now she smells like me. Like my kitchen. My business. It makes me want to kiss her.

Clearing my throat, I make sure my hands are still shoved in my pockets to keep from reaching out. "What brought you in to Burgers and Brew tonight?"

She shrugs her shoulders and moves away, finishing up her trip around the kitchen. "Dustin had gone home already. He was super tired from the day and wanted to rest, so I said I'd bring home dinner after I finished up at the bakery."

My heartbeat kicks up a few notches as guilt sweeps in. "That was hours ago," I state, noticing it's already nearing eleven.

"It's okay. Jameson ran a sandwich to him earlier," she says. "When I was out by the entrance, preparing to place an order with your hostess, Jameson came out and saw me. We were chatting for a few minutes before he left me to order. A few minutes later he came back and asked if I could help out in the kitchen. He promised to check on Dustin and make sure he had food, so I agreed to help you."

I'm not sure which I'm annoyed at more: the fact he was, again, all chummy with Lyndee, or the fact he asked her to help when it wasn't his call to make.

We finally make our way back to the doorway. "I think Jameson put my coat somewhere," she states, glancing around.

"I bet I know," I reply, heading to my office. As I go to get my own coat off the hook behind my door, I find a much smaller, feminine one hanging on top of it. I grab it, the familiar scent of sugar and cinnamon wraps around me like a warm blanket. When I bring it to my nose and inhale like some creepy pervert, my cock notices and springs to life.

Returning to the main kitchen, I hand her the coat and watch as she slips it on. Realization sets in. She's about to leave, and I don't want that to happen. I want to spend more time with her. "Do you want to come over to the bar with me? Jameson is playing, and he's pretty good. You can have a drink before I take you home."

She finishes shrugging on the coat and faces me. "You don't have to take me home," she counters, starting to zip the fluffy outerwear closed.

"You're not walking, Lyndee. It's late."

"I only live a short distance, Jasper. I don't need an escort." She lifts her head, meeting my gaze head on. What's crazy is the way my cock stirs to life by her firmness. It's a huge fucking turn-on, even if I want to paddle her ass for being so cavalier with her safety at night.

"Maybe not, but you're getting one," I argue, placing my hand on her back and guiding her through the kitchen, out the back door, and down the hallway. We don't allow just anyone back here. The employee break room, staff restrooms, and bar storage is this way.

We pass the stairs leading to Isaac's office, as well as the spaces for Walker and Jameson, the sound of my friend playing Eric Clapton on his guitar growing louder with each step we take. I open the door that separates the back area from the bar and am greeted with a standing room of patrons, their eyes all cast toward the small stage where Jameson plays.

At the bar, I find Isaac sitting on the stool at the end and Walker pouring a draft beer. Lyndee's attention is automatically pulled in the direction of everyone else's, even after we stop beside Isaac. "Wow," she mumbles to no one in particular.

"He's pretty damn good," Isaac replies, sipping a glass of amber liquid and pulling her attention from where Jameson plays.

"He is. I love this song," she adds, a soft smile playing at the corners of her lips.

And I love watching her. I find myself mesmerized by her eyes and the way they widen ever so slightly when she's excited. The way she nibbles on her lips when she's concentrating. The way her cheeks flush the most gorgeous shade of pink when she's nervous. And the way her mouth looks ripe for kissing under any light.

"What can I get you?" Walker asks, his eyes flicking between myself and the woman beside me.

"Just a Coke, please," Lyndee replies with a flash grin before returning her gaze to Jameson.

"I'll just have a water." Walker gives me a questioning look before grabbing two glasses, filling one with pop and the other with ice water. He pops a straw in each and slides them across the bar.

We listen to two more songs, and as much as I try to ignore the way her slender body brushes against mine as she sways to the music, it's hard.

As am I.

Lyndee yawns for the fifth time in a matter of minutes, which has me sliding my half-empty glass toward the edge of the bar and reaching into my coat pocket for my keys. "We should get you home. You're about to fall asleep standing up."

She doesn't argue, just places her glass down on the counter and turns to face Numbers. "It was nice to see you again," she says politely.

"Hey, thanks for helping out tonight. I want to pay you for your time," he says, reaching for an envelope in his dress shirt pocket, but Lyndee is already holding up her hands in protest.

"No, absolutely not. I was helping friends."

He hesitates, clearly not happy with her not accepting the cash in the envelope.

She reaches over and places a hand on his forearm. Jealousy gurgles in my stomach like bad sushi. "Please. I was happy to help."

Numbers slips the envelope back into his pocket and smiles. "Anytime you need help across the street, just holler."

Now she grins, a breathtaking smile that transforms her already gorgeous face into something so stunning, an ocean sunset would be envious. "I will."

While Lyndee steps away, I slap him on the back, a little harder than I probably should. "I'm running her home. Be back later."

His smirk is all-knowing. "Jameson and I will help close. Don't worry about it. Take the night and...relax."

I don't acknowledge his comment or the teasing innuendo behind it. Instead, I guide Lyndee toward the way we came. As I push out the back door, I click the fob in my pocket, starting my car. The air is chilled and crisp and feels good against my warm skin. Maybe it'll help calm the raging desire I seem to be carrying around like a backpack whenever she's near.

"I can walk, Jasper, really," she counters, her gait hesitant as we approach my ride.

"Don't argue with me," I state, unlocking the doors and opening the passenger one. "Please just get in the car."

She sighs and gives me an incredulous look. "Fine, but only because you have heated seats."

I chuckle as she slides down into the front seat and runs her hand over the buttery soft leather. I watch as she leans her head back, resting against the headrest, and closes her eyes. There's the faintest smile on her lips. I want to kiss them more than I want my next breath.

I'm in big trouble.

Lyndee

A girl could get used to this.

The ride is too short, and before I know it, we're pulling into my driveway and I have to get out. But I don't want to. The seats are the most comfortable seats in the world, conforming perfectly to my butt. And the heat? I've never actually sat on heated seats before, and I'm pretty sure I'll never be happy with the regular old cloth seats in my Malibu again.

"Thanks for the ride," I say.

"You're welcome. I'm glad you're home safe and sound."

I can't help but roll my eyes. "I would have been fine walking."

Jasper shrugs. "Maybe. Now we don't have to worry about it."

I start to reach for the handle, but something gives me pause. "Do you want to come in for a drink?"

Even in the darkness of his car, I can see the surprise on his face. "Oh," he replies, seeming a bit confused, which tells me one thing.

He's trying to figure out how to let me down easy.

"Never mind," I blurt out quickly with an awkward chuckle, reaching again for the door handle. "It's late. I'm sure you're busy."

Yeah, busy trying to come up with a getaway excuse.

I practically throw myself out of the car, only to be stopped by the still-fastened seat belt. A whoosh of air leaves my lungs in a very clumsy fashion as it tries to hold me against my will inside this fancy Mercedes. Could this get any more humiliating? Rejected by the owner and the car itself.

"Let me help you." Jasper suddenly appears at my door, crouching down and reaching for the buckle release. I can feel the warmth of his imposing body as he reaches across my lap and presses the small button. He meets my gaze as I feel the restriction of the belt relax, but for some reason, I still can't breathe. It's almost worse now, staring into his deep brown eyes. They practically swallow me whole with their power and need.

Maybe I'd be better off taking my chances with the seat belt.

I stand up, barely feeling the cool air around me. The night is silent as he shuts the passenger door and escorts me toward my condo. "What are you doing?" I ask, realizing for the first time that his car is off.

Jasper stops, a look of uncertainty flashes across his features. "Well, you invited me in. If you'd rather not now, that's fine," he says, taking a step back and dropping his hand.

"No!" I insist, reaching for his coat. I don't know why I grip it in my hand, to keep him from leaving, maybe?

His leisurely smile turns a bit too cocky for my liking, and I can't help but roll my eyes again. "Then I'd love to join you inside for a drink."

Something in the way he says *inside* sounds way too dirty and way too good.

I quickly unlock the front door and usher him inside. We're both quiet as to not wake up my brother, even though I know my brother could sleep through a freight train running through his bedroom. Dustin's always had this uncanny ability to sleep through anything.

"Throw your coat on the chair, if you'd like," I whisper, toeing off my sneakers and tossing my own coat over the arm of the couch. Four in the morning comes too early to worry about hanging it up in the closet.

Jasper does and kicks off his own shoes before following me into the kitchen. Our condo is fairly open, with wide doorframes and plenty of moving space, but for some reason, having Jasper in my kitchen makes it feel small. He's close, hands shoved in his pockets, as he looks around at the space.

"What would you like to drink? I have water, orange juice, Dr. Pepper, and some milk that might be questionable on the date. Oh, and chamomile tea," I say, glancing in the refrigerator.

"What are you having?"

"Tea. I love warm tea before bed."

His eyebrows arch upward, and another smirk spreads across his lips. I can tell he took that whole *bed* comment the wrong way. It's in the way his eyes dance with something naughty. I feel a fierce blush creep up my neck, and I try to hide it by sticking my face back in the fridge.

I hate that he has this schoolgirl crush effect on me.

I shut the door a little too hard, causing the condiments in the door to rattle. "I just mean it helps me relax after a long day," I add, crossing my arms over my chest.

Jasper leans a hip against the counter, mimicking the way I hold my arms. "I prefer *other* activities at bedtime to help me relax." He wiggles his eyebrows suggestively just to punctuate his point.

And now my blush feels like someone lit my face on fire.

"Umm," I stammer, clearly flustered. I reach for the tea kettle and notice the slight shake of my hand. I don't know if it's the embarrassment or the fact I can't stop picturing Jasper doing *other* things, but I'm completely out of sorts right now. Maybe it's best if I just offer an excuse to end the evening, run to my room, and come out in the year 2055. Surely I'll have forgotten all about this moment by then, right?

"Tea would be great, thanks. I actually prefer coffee, but I don't see a pot on your counter," he says, glancing around.

"Oh, uh, yeah," I stutter, awkwardly laughing. "I don't have one. I can't drink that stuff at night, or I'd never go to sleep," I add, turning on the stove and filling the kettle.

"It doesn't bother me," he informs, taking a seat at the small table in the corner.

"You drink it at night?"

Jasper shrugs. "I have insomnia, so it doesn't really matter. I don't sleep whether I drink coffee or not."

Pulling two mugs from the cabinet, I place a teabag in each and pop a hip against the counter. "Insomnia? What's that like?"

Jasper seems to contemplate my question, gently leaning back in the chair. "Well, it started in college. It was like overnight I went from a solid eight hours of sleep to like four. At first, I just thought it was because I was in college, drinking like a typical twenty-year-old student and occasionally smoking pot in someone's dorm.

"But then I was done with school and working full time. My stress level was off the charts, so that didn't help. I went to a doctor, who prescribed a sleep aid. All that did was make me groggy and grumpy."

I can't stop the snort.

Jasper glances up and grins. "Fine, *more* grumpy than normal. Anyway, over the years, I learned to live with it. I come up with some of my best recipes after midnight."

The whistle sounds, so I turn to fill our cups, letting the tea steep for a few minutes. "Well, good news for you. Chamomile tea is supposed to be a great sleep aid. I bet, one cup of this, and you'll be sound asleep in no time," I tell him, carrying the cup over to where he sits.

"I guess that's okay. You know, since the thing I do to help me sleep hasn't been thrown on the table yet." His eyes are playful as they meet mine. "Unless you want me to throw it on the table." Jasper waggles his eyebrows suggestively.

I burst out laughing, causing my tea to slosh over the rim of my cup and burn my hand. Quickly, I place it on the table and reach for a napkin. "Ouch."

"Are you okay?" he asks, jumping up and grabbing the hand towel from the counter.

"I'm fine," I insist, pulling my hand back as he reaches for it.

"You burned your hand."

I have no choice but to follow as he takes my hand and pulls me toward the sink. Jasper turns on the cold faucet and moves it under the running water. It's uncomfortable, but not horrible. It's not even really a bad burn. I've had worse, usually grazing a knuckle or a fingertip against a rack in the oven.

"Hold still."

"I'm...fine. It's just a little burn. Happens all the time," I insist, giving my hand one more tug. But Jasper's Herculean strength is no match for my slight physique. He carefully holds my hand under the cold water for a full minute before he gently pulls it back.

Jasper examines my hand, taking in the slight pink coloring on my thumb and index finger. Those don't hurt. What does sting a little is the tender skin between them. It's a touch redder, the burn more sensitive. He runs his thumb over the angry flesh. "You should put something on this." He continues to hold my hand, his fingers soothing the burned skin.

My heart hitches in my chest. "I have some ointment in the bathroom."

"I'll get it," he quickly states, releasing his hold on me and heading for the short hallway. I should go with him, to assist him in finding the burn ointment, but I'm so stunned by the tenderness he displayed, I can't seem to force my feet to catch up. "Here." Jasper returns just a few seconds later with the small jar of ointment.

I reach for the container, but he shakes his head.

I watch in wild fascination as Jasper gently grasps my wrist and brings my hand to his mouth. He softly blows on the burn, making sure it's dry. Why he's not using the hand towel is beyond me, but I'm not about to complain. His warm breath is intoxicating, his touch mesmerizing, and I find myself not wanting it to end.

Once he's certain the flesh is dry, Jasper reaches for the jar of cream and spreads a generous amount on the reddened area. His steady fingers are gentle as he makes sure to apply the medicine to all affected areas, his eyes concentrating on the task at hand. I know this because I'm watching him. My eyes are fixed on him, taking in the way his dark eyes study my skin and makes sure to spread an even coat. Even when he's doing something as mundane as applying ointment to a burn, he's simply stunning.

He glances up, meeting my gaze. There's a moment where time stops. Where the sounds of us breathing together in such a close space makes everything else just fade away. Where the burn doesn't hurt and all I can feel is his hand wrapped around mine, softly caressing my skin. Where all I see is deep chocolate eyes and the slight stubble on his jaw from the day.

I bet that would burn against my cheek...

And *other* places...

It's as if he knows exactly where my mind wandered. I see the desire pooling in his eyes, followed by hints of resignation, as if he knows he can't fight whatever happens next.

Jasper takes a step forward, our bodies a whisper away, and his gaze drops to my lips. A hushed gasp spills from mine as I inhale, anticipation and excitement coursing through my veins.

He's going to kiss me. I can feel it.

Our eyes remain locked as his mouth slowly moves toward mine. My eyelids flutter closed just as his lips press firmly against mine. This isn't a sweet kiss. Not the kind one would expect for a first kiss. There's something so...possessive about the way he plies my mouth open with his tongue and takes what he wants. All I can do is hang on and enjoy the ride.

I press my body against his, reveling in the head-to-toe hardness, the slight discomfort of my hand a distant memory. All I can think about—all I can feel—is him.

His tongue dances with mine, his expert lips taking me for a ride to Ecstasy Land. The hand not holding my own comes up and cradles my jaw, his thumb stroking my neck and sending shock waves of lust through my extremities. We rock together. I'm not sure who moves first, but I can feel the very hard, very large length of him pressing against my stomach. A moan of pleasure fills the space. Did it come from him? Me?

Probably both.

This kiss is everything that's always been missing from kisses in the past. It's passionate, it's powerful, it's all-consuming.

It's infinite.

I'm mere seconds away from climbing up his lean, muscular body as if he were a tree, when a throat clears behind me. I jump back, ripping my lips from Jasper's and trying to put as much distance between us as possible. Unfortunately, all I do is connect with a wall, bumping my head.

Jasper's eyes dance with shock and a touch of humor before he glances toward the doorway. "Hey, Dustin."

"Jasper, hi. Wasn't expecting to find you in the kitchen," he says, grinning widely.

"Lyndee invited me in for tea," Jasper replies, still standing directly in front of me.

"Yeah, tea. We were having tea!" I blurt out, causing two sets of eyes to land on me.

Dustin smirks. "Why are you being so weird?" he asks, moving to the cabinet by the sink. My brother retrieves a glass before heading for the fridge and pouring a glass of orange juice. After taking a sip he adds, "You act like I've never seen you making out with a guy before."

A gasp spills from my lips. "What? I've never...when?" I ask, my voice shaky.

Dustin just laughs. "Right after you moved home after college. You were dating that guy with the bad bowl cut. What was his name? Gary?"

"Jerry," I correct, clearing my throat. "I, uh, didn't realize you saw us."

"Mom did too," he replies with a shrug. "You were on the front porch after a date, and we were coming back from a walk. I remember Mom commenting on him trying to swallow your face."

I can feel my face bursting into flames, and it only gets worse when Jasper starts chuckling. "He tried swallowing her face?"

I recall the kiss my brother is referring to. It was…bad. Jerry was very scholarly, but not so knowledgeable about kissing. It was horribly sloppy with too much tongue, and I remember being a tad grossed out by the kiss. So much so that I declined his request for another date a few days later.

"Oh yeah," Dustin confirms, taking another sip of his juice. "I think he didn't realize his tongue was supposed to go *in* her mouth."

My brother and Jasper laugh hard, at my expense, nonetheless. "Why are we talking about this?"

"Because I just walked in and caught you sucking face with Jasper," my brother points out.

"He was helping me with my burn!" I insist.

He looks at me skeptically. "You burned your tongue?"

I sigh dramatically. "No, my hand." I hold it up to prove my point. "But it's fine. It's only a little burn."

"Good thing Jasper was here to help you," Dustin says, nodding toward the man standing with me. "I mean, at least you know your tonsils are good."

Jasper barks out a laugh and shakes his head. "I should head out. You have to get up early in the morning," he says, finally stepping out of my personal space. The only problem is I miss him there the moment he's gone.

"Thanks for driving me home," I blurt out quickly, following behind as he heads for the front door.

"It was the least I could do. Thanks for helping out in the kitchen." Jasper toes on his shoes, bending over to tie the laces, his ass pointed my way and looking very nice in his khakis. When he stands back up, he adds, "We make a great team."

I feel a ball of something lodge in my throat. We did work well together today, preparing dishes on a busy Friday night. It didn't take me long to figure out his system. It was efficient, much like the man himself. He definitely knows his way around a kitchen.

And his way around your mouth...

"We do," I agree as he slips his coat on and reaches for the doorknob.

"Good night, Dustin. Sorry if we woke you," Jasper says over my shoulder, offering my brother a friendly grin.

"Good to see you again, Jasper, even if you were making out with my sister."

Kill. Me. Now.

But Jasper just takes it in stride, not even appearing the least bit sorry for being caught kissing me. He steps forward, once again invading my personal space, and whispers, "Take care of that burn. Make sure you put more ointment on it again." His eyes are intense and full of desire, something I will forever associate with this man. Just one look, and he turns me into a puddle on the floor.

My throat is so dry, as if I've spent days in the desert without a lick of water. "I will," I finally spit out.

He leans down and brushes a soft kiss across my cheek. "Your tonsils are definitely good," he murmurs, referring to my brother's earlier comment.

And...cue the blush.

Jasper walks out the door, heading for his car, and waves before slipping inside. Once it's started and backing out of the driveway, I close the door, making sure it's locked securely. As I turn around, I startle, coming face-to-face with Dustin.

And he's smiling.

"What?" I ask grumpily.

My brother is leaning against the doorjamb, wearing a big, goofy grin. "Nothing."

I roll my eyes and walk past him, eager to clean up the tea mess so I can go to bed. Not that I'll be doing much sleeping tonight. Not with that kiss still replaying in my mind.

After wiping up the spilled tea with a wet cloth, I toss it in the hamper and flip off the lights, only to find Dustin still standing in the doorway, watching. I can practically see the wheels in his head spinning. "Say it."

"Say what?" he asks, the corner of his lips twitching.

"Whatever it is you want to say. I've been up since three thirty, and I'd really like to go to bed."

"Go," he replies, taking a step back from the doorway.

"Thank you," I mumble, stopping and giving him a kiss on the cheek as I pass. "Good night."

"Night," he practically hums behind me. As I reach my slightly ajar door, he asks, "Hey, Lyn?"

When I turn to look his way, he gets this huge grin on his face and sings, "Jasper and Lyndee, sitting in a tree…"

Jasper

The bell above the door chimes, signaling my arrival. As I step into the bakery, I'm assaulted with the familiar scents I will forever associate with Lyndee. Cinnamon and sugar. The space in the front of the bakery is busy, with all tables filled with locals enjoying donuts, pastries, and cups of hot coffee.

I step in line and watch as the girl at the counter, Dustin, and even Lyndee bustle around, filling orders. Dustin glances up to check the line and notices me. He offers a quick wave before moving to the display case to retrieve something sweet from within. I notice the limp as he slips around the space with the use of his walker, wondering how long it'll be before he needs to move to his wheelchair. I've only seen him use it a couple of times, but I know Lyndee keeps one here if necessary.

We slowly move forward, and my eyes can't help but seek her out. It's not the rolls or the fresh bread that calls to me. It's the woman in khaki pants and a light green shirt. Her brown hair is pulled tight and fastened high on her head. Her brown eyes sparkle as she converses with customers, pouring a cup of coffee and grabbing a carton of chocolate milk from the small cooler on the back wall. My eyes can't help but drop to her ass when she bends over.

I almost groan out loud, her ass is so fucking nice.

"Can I help you?"

I glance up and realize the girl behind the counter is talking to me. She offers me a shy smile as I step up. "Hi. I'll take a large black coffee and one of those blueberry fritter things."

"Hi." Lyndee is standing beside her employee, a hesitant little grin on her lips.

Lips I kissed just last night.

Lips I want to kiss again as soon as possible.

"Morning," I reply, returning her smile. "How's your hand?" I ask casually and quietly.

"Oh, it's good," she answers, holding up her hand. "See? No pink."

I chuckle as she turns to pour my cup of coffee. "Careful or you'll burn yourself," I instruct, more out of mischief than worry she'd really burn herself a second time.

Lyndee glances over her shoulder and narrows her eyes. "I got it."

Her sass makes my dick hard.

"I got it," she says to her employee as she moves to the register and sets my cup on the counter, securing the to-go lid on the top.

"How much?" I ask when she makes no move to ring up my purchases.

"On the house," she whispers, sliding the bagged pastry and my coffee toward me.

"Business 101, sweets. Nothing is ever on the house," I state, reaching into my pocket for my wallet.

"You tried giving me food last night," she counters, crossing her arms over her chest. My eyes are instantly drawn to the way her tits push up and against the material.

"Yes, but that was because you worked in the kitchen. It was the least I could do," I point out, pulling out a twenty.

"Potato, po-tah-toe. You helped me before I opened. Plus, you took me home last night," she counters, refusing to take the twenty I hold out.

My mind latches on to the *took her home* part, wishing it had ended with a much happier ending than it did.

But I'm not complaining. This *thing*—whatever the hell it is—with Lyndee is complicated, but enjoyable. I've never expected to have this much fun with a woman, especially one I found utterly annoying in college. Not like Janice from *Friends* annoying, but her continual need to one-up me, always trying to get the best.

Now, I find her fascinating.

And sexy as fuck.

I grab the ink pen on the counter, realizing I'm holding up the line. She's still making no move to take my money, so I pull a business card from my wallet, jot my number and a brief note on the back, and drop it, along with the twenty, into the tip jar. "Thanks for breakfast, sweets. See you tomorrow night at my place," I say as I grab my purchases. The employee is standing directly beside Lyndee now, so I throw her a wink, watching her cheeks blush.

"Have a nice day," the young woman hollers as I turn around, making me chuckle. No, I'm not interested in her—she's way too young for my taste—but I'm a natural flirt, and I did actually enjoy witnessing the flash of annoyance dance through Lyndee's eyes.

"Later, Dustin," I bellow as I reach the door, throwing a wave to my new friend and smiling when he returns the gesture.

Outside, the cold air hits me square in the face, but I barely feel it. Instead, I feel lighter, happier now that I've seen Lyndee. I fully expect a busier than hell Saturday, but for some reason, just spending a few minutes with her before work has me anxious and ready to tackle the day.

I'm sure it has nothing to do with the fact I'll be seeing her tomorrow too, when she and Dustin come to my place for dinner.

Nothing at all.

Keep telling yourself that.

"Hey!" Numbers hollers as the front door closes. A few seconds later, he adds, "Damn, it smells amazing in here," as he enters the kitchen.

"Thanks." I glance up and give him a smile, only to have it falter just a touch when I see the woman at his side.

"You remember Savannah, right?" Numbers asks, knowing full well I do. He reaches for her coat and takes it once she removes the outerwear.

"Yes, of course. Nice to see you again, Savannah," I reply cordially, doing everything I can to not actually roll my eyes.

I love Isaac like a brother. He's one of my best friends, and I'd trust him with my life. But he's unable to see how unfit Savannah is for him. It pisses me off how she uses him, and he gets his hopes up that their relationship will stick this time around. Like Jameson said before, we're tired of watching him get his heart broken time and time again.

Speaking of, I wonder if Jameson knows she's coming. I mean, no one needs approval to bring a woman to one of our small gatherings, but I find it odd that Numbers didn't at least mention it prior to tonight. Unless he knew we'd give him a hard time about her presence, especially after the spat he had with Jameson over her.

"Thanks for inviting me," she states with a little too much sugar behind her words.

I glance at Numbers as he returns from hanging their coats in the foyer closet, my eyebrows drawn up in question. He gives me a look, one that says to be nice and not start shit with her. I, of course, ignore the look and reach for my beer. "So, Savannah. What have you been up to lately?"

"I just finished decorating the Masters mansion on Park Place. You know the one, right?" she asks, taking the glass of red wine Isaac pours for her.

"I do. Nice place. Isn't that caught up in a nasty divorce right now? The one with the cheating husband?"

The color falls from her face. Sure, I'm being vindictive, but I don't care.

"I hope you got paid before everything blew up with that scandal," I add for good measure.

Numbers sighs.

Savannah looks like she's going to throw up.

I want to laugh in her face and apologize to my friend at the same time for bringing it up.

Four months ago, Savannah pulled another of her famous "I just don't see this going anywhere long term" bullshit excuses and ran straight into the arms of a married man. The very one she was working for. John Masters. His wife found out her husband was screwing the designer she hired to redecorate the entire first floor of the seven thousand square foot home, and promptly filed for divorce.

Especially since there was no prenup.

Unfortunately for John, he made his fortune after marrying the young Miss Ohio in 1986, leaving himself wide open for sharing everything he made right down the middle. Rumor has it, once the affair came to light, he dumped Savannah in hopes of reconciling with his wife. I haven't heard whether or not that happened, but the fact remains: Savannah's only into Isaac until something bigger comes along.

And I hate her.

Another knock sounds on the front door, saving us from the awkward conversation we were embarking on. My first thought is Jameson, until I near the little feet pounding on the hardwood. A smile instantly spreads across my face, and I set my spoon down on the counter.

"Lizard!" I holler the moment her small body breaches the doorway and launches at the first unofficial uncle she finds.

"Is it time for pwesents?" she asks Isaac, big hopeful green eyes cast his way.

"I told you we have to eat dinner first," Mallory reminds her daughter, giving her a stern look.

"I don't understand why we have to wait. I mean, if Lou wants to open presents, why not just get them out of the way?" Walker asks, following behind his girlfriend.

Mallory sighs, closing her eyes and taking a deep breath. "Because it's a strategic parenting technique to ensure a child eats all of his or her dinner. We went over this, Walker. If she opens presents first, then she'll refuse to eat any food."

"I not!" Lizzie proclaims, reaching for me next. The moment she's in my arms, she whispers, "Pwease, Uncle Jasper? I've been weally dood all day!" Little hands wrap around my neck as she brushes a kiss on my cheek.

My heart literally turns to mush—in a very manly way, of course.

"Awww, why you gotta be so mean to Lizard?" I ask her mom, earning an eye roll.

"You men are all the same. She has you completely wrapped around her fingers," Mallory grumbles, heading over to the fridge to grab a bottle of water.

I glance at Lizzie, who bats her little eyelashes at me, and I know I'm completely smitten. "One wouldn't hurt, right?" I whisper.

Her eyes light up instantly as she shakes her head, little blonde ringlets flying about.

"Come on, little one. Let's go see what's in the office," I murmur.

"Where are you going?" Mallory asks, eyeing us suspiciously.

"Nowhere."

"To duh office!" Lizzie proclaims, pointing down the hallway.

I have a handful of gifts—okay, way more than I probably should—under the tree, but I knew I wouldn't be able to resist giving her one gift early. Once we're in the room, I set her down and grab the wrapped item on my desk and hand it to her. I drop to my knees and watch as she holds the gift in her hands, her eyes so full of young wonder and amazement. "Tan I open it now?"

"Of course! That's why I brought you in here," I tell her.

Lizzie drops to her butt, the small package on her lap, as she rips into the paper. She looks down at the book about princesses and grins. "Tan you wead it to me?"

I give her a big smile. "I'd love to after I finish cooking dinner, okay?" The front door opens and closes, heavy boots falling on the hardwood floor. "Actually, Tank just got here. I bet he'd love to read it to you," I tell her, referring to Jameson. Lizzie can't say his first name, so she refers to him by his nickname.

"Yay!" she bellows, jumping up and taking off running, book in her hand. "Tank!"

Chuckling, I hop up and follow in her wake. Just as I step into the hallway, there's a gentle knock on the front door. A smile instantly spreads across my face.

Making my way to the door, I pull it open and find my two guests standing on the stoop. "Welcome," I greet, stepping back so Lyndee and Dustin can enter.

"It just started to snow," Lyndee states, shaking the snowflakes out of her hair and stomping her boots onto the mat, even though there's no snow gathered yet.

"Let me take that," I offer, reaching for the large containers of sweet treats. I can tell by the scent of sugar wafting from within.

Dustin steps in, carrying his walker in his hands. I'm assuming it was so he wouldn't coat the wheels with wetness. "Hey, Jasper. It smells amazing in here," he says, stepping out of the way and taking off his coat.

"Throw your coats in that closet," I say, nodding to the space behind me. "We're in the kitchen."

They both take off their winter coats and hang them up before following me to where all my friends are gathered. "You guys remember Lyndee and Dustin, right?"

"Hey!" everyone cheers, a few heading over to greet her with a hug.

My friends are assholes.

"Lyndee, Dustin, this is Savannah," Numbers says, holding out a hand to the woman beside him. Clearly, she's too busy on her phone to stop typing for one second to greet the last guests to arrive.

"Nice to meet you," Lyndee says pleasantly.

"You too," Savannah replies, barely glancing up to offer a smile.

Dustin heads over to Jameson, who's seated at the kitchen table, Lizzie on his lap. She instantly starts telling him all about her new book, pretending to read him the story, even though she can't read the words.

"I think you know everyone else, right?" I ask Lyndee as she steps up beside me and starts opening the containers I placed on the counter.

"I think so," she says, a hint of nervousness in her reply.

"Well, make yourself at home. Anything you want, it's yours. I was just going to put the appetizers on the island. There's wine and beer in the fridge."

"I probably shouldn't drink," she mumbles, more to herself than to anyone in the room.

"Hey, go ahead and have one. There'll be plenty of time between now and when you leave. Plus, you'll have appetizers and dinner. One drink won't hurt. Everyone will have a few early and then switch to something non-alcoholic later."

She considers my words, and I can't help but wonder if she'll actually do it. According to Dustin, she never drinks if there's a chance she'll have to get behind the wheel.

"And if you don't feel comfortable driving home, you guys can stay here. I have a guest room upstairs and a fold-out couch in my office," I state, trying to hide any excitement I might feel at that prospect. Of course, in my mind, she's curling up under the comforter in my bed, not in the guest room.

"I suppose one won't hurt," she concedes. "It's still early, and I'll have plenty of food in my belly before I leave."

"Right," I nod, reaching into the fridge. "What's your pleasure? Wine or beer?"

Her eyes flare with something that looks a lot like desire at my reference to pleasure. Though, if I have my pick, the pleasure she receives won't be from alcohol, but from me. My mouth. My tongue. My hands. My cock.

"Beer, please," she whispers, swallowing hard and making my cock twitch.

"Dustin?"

"Beer is good," he hollers, barely looking up from the book he's being shown.

I grab two bottles of my favorite brew from the refrigerator shelf as Mallory comes up beside me. "Really? You gave her a gift before dinner? You're just as bad as Walker."

I hold up my hands—with a bottle in each one—in surrender. "Hey, it was just one little gift. A book, Mal. I mean, you can never go wrong with books. They're educational. If anything, it's not really a gift, but more of a tool to unlock the imagination in her mind."

She gives me a look and crosses her arms. "Really?"

"Really. I was totally thinking about her future," I reply, somehow keeping myself from smiling.

She moves her hands to her hips and narrows her eyes. "So that big gift beside the tree isn't the big kitchen playset you hinted about last week?"

I feign innocence. "Of course it's not. You told me not to get it because there are tons of pieces and you'd forever be picking them up."

She rolls her eyes so big I can only see white. "You're such a liar."

I bark out a laugh. "You love me."

"I don't know why," she mutters, reaching into the fridge and grabbing a second bottle of water.

"You know. Hey, I bought that weird girly beer, just for you," I inform her, handing Lyndee the two beers. Our fingers touch as she takes them, causing heat to shoot through my veins.

"Oh, uh, yeah. Thanks. I'm not in the mood for that right now," she mumbles as she quickly looks away, seeming a little uncomfortable all of a sudden.

"What? I bought that nasty fruit beer just for you," I tease, pulling the trays of finger foods from my fridge.

"I'm just not drinking," she whispers, taking a quick sip of her water and stepping away.

"Why, are you pregnant?" I ask with a snicker, a little too loudly.

Suddenly, the entire room goes silent, and Mallory looks like she touched a spider. The color drains from her face, her wild eyes landing on Walker. You could hear a pin drop as everyone looks around, no one really knowing what to say.

Walker doesn't look nearly as freaked out as Mallory does. In fact, he seems downright happy. Even though our friend is smugly grinning, his next words still shock me and everyone in the room. "Surprise! We're having a baby."

Lyndee

My eyes are wide as I glance around the room. Something major is happening, and I have no clue what I should do or say. I mean, I barely know these people, and a pregnancy announcement seems like a pretty big deal.

"Are you shittin' me?" Jameson breaks the silence, a big grin spreading across his scruffy face.

Mallory groans. "Let's not make a big deal about this," she argues, chugging her water.

"Not a big deal? This is huge," Jasper declares, pulling her into a hug. "Congratulations."

Walker grumbles as Isaac moves her way and hugs her too. "Keep those hands at a respectable ten and two position."

I arch my eyebrows in question, glancing at Jasper. He seems just as curious about his statement. "Ten and two? She's not a car."

Jameson stands up from the table, Lizzie in his arms, as he approaches Mallory and gives her a hug too.

I can't help glancing at Walker, looking for an explanation. "No, but ten and two are the perfect positions on her back so you don't get your ass beat," Walker states his eyes focused only on Mallory.

Feeling like I'm an outsider in a very private, family moment, I move around Jasper and start taking care of the appetizers. Most are already prepared, and all I have to do is take them from the oven warmer or the refrigerator. Platters of smoked salmon and cheese, mini beef tourtières, shrimp bruschetta, and veggie tartlets with what looks like a Greek cheese on top. Plus, fruit skewers, perfect for little hands. I smile as I help arrange the food on the counter.

"I can do that," Jasper says as he approaches.

"You were busy, and I wanted to help. That's some news, huh?" I ask, changing the layout of the food twice before I settle on the way I like. When he doesn't reply to my question, I finally glance his way, only to find him smiling.

"Yes, it's huge news, I'm happy for them," he whispers so only I can hear. "He's going to make an amazing dad. He's already one to Lizard."

I watch as his gaze moves to his friend, who's holding Mallory closely, his eyes on the little girl sitting at the table. "They're not married though, right?"

"No," Jasper replies, glancing to the little girl at the table. "They've only been together a handful of months, but that doesn't matter. They're perfect for each other."

"Is Jasper Kohlmann a closet romantic?" I tease, picking up a tartlet and taking a bite. The flavor exploding on my tongue.

Jasper snorts. "Uhh, no. You don't get romance with me, sweets."

"No?" I ask, slowly chewing the delicious food.

"Nope. No wine or roses here. But if you want mind-blowing orgasms, and lots of them, I'm your man." He throws me a wolfish grin just to punctuate his statement, causing my core to clench with need. I remember his lips and the wicked kiss we shared Friday night. The man was born to kiss, and I can only imagine what he can do with that mouth on *other* parts of my body.

I almost throw my hand in the air and ask where I sign up for the orgasms.

Almost.

"What do we have here?" Mallory asks, approaching the counter and diving into the platters. "Ohhh, is this beef in these little flower petal things?"

"It is," he answers, pointing to each dish and giving a list of ingredients. My brother comes over and takes a few appetizers, quickly followed by Jameson and Lizzie. Jasper moves to the oven, leaving Mallory and me alone by the refrigerator.

"I'm not sure I like her much," she mumbles, nodding to where Savannah stands off to the side, typing away on her phone.

Come to think of it, she's been off to the side on her phone since I got here. She's barely given Isaac, let alone anyone else in the room, a second glance. But I don't know her. Maybe she's a workaholic and in contact with her job or a client. Or maybe she has a sick family member needing her attention. Either way, I don't feel I can judge her completely, even if my gut tells me she's not someone I'd consider a friend.

"Oh, well, I don't really know her," I reply diplomatically.

She chuckles. "Me either, but I can tell she's no good for Numbers. Walker says he's completely hung up on her too, but she keeps jerking him around. For that, I hate her. He's my friend, the first person to help me when I moved to town, and I don't like her screwing with his head."

What do I say to that?

"How are you feeling?" I ask, trying to change the subject to a more manageable topic.

She sighs and pops a hip against the counter. "Okay, I guess. I mean, I'm not sick yet, even though I've been nauseous the last few days. It's still early though," she says with a shrug as her eyes move to her daughter.

"Are you okay?" I ask, noticing a slight melancholy in her gaze.

She looks back and smiles. "Yeah, I am. I guess this just hasn't sunk in yet. Yesterday I was shopping with Walker, picking out Christmas gifts for Lizzie, and today I'm pregnant with another child." She gives me a sad look. "It's been a wild twenty-four hours."

I bark out a laugh. "I bet."

She glances to Walker, the softest smile playing on her lips. "I always wanted another baby, maybe even two more. I guess I just thought I'd be married this time around when it happened, you know?"

It's as if Walker has supersonic hearing, and suddenly he's moving our way. He stops and grabs Lizzie off Jameson's lap before he approaches where we stand. There's something in his eyes, so assuring and resolute. "Lou, it's showtime."

The little girl beams with excitement as she's placed on her feet in front of her mom, smiling like the cat that ate the canary. "We dot a prize for you, Mommy!" she exclaims, her blonde curls pulled into pigtails.

"A prize?" she replies, grinning at her daughter.

"Surprise," Walker states, handing something to Lizzie.

I take a step back, so I'm not in the middle of whatever moment is happening, only to run directly into Jasper's hard body. He places his hands on my upper arms to keep me from stumbling and pulls me back against his chest. I don't complain. How can I? It's a really nice, muscular chest.

"Mommy, Daddy Walk has a kestion for you. I already tolded him yes. I wanted him to be my daddy forever," she announces, handing her mom a folded piece of paper.

With shaking hands, Mallory opens the note and bursts into tears. She drops to her knees and throws her arms around Lizzie and Walker, who has remained on his knees. One knee, in particular.

"What's on the paper?" I whisper, my eyes glued to the scene playing out before us.

"I don't know, but I have a pretty good idea," Jasper murmurs, his warm breath tickling my ear. We're so close.

I glance around and find everyone watching, waiting, and smiling. Even Savannah seems to have pulled her attention away from the phone in her hand to witness this beautiful moment.

"Mallory Sargant, you are the most extraordinary woman I've ever known. You are kind and loyal and have the biggest heart." He glances at Lizzie, who's still standing at his side, smiling. "The day you and Lou came into my life was the day I finally found my happiness."

He takes a deep breath and pulls a ring from his pocket. "This morning, we found out a pretty shocking surprise, but it doesn't scare me. How can it when I've seen how amazing your daughter is? Our son or daughter will be just as blessed to call you Mom. I'm not scared. There's no doubt in my mind that you were put on this earth for me. You and Lou," he adds, smiling down at the little blonde.

"So, Lizzie and I have a question for you. Lou?"

"Mommy, will you marwe Daddy Walk? Pwease say yes!" the child proclaims, bouncing up and down with excitement.

"Yes," she whispers, swiping at the tears streaming down her face. "Let's become an official family."

I sniffle as I watch Walker slip the ring onto her finger and pull her in for a long kiss. The room erupts in cheers once more. I glance up at the same time Jasper looks down, and I can't help but smile at the wetness I see gathered in the corner of his eye. "That was amazing," I mutter as he pulls me closer and hugs me tightly.

"It was. No one deserves a happy ending more than him. He's long overdue," he replies, smiling as one of his best friends receives another round of congratulatory hugs.

I step up to congratulate my new friend. Mallory quickly pulls me into a hug. "We're friends now," she states with a sniffle. "That means we hug."

It takes a second, but I return the gesture right away. How long has it been since I've truly had friends? A long time. So to be on the receiving end of one of her hugs and a declaration of friendship, I can't help but smile happily. "Congratulations," I tell her, dabbing at my eyes once more.

"Thank you. I can't believe he just did that. We practically stole your and Jasper's thunder."

"Our what?" I ask, laughing.

"Your thunder. You know, like in *Friends*? We didn't even get to discuss the fact you're here, as his date."

I open my mouth, but nothing comes out. Finally, I stutter, "This isn't...it's not...like that."

Mallory rolls her eyes. "Whatever. In the months I've known Jasper, he's never once brought a woman to a gathering. That means you're special."

Now it's my turn to roll my eyes. "We're just old friends who went to school together a long time ago."

She laughs in my face. "Sure. Keep telling yourself that," she says, nodding to my left.

I glance over, only to find Jasper's gaze locked on me as he chats with Isaac. There's something raw, something primal in his eyes that makes me squirm a little in anticipation. I don't know what it is about him, but I find myself completely under his spell whenever he's near.

Like now.

I'm drawn to him, this pull is too much to fight.

So I don't.

I won't.

I can't.

He smiles, as if he knows I've conceded. As if he knows I'm his. At least for now. I'm too weak to fight it.

"Dinner's ready. Let's eat."

"She's out," Walker whispers, rocking a sleeping Lizzie in the recliner.

"You ready to head home?" Mallory asks, glancing outside. "It's starting to really come down out there again."

"Sure," he replies, kissing the crown on the little girl's head before slowly and carefully standing up. Lizzie squirms, but gets comfortable on his shoulder, the new doll Jameson got her tucked under her arm.

"How are we going to get all of that home?" Mallory asks, pointing to the mountain of opened gifts scattered around the living room.

"We can get them tomorrow," Walker replies, glancing to Jasper for confirmation.

"They're fine here until you're ready," he states, running his finger along the back of my neck. We're seated on the couch with my brother, Isaac and Savannah are on the loveseat, and Jameson on the floor. "Though I can't guarantee I'm not putting that kitchen set together and whipping up some plastic meat and carrots in the microwave."

I smile. I'm not sure who was more excited when Lizzie opened that massive gift. The little girl or the man who gave it to her.

"Lou's going to be pissed when she wakes up in the morning and all this stuff isn't there," Walker adds as Mallory retrieves their coats from the closet.

"Here, I'll put together a bag so she has some of her new toys when she wakes up," Jameson says, reaching for one of the large gift bags and filling it with some of the smaller gifts. Even then, it barely makes a dent in the number of gifts the three guys gave her.

I glance over as Savannah pats Isaac on the leg and taps at her watch. She's been fairly quiet all evening, spending a big part of her time on the phone. It also seems like Jameson has been avoiding her. He's been cordial, but I can practically feel the animosity rolling off him in waves.

"Yeah, we're gonna head out too," Isaac announces as he stands up and offers Savannah his hand.

Each friend retrieves their coats and offers their appreciation to Jasper. The meal he prepared was downright amazing. I forgot how great of a chef he was. The man is a magician in the kitchen.

Jameson's the first one to pull me into a hug. "Those mini cherry cheesecake pies were to die for," he whispers, kissing my forehead.

I snicker. "There's a baggie of leftovers on the counter. If you hurry you can get them before Walker finds them."

Jameson lets go and practically sprints to the kitchen. "Where's he going? Jasper asks.

"To get the pies."

His grin is mischievous. "Good luck finding them," he mumbles, looking awfully proud of himself.

I gape at the handsome man before me. "You hid them? That's mean," I state with a giggle.

"Where'd you put them, Kohlmann?" Jameson demands as he reenters the room.

Jasper just shrugs. "I don't know what you're talking about."

"Fine," he argues, holding up a Tupperware container. "I'll just take all of these," he adds, referring to the leftover appetizers, as he walks past us and heads straight out the door.

Isaac is next, pulling me into a hug. "I'll see you in the morning. I can't wait to try one of those new scones you were talking about earlier."

"I'll save one just for you," I tell him with a wink.

He takes Savannah's hand as they head for the exit. I can tell how much he really cares for her. As everyone steps out the front door, I feel my cell phone vibrate in my pocket. Usually, I'd ignore it while with friends, but I can't imagine who would be calling me at ten at night. I'm concerned the moment I see Mr. James, my landlord's name, on the screen.

"Hello?"

"Good evening, Lyndee. I'm so sorry for calling you this late. I just knocked on your door, but it doesn't appear you're home."

"No, Dustin and I are visiting friends but will be heading that way shortly. What's up?"

"There's a slight problem with the condo next door."

"What kind of problem?"

"A pipe burst in her bathroom. We're praying for minimal damage, but some of the water did seep through the wall into your bathroom. We're going to need a few days to get it all fixed."

"Oh no," I whisper, closing my eyes and placing my forehead against my palm. "So we need to stay somewhere else?"

"Yes, unfortunately. We can help cover the cost of a hotel room, but I have to be honest, Lyndee, with only a couple of days until Christmas, I'm not sure we'll get the job complete before the holiday."

I sigh, hating the thought of living in a hotel, especially over Christmas, but what choice do I have? "Okay, thank you for letting us know. Can we get in there and grab some of our personal items?"

"Yes, of course. I'm here now getting things sopped up."

"Okay, we'll be there in a few minutes. Thank you." I sign off, trying to wrap my head around what Mr. James just said.

"Everything all right?" Jasper asks, drawing my attention to where he stands with my brother. Everyone else is gone.

"Oh, uh, no, not really. A pipe burst in the condo beside ours, and we have water. Dustin and I have to head to a hotel for a few days."

"Well, that sucks," Dustin mumbles, using his walker to head to the closet to retrieve his coat. He hands me mine, my brain running a million miles a second as I try to make a plan. A list of all the things I need to grab, especially if we won't be back home for a handful of days. Plus, there's a bit more of a commute with staying at a hotel. There are two in town, but both are on the opposite end, closer to the highway.

I turn to Jasper, ready to thank him for a lovely evening, when he stops me in my tracks with his offer. "Stay here."

I gasp, clearly hearing things. "What?"

"Yeah, why don't you stay here? I have plenty of room. There's the guest room upstairs and a foldout couch in my office. Hell, I'd even give you my bed and take the pull-out," Jasper insists. "You'll have plenty of space here, and your own bathrooms. You won't even know I'm here."

I almost snort.

Fat chance of that.

"I don't know," I argue, but unable to continue.

"Really, Lyndee, it's no problem. I'll be working late most nights and you get up early for work. We probably won't even see each other." Then he goes in for the kill. "Plus, who wants to be in a hotel room for Christmas?"

I sigh, feeling my resolve fly straight out the window. With his work schedule and mine, there's actually a good chance we'll barely see each other. We'll be like two ships passing in the night, which might not be too bad. Then I'm less likely to act on the kiss replays that keep running through my mind.

"And it would be kinda cool to hang out with Dustin too," he adds, hitting me with a final bullet to the heart.

I glance at my brother, whose eyes are full of excitement and pleading. He's practically begging me without even saying a word.

This is a bad idea.

I can feel it.

Yet, it really is the best option for us.

"Okay. We'll stay here."

Jasper

She's been gone for thirty minutes, and I can't stop pacing. I offered to go with her to her condo, but she refused. Instead, I stayed behind and make sure the guest bedroom was ready for an occupant, and that my office bed was loaded up with extra blankets so you don't feel those uncomfortable bars across your body.

No, it's not ideal, but it'll work.

Even if I have to sleep on it.

I see the headlights from her car streak across the front window and hurry to the garage to open the second bay. At least while she's here, she can park inside, right? There's a hesitation once the door is open, but eventually she pulls in. I meet her at the driver's side and notice the back of her car is packed with bags. "Let me help."

I start pulling bags from the back seat but notice right away how tired Dustin looks. He's not moving nearly as well as he was earlier, which tells me he's overdone it for the day. I remember Lyndee talking about him using his wheelchair when he gets exhausted, and it looks like his strength is depleting right before my

185

eyes. "Hey, Dustin, I got this stuff. Why don't you head into the kitchen while I bring it in," I suggest.

He looks as if he wants to argue, but there's no fight left in him. "Yeah, okay. Do you mind if I grab a bottle of water? I need to take my medicine."

"You don't have to ask my permission. If it's there, you're welcome to it," I tell him, watching as he limps with his walker toward the doorway between the garage and the mudroom.

"It's been a long day for him," Lyndee whispers when her brother is out of earshot. "Thank you for that."

"It's no problem. I'm happy to help," I reply, grabbing the rest of the stuff from the back seat. "How bad's the damage?"

She sighs. "Not horrible, but the floor was still wet in the bathroom, and you can tell the drywall is bubbling out on the wall between the two condos. Mr. James said it's all going to come out tomorrow to make sure it dries. He's still hoping for five to seven days, but I'm not sure. Poor Mrs. Anderson will be out even longer, but fortunately, she has a daughter she can stay with for a few weeks. I don't want to overstay our welcome, Jasper. We can go to a hotel for a few days," she frets nervously.

"I've already told you, sweets. Not necessary. You're both welcome here as long as you need to be," I insist, carrying the bags toward the mudroom.

"You may say that now, but maybe not so much when you find me dancing in the kitchen to Aerosmith, with flour covering every conceivable surface," she states with a laugh, following me into the house.

As I step through the doorway, I pause and glance over my shoulder. "Aerosmith? What song?"

"'Love In An Elevator,' of course." She winks and steps around me, her hair brushing against my arm and the sweet scent of sugar surrounds me like a blanket.

I'm so hard right now I can barely see straight.

When all their belongings are in the house, I make sure the garage is locked up and return to the kitchen. "I'm more than willing to let one of you take my bed. I changed the sheets while you were gone."

"Actually, I'd rather stay down here," Dustin states from his position at the island counter. "I don't like stairs on a good day, but I definitely don't want to try them tonight when I'm so tired."

"That sleeper sofa probably isn't the most comfortable," I quickly remind him. "It has an upgraded mattress and I have a thick Posturepedic pad on top which helps, but it's still not great."

He waves off my concern. "I'll be fine. It's not the first time I've slept on a couch," he replies with a shrug.

"Well, if you insist. I really don't mind taking the downstairs couch though."

"And I appreciate that," Dustin says, glancing to his sister. "I'm going to head off to bed. Tomorrow morning's gonna come early."

"Let me help you get your things in there," she responds, hurrying to the big pile of belongings on the floor.

"This way." I wave to Dustin, standing beside him, ready to help if needed.

I show him the half-bath in the office, never more grateful for that small toilet and sink than I am right now. "The full bathroom is directly across the hall. You're the only one to use that shower, so feel free to keep anything you need in there."

Dustin walks to the wingback chair and takes a seat as his sister brings in his bags. "This is a great room," he says, glancing around.

"I barely use it, honestly. Most of my work is done in the kitchen, not an office. What time do you have to go in?" I ask, looking from brother to sister.

Lyndee yawns. "I did a lot of my prepping today while we were closed, but I'll still need to be there by four thirty."

"What about you?" I ask, my gaze on Dustin.

"I'll need to go with Lyndee. She's my ride."

"What if I take you a little later so you can sleep in a bit? Do you have to be there so early too?"

The exchange a look. "No, he doesn't, but I can't ask you to do that," she says.

"You didn't ask. I offered."

She doesn't reply right away, just helps put some of her brother's things in the small half bath, but I can tell she's thinking. She's probably used to doing a lot of this by herself. Since her mom passed, she's been the caregiver to her brother. To be honest, I respect the hell out of her for it, for taking on this extra task of making sure he has exactly what he needs in this life.

I just want to help alleviate the load just a bit.

That doesn't scare me as much as I always thought it would.

I'm a selfish man, always have been. Thinking of others isn't exactly my strong suit. I'm a complete dick to boot, which puts me solidly in the asshole category. I know this. Sometimes even embrace it. It's who I am.

Yet here I am, ready to do whatever I can, and not only for Lyndee, but Dustin too. I really like spending time with him, so hanging out a little bit before work tomorrow isn't going to be a hardship. Especially if it helps him get a little more rest before he goes to work.

She rejoins us in the office. "Thank you. If you don't mind bringing him to the bakery in the morning, I would appreciate it." A whole heap of emotions passes through her eyes. Appreciation for sure, but also resignation and maybe weariness. She knows she needs the help, even if it's hard to admit.

"What time do you want him there?" I ask, forcing myself to stand where I am and not pull her into my arms.

"Is seven too early? That way he'll be there to help with the morning rush that usually hits around seven thirty."

"Seven is fine."

"But if you're not heading into work at that time, it can be later. Whatever's easiest for you."

"Lyndee." When she looks up, I continue. "It's fine. I'll have him there at seven. There's plenty of stuff for me to do at work before I start prepping for lunch."

She nods. "Thank you." Once everything is in place, she looks to her brother. "We'll let you get ready for bed. If you need anything, holler. Or text. I'll have my phone with me."

Her brother just rolls his eyes. "I'll be fine, sis, but thank you. See you both in the morning." Dustin heads for the bathroom with a pair of sweats and a T-shirt.

Lyndee and I slip out of the office, carefully shutting the door behind us as we go. "Let's get your things upstairs."

I'm able to carry her bags, leading the way up to the second floor. "The guest room is here, but you're more than welcome to take my room. The bed is much bigger and a hell of a lot more comfortable."

"This is fine," she insists, setting her purse down on the full-sized bed. "I just appreciate having a place to stay."

I deposit her belongings onto the floor beside the dresser. "There's a Jack and Jill bathroom through there," I add, pointing to the open door, "And you're welcome to use the dresser. There should be plenty of space in the closet too. Though, I'm not sure what might be in there." I run my hands through my hair, feeling a bit off-kilter. What is it about this woman that gets under my skin? Makes me all antsy and anxious.

I'm not even sure when she moved, but the next thing I know, she's standing directly in front of me. She reaches out and places a small hand on my arm. I almost jump from the shocks of electricity, but make sure to hold completely still as to not dislodge her touch. "Thank you. From the bottom of my heart, I appreciate it more than you know."

I clear my dry throat. "You're welcome. I'm happy to help, Lyndee."

She tosses a small smile my way like a grenade. I'm not prepared for the effect it has on me. My heart starts to hammer in my chest and things start to stir to life in my pants. It's not just an attraction I feel, but something headier. Deeper.

"Well, I'll let you get to it. Good night," I say, backing away and running into the dresser.

Smooth, Jasper.

"Night," she murmurs, watching as I practically stumble out of the guest room and make a beeline for my bedroom down the hall. My space takes up the entire back side of the home, with the smaller two bedrooms and the Jack and Jill bathroom on the other. While the door for the gym in the other upstairs bedroom is closer to my door, I've never felt her presence this near before.

Even with my bedroom door closed and locked.

It's like my body knows she's just a few walls away, calling out and drawing me in.

I opt for a quick shower instead of going over and fucking her. Let's be honest. That's exactly what I'd prefer to do, but that's not what's going to happen here. She's a friend. She and her brother needed help, and I offered. Who cares if it's the first time I've ever really done that. My point is I'm being nice, and the last thing either of us needs right now is to complicate things with sex.

Oh, but doesn't that sound like the best night ever.

Throwing open my closet door with a little extra force, I gather some shorts to put on after my shower. I usually sleep naked, but I don't think this is the time to be free-balling in bed when Lyndee Gibson is just a few thin walls away. It's going to be hard enough— pun intended—to keep my hands to myself, especially when I keep replaying that kiss over and over again. The last thing I need is to give my cock any ideas.

Shower. Bed. Sleep.

Nowhere in that equation should I be thinking about kissing Lyndee.

Should be easy enough.

I've been tossing and turning for a good hour.

Glancing at the clock for the hundredth time, I notice it's just after midnight. I was able to steal a little sleep, but now my insomnia is wide awake and refusing to let me settle. I reached the point thirty minutes ago where I would have gotten up, but with houseguests, the last thing I need is to be banging around in the kitchen. Dustin was exhausted when he went to bed, and I refuse to be the asshole who wakes him up.

I throw my comforter off, hating the way the shorts restrict my movements. Okay, they really don't, but when you're used to not wearing them to bed, they feel stifling when you do wear them.

I start to pace, willing my mind to settle and sleep to return, knowing it's completely futile at this point. I flip on the TV, making sure the volume is down low. A documentary on Michael Jordan is playing, but I've already seen it. Even so, I still try to focus on the basketball legend's career, only to find I can't concentrate. Television has never been my thing.

Cooking, yes.

Working out, sure.

Sex, absolutely.

Since the first and last on that list aren't an option, I guess I can slip over to my home gym and try to run myself into exhaustion. That's still no guarantee I'll be able to sleep, but maybe it'll help.

I forego throwing on a T-shirt and grab socks, running shoes, and my earbuds. I won't be able to do much, in hopes of keeping the noise down, especially with Lyndee sleeping just a short distance away.

Quietly, I tiptoe across the hall, stopping to make sure I haven't disturbed anyone. When I'm met with silence, I slip inside, shut the door, and bathe the room in light. Then, I get to work. As soon as my shoes are on and my buds are in my ears, I do a few stretches and hit the treadmill. I set a demanding pace, letting Mötley Crüe fuel my drive. I blow through one mile, then two, and quickly three. Sweat soaks my body, running down my face and blurring my vision. Even then, I keep going.

One grueling hour later, I finally slow the machine, praying my legs have enough strength to carry me back to my bedroom. I chug a bottle of water from the mini fridge and do one final stretch, making sure my quads and hammies are loose.

I'm on the floor, my legs spread wide as I grab my toes when movement catches out of the corner of my eye. I glance over and find Lyndee standing in the doorway of the bathroom, her wide eyes glued to my chest. "Lyndee?" I ask, whipping out my earbuds. "Is everything okay?"

"Huh?" she asks, her eyes dropping to my legs.

I can't help but take in her own appearance. Her hair is mussed, her face void of any makeup, a T-shirt, and the cutest fuzzy lounge pants with Christmas presents all down her legs. She's positively adorable.

And so fucking sexy.

I can't help but grin. She has yet to look up at my face. "I asked if everything was all right."

Finally, my words seem to register and her deer in the headlight expression meets mine. "Oh. Uh, yeah. Fine. All…good." Her eyes flash quickly down to my chest once more before settling on my eyes.

"Okay," I start, hoping she'll finish. Then it hits me. "Did I wake you?"

"I couldn't figure out what the sound was. I laid there for a few minutes and listened to the low hum and pounding. Was that you running? Are you training for a marathon?"

I snort, carefully getting to my feet on wobbly legs. "No, I actually hate running."

"But you do it because of your insomnia," she surmises.

I nod and stretch my arms over my head, her gorgeous brown eyes slowly dropping to take in my movement. I'm helpless against their power as they pool with dark desire and desperation. A desperation that lands squarely in my balls, causing all of my blood to pool in one concentrated area. Before I can even try to reason with myself, I'm moving.

Toward her.

Threading my fingers in her hair.

Claiming her lips with my own.

Nothing this wrong has ever felt so right.

Eighteen

Lyndee

When Jasper's demanding lips meet mine, I'm helpless against them. He coaxes my mouth open, his tongue claiming my mouth with fervor and need. His chest is soaked with sweat, but I don't care. Jasper without a shirt on is a masterpiece. A work of art. The most amazing thing I've ever had my hands on.

My nails claw at his flesh, trying to get him as close as possible. I can feel his erection pressing firmly against my stomach, hard and long. My core clenches and aches with a need that he seems to evoke from my soul.

He gently moves me back until I'm pressed against the door, and then he devours, gently lifting me against the hard wood and stepping into the apex of my legs. My ankles lock behind his back and my hands around his shoulders lining us up intimately. I grip at his hair, raking my short nails across his scalp and drawing a hiss out of his mouth. Jasper thrusts forward, his hardness rubbing at the exact spot I need.

I cry out, throwing my head back against the door. He takes the opportunity to nip at my neck before replacing his teeth with his tongue. It's a delicious pain that only seems to make me wetter. At this point, my panties are drenched, and I'm sure he can feel it soaking through my thick flannel pants.

But I don't care.

I need...more.

"Fuck, why is it I feel so completely reckless and helpless at the exact same time when I'm around you?" he whispers, sliding his lips across my skin, the roughness of his stubble causing goosebumps on my entire body.

I try to reply, but no words come out. I can't think. I can barely breathe. All I want is for Jasper to relieve the ache that's consuming my entire being. Since the first time I saw him standing in my kitchen, it's been building, steadily growing inside of me like a living entity, waiting idly for Jasper to come and unleash it.

He rocks his hips and bites my collarbone. "Why can't I stay away from you?" he mutters, almost to himself rather than to me.

"Why do you want to?" I murmur back, as he takes my wrists in his big hand and holds them against the door above my head.

His eyes lock on mine. They're blazing with a darkness I've never witnessed before. They're animalistic and raw, like I'm the prey and he's the wild animal ready to pounce. This is a new side I've never experienced before, but I'm not afraid of it. If anything, I anxiously welcome it.

When he doesn't move, I find myself pleading, "Please," squeezing my legs tightly around his waist.

He seems completely torn. Desire and confliction collide, radiating from those dark orbs. "This is a bad idea."

"Why? It feels like a really good one to me," I state bluntly, rocking my hips up and grinding against his cock.

He takes a deep breath, releases my wrists and cradles my jaw in his warm hand. "Because you deserve more than a quick fuck against a damn door, and that's all I can give you."

My heart is racing in my chest. "Who are you to decide what I want or need?"

Jasper sighs, closing his eyes and leaning his forehead against mine. "I'm not the hearts and flowers kinda guy, sweets." His words almost seem remorseful.

"Good thing I hate flowers then, huh?" The corners of my lips turn upward, but I can still see the battle he's waging with himself. Reaching up, I place both palms on his cheeks, not missing the way his eyes widen at my touch. "Jasper, I'm here right now because I want to be. I don't care about tomorrow, if I'm being honest, because it's been a really long time since I've had anyone look at me like you are."

His voice is hoarse and hushed as he asks, "How am I looking at you?"

"Like I'm a desirable woman." The words rush out in a heap, the confession sensitive and real.

"What are you talking about? You're the most desirable woman I've ever known," he murmurs, confusion flashing across his face.

Feeling bolder than ever before, I press my chest firmly against his and demand, "Then prove it. I'm not asking for tomorrow. I'm asking for right now. Please, Jasper."

I watch as all control flies right out the proverbial window. "You want me to prove how much I want you?" He flexes his hips, driving his erection against my clit. "You feel that, sweets?"

A moan of pleasure spills from my lips. "Yes," I gasp.

"That's what you do to me." His hand grips my ass, kneading the soft flesh and rolling my body against his. "I can't stop thinking about you." He bites my jaw. "About fucking you." He runs his tongue over the rapidly beating pulse in my throat. "All I want is to rip these cute as fuck Christmas jammies off your sexy body and bury myself so deeply inside you, you'll feel me for days."

My eyes roll back in my head.

Then, we're moving. With his big hands gripping my ass, he walks to the door, somehow gets it open while giving me a bruising kiss on my already-swollen lips, and marches across the hall to his bedroom. The door shuts with a bang, but neither of us seem to care. There's only one sole focus for both of us, and that's getting naked.

He lies me down on his bed, my body sinking into a plush mattress and luxurious bedding. Jasper comes down on top of me, his body still covered in sweat from his workout. It doesn't bother me though. It's not disgusting or a turn-off. If anything, it drives this desire further, pushes it closer to the edge of reason and recklessness.

"As much as I really love these pants, I think we should get rid of them," he mumbles, his mouth tracing my collarbone.

"Yes, I agree," I huff.

Jasper chuckles at my urgency, pulling himself onto his knees and reaching for my waistband. "Put your hands against my headboard."

My eyebrows draw together in question, but it's the wicked grin that spreads across his lips that has me reaching above my head. The headboard is solid wood with nothing to grab onto, so I place my hands against the cold, hard surface and hold my breath.

He slips his hands under the band of my pants and slowly pulls them toward him. I watch as his eyes drink in every square inch of exposed flesh. When the pants hit mid-hips and reveal the fact I'm not wearing panties, he makes a choking sound deep in his throat and closes his eyes. "You haven't been wearing panties?"

I shrug a shoulder, even though he isn't watching me. "I don't like to sleep in them."

When he opens his eyes, they're locked on the apex of my legs and on every inch of bare skin he reveals. Finally, after what feels like the longest undressing ever, I'm left naked below the waist. "Fuck, you're even more gorgeous than in my fantasies," he states, his gaze meeting mine. "And I've been fantasizing...a lot."

"What do you think about?" I ask as he drops to his elbows and positions himself between my legs.

"Eating your pussy." His words are blunt—dirty—and make me even wetter. "Don't move your hands. You hear me, sweets? You move those hands, and I stop." He sticks out his tongue and swipes it through my folds. "Do you want me to stop?"

I gasp. "No, God, no, don't stop."

Jasper smirks.

And devours.

He licks and sucks on my swollen, wet flesh, setting my entire being on fire. I rock my hips, gyrating against his face, and seeking out more. Jasper adjusts his position, bringing his fingers into play. His index finger toys with my clit before slipping down and sliding into my pussy. Just as he pushes all the way inside, he sucks at my swollen clit, drawing it into his warm mouth.

"Oh my God!" I gape, pure pleasure coursing through me. I reach down and thread my fingers into his hair, needing to touch him.

As suddenly as the gratification started, it stops.

"What did I say?" His question is full of authority, and surprisingly, instead of turning me off, it does the opposite.

"I just wanted to touch you," I argue, moving my hands back into place.

His eyes soften just a smidge, and the corner of his mouth ticks up. "If you touch me, I won't be able to control myself. I'll be balls-deep inside you in less than a second."

"So?" I ask, holding my breath as he lowers his mouth. "I don't think that sounds so bad at all."

He chuckles, low and deep, against my clit, the sound vibrating through my body. "I'm going to make you come on my face before I bury myself inside this sweet pussy."

Jeezus, this man can dirty talk. He's like the gold standard of saying all the naughty words and making me lose my damn mind.

But dirty talking isn't the only amazing thing he can do with his mouth. In under a minute, he has me racing toward the finish, teetering on the edge of euphoria. Jasper presses two thick fingers into my body and sucks my clit between his lips. The combination causes me to erupt like a volcano, blinding white light bursting behind my eyelids. Wave after wave of release rushes through my veins as my hips continue to rock and ride out the pleasure.

When my orgasm finally ebbs, I feel boneless against the soft bedding. My eyes are closed, and I'm pretty sure I'm smiling. My first orgasm in nearly two years that wasn't induced by myself, and I'd say it was pretty magnificent.

Speaking of magnificent, I feel Jasper moving and crack open my eyelids. His hard chest is on full display, no longer wet with perspiration. His face, however, glistens like the night sky. As if sensing where my thoughts are directed, he grins wickedly and crawls up my body, placing his lips against mine. "You can move your hands now."

My arms tingle as they lower and wrap around his shoulders. The kiss turns ravenous quickly, as I hitch my legs up on his hips, spreading myself wide open for him. His tongue delves deep into my mouth, an action mimicking sex. At least it feels like it to me. He's making love to my mouth.

Except Jasper doesn't make love.

He fucks.

And right now, his sights are set on me.

Jasper rips his lips from mine and slowly gets off the bed, in long, fluid movements, like a cat. He toes off his shoes, ripping his socks off and tossing them aside. "I really should take a shower," he starts, but holds up his hand when I start to shake my head. "But I don't think I can wait to be inside you." Then, he hooks his long fingers under the waistband of his shorts and yanks them down in one swoop.

His cock is glorious. Long, thick, and hard, with veins running down the sides that make my mouth water. He reaches for the drawer in the nightstand and pulls a condom from within. Honestly, my brain is so scrambled right now, I wasn't even thinking about protection. Thank God he had the forethought to make sure we're prepared.

Once he's sheathed, he returns to the bed, crawling between my legs and sitting on his haunches. His eyes move to the apex of my legs, his tongue slipping out and licking his lips. When he glances back up at me, his eyes are molten.

A shiver sweeps through my body in anticipation.

He helps me remove my pajama top before he grabs my wrists once more and places them over my head. "Hands up here, sweets. Remember, if you move them, I stop."

With my arms up, he takes his position, running the head of his cock through my wetness. When he presses forward, inch by glorious inch, there's a tinge of pain as my body stretches to accommodate him. He takes slow, skilled strokes, each one pressing farther into my body, until he's finally fully seated. It borders on painful, but there's no way I want him to stop.

"Breathe, sweets," he whispers against my ear. As he runs his tongue along the shell, I gasp, greedily. "There. That's better."

I feel myself relax a bit, allowing him to move a little more freely. Jasper pulls himself back until just the head remains before thrusting forward once more. He fills me so completely, so perfectly, with one fluid motion it steals more than just the air I breathe. It steals my sanity and all control.

"Jesus, Lyndee," he groans, methodically pushing inside my body and doing a little grinding move, putting pressure against my swollen clit. "You're so fucking tight."

There's something about his words and the naughtiness they contain, that causes my core to tighten once more. I've never experienced dirty talk like this. Most guys from my past never said a word during sex, except one who grunted a lot and would yell "Yeah, Mama" when he came. After the second time of mid-sex awkwardness, and the fact that my own orgasms came later (after he left), we broke up.

I keep my hands over my head and rock my hips in rhythm, keeping pace with Jasper. He adjusts his position, moving my legs to his shoulders. My ankles barely lock around his neck, but the angle…oh God, the angle is heaven. I swear I can feel him all the way back to my spine.

"You have to be the sexiest woman I've ever seen," he proclaims, holding my hips and thrusting into me. "I could watch your tits bounce all day, every day, and never get tired of it." He reaches up and cups one, tweaking the nipple with pressure before bringing his mouth down to lick and suck.

The movement causes my knees to practically hit my arms, sending him even deeper inside of me. Our joint groans of pleasure fill the room, as he pumps his hips with short, fast strokes.

I can feel another orgasm starting to build. Never in my life have I had two in one night, but never in my life have I ever experienced something so toe-curling, so all-consuming as getting naked with Jasper Kohlmann.

"You getting close again, sweets? I can feel you gripping my dick," he mutters without breaking stride. There's a fine sheen of sweat on his chest again, and my fingers itch to touch. But I also don't want to move my hands and risk him stopping. With each thrust, I'm drawn closer and closer to coming for a second time in a short period.

"So close," I whisper, closing my eyes and just feeling. I can feel everything. His hands, his cock moving methodically in and out of my body, the way he grinds down on my clit with each pump of his hips.

"I want to feel you come," he demands, gripping my hips in his big hands and thrusting hard. "Strangle my cock." He reaches with one hand and swipes his thumb across my clit, causing the most glorious orgasm to sweep through my body.

I cry out, white light filling my vision, as I come for a second time. I can feel my body gripping his shaft, but he continues to move, drawing out my release until I'm boneless and completely spent.

But I'm given no time to rest.

Jasper still moves inside of me, and it's only then that I realize he didn't get off. When my eyes crack open and meet his, they're still full of fire and passion, and that's when I know.

We're not finished.

Not even close.

He pulls out, causing me to whimper at the loss of his body inside of mine. He covers me from head to toe with his much bigger, much stronger body, and takes my mouth in a bruising kiss. Every ounce of energy I lost during that second orgasm returns with a fervor and a demand. I've barely come back down from the clouds, and I need more.

When he finally releases my mouth, it's to help me move. I'm on my elbows and knees before I even know what's happening, my legs automatically parting for him. He takes his place behind me, and any qualms I have about being in this position fly right out the window when he pushes forward.

Big hands grip my hips tightly as he moves fast and hard. I try to stay quiet, really I do, so I bury my face in the pillow to help conceal my moaning. Our bodies make a slapping sound as he pumps into me, his grunts barely muffling the noise, but I don't care. I can't think about anyone hearing us right now.

All I can do is feel.

And what I feel is a third orgasm building.

He's so fucking deep, hitting that magical spot inside my body over and over again until my third release starts not long after the second one ended. I can't breathe. I'm flying, euphorically and blindly.

I feel his cock grow thicker moments before he slams into me and pauses. I swear I can feel his orgasm ricochet through me as he comes, my name spilling from his lips.

Eventually, his hips finally stop moving. We fall together in a heap of limbs and heavy breathing onto the bed, my body spent. My brain doesn't work.

I'm officially too sexed to think.

After several minutes, I feel Jasper adjust his position and get off the bed. I know this is the part where I need to get up myself and head back to the guest room, but I can't seem to make myself move. Soon. I'll get up soon.

He returns a few minutes later and wipes off my thighs with a towel. I crack open my eyes, expecting to be escorted back to where I belong, but am surprised when he slips back into his large, comfy bed. Instead of asking me to leave, he practically lifts me off the comforter and against his hot body. Jasper adjusts us so my head rests on his chest before wrapping us in warmth.

I sigh in contentment.

"Why do you call me that?" I whisper, exhaustion knocking on the door.

"What?"

"Sweets."

I can practically feel his grin as he slides his hand down my side. "Because you always smell like sugar. Plus, now that I've tasted you, I can confirm you taste as sweet as sugar too."

"Oh."

Wow.

Jasper swipes hair off my forehead and settles his hand on my back, and that's all it takes. I'm drawn into sweet slumber with my body securely pressed against his. I know it's wrong. I know I should leave. But I don't.

I can't.

All I want is to grab on to whatever moments he's offering and hold on with both hands.

I'll deal with the rest when we wake.

Jasper

I wake up at four, fully rested. I expect the familiar fatigue and drowsiness to appear, but it doesn't. Even after my grueling run just a few hours ago, I find myself feeling refreshed, my battery completely recharged.

And I know why.

I turn and catch a glimpse of the woman still snuggled in the crook of my arm. Even in the darkened room, I can see her dark hair fanned out across the pillow and the way her mouth forms the cutest little "O" as she sleeps tranquilly. My cock actually jumps with anticipation as images of it filling that sweet little mouth come to mind.

Except now's not the time.

She needs to get ready for work.

Instead of waking her, however, I find myself watching her sleep and replaying every second of our time together, from the moment I looked up and found her standing in the doorway, watching me, to the view I enjoyed of watching her perfect, round ass bounce as I fucked her from behind. That's an image I won't forget anytime soon.

It wasn't just the sex that contributed to my restful sleep. It was the woman. Holding her, watching her drift off, was the most peaceful I've felt in years, if ever. There's no doubt in my mind that Lyndee was the reason I was able to get a couple of hours of good sleep.

Glancing at the alarm on my nightstand, I realize she's out of time. Hell, she's probably already running behind. I gently roll to my side, carefully dislodging myself from beneath her. Brown eyes slowly open, and there's a moment where she startles before recognition settles in. "Hi," she whispers, her voice gravelly and low.

"Morning. I didn't want to wake you since you were sleeping so peacefully, but it's after four," I tell her, reaching over and swiping a strand of hair from her cheek. The warmth of her skin sets my blood pumping.

"Shit," she mumbles, closing her eyes for a brief second. "I need to go."

"I figured," I reply, though make no move to get up out of bed. I also don't try to think too hard about why I like waking up beside her as well.

She jumps up, her nipples instantly pebbling the moment the comforter drops. My dick twitches and gets all excited as I take in the bounce, recalling the way they filled my hands very early this morning. "I should," she starts, waving her thumb toward the door.

"You could shower here, if you wanted."

She seems to consider my offer, but only for a second. "Actually, all of my stuff is down the hall. It would probably be easier to just go shower there."

Ignoring the disappointment that creeps in, I cover it with a quick nod. "That makes sense. I'll run down and start a pot of coffee," I state, slipping out of my bed and walking toward the closet.

Lyndee pauses halfway to the door, her eyes watching me. Specifically, on my cock. It's half-hard and only getting harder with each passing second.

"If you don't stop looking at me like that, you'll never get to the bakery." There's heat in my voice, a desire that can't be masked.

She glances up, her cheeks blushing a cute pink. "Sorry."

I chuckle. "Don't apologize, sweets. Clearly, I want you just as badly," I state, pointing down at my ready-to-go dick.

She scurries from the room, grabbing her pajama pants and top on her way, leaving me standing naked in my closet. I toss on a T-shirt and pair of flannel pants and tie the drawstring around my waist. Once I'm dressed, I head to the bathroom to relieve myself and brush my teeth.

In the hallway, I hear the sound of the water running coming from the gym. Lyndee didn't shut the door she left open early this morning. The thought of her naked and wet in the shower has my cock right back to full-mast, ready to strip out of my pants and join her underneath the hot spray. I can just picture it now, me holding her against the tile wall and burying myself balls-deep in one stroke.

Adjusting myself, I forego that brilliant plan and continue down the stairs. She really does need to get going or she'll be late and most likely be behind all day. As a chef, that's the worst feeling in the world. Those are the days where you never seem to catch up, always feeling one step behind, and I refuse to do that to Lyndee.

I turn on the coffee pot, but then remember what Lyndee said about preferring tea. I dig out the kettle, fill it halfway with water, and turn on the burner. I check my pantry and find a few varieties of tea, all of which I purchased when I was trying anything and everything to help with my insomnia.

In the variety pack, I find a chai called Good Morning and drop two bags into a travel mug. I'm just pouring the water into the mug when I hear her soft footfalls on the stairs. I grab the lid just as she walks around the corner, looking fresh and gorgeous on this Monday morning.

"That smells good," she says, setting her purse on the counter.

"I made you tea. I don't know if it's any good, but it has all the good shit you need to start your day," I reply, carefully removing the teabags and screwing on the lid.

She grins as I hand her the mug. "Thank you. I can't believe you remembered."

I shrug off the compliment and walk her to the garage. I grab the spare opener off the shelf and stick it on her visor. "Just pull back in when you get here tonight."

"I don't mind parking outside," she replies, throwing her purse onto the passenger seat.

"No need. I have the space and now your vehicle is already warm."

She goes to pull her door closed but stops. "Thanks for bringing Dustin in a bit. I really appreciate it."

"I don't mind, sweets, really. He gets to rest a little longer, and he's a pretty cool guy. I like hanging out with him," I state with a smile.

She returns the gesture, her brown eyes sparkling with happiness. "He likes you too."

Something passes between us, but we leave it unspoken. Whatever it is, it calms and roots me. "I'll see you later," I say, helping close her door.

I watch as she starts her vehicle, opens the door, and slowly backs out. Once the front end is clear, she presses the button and lowers the door. When I'm left in silence, I finally head back inside, suddenly anxious to start my day. Usually, this is the point where I start to plan and prepare for a busy Monday at Burgers and Brew, complete with the owners' meeting in the afternoon, but all I can think about now is getting through the day and coming back home.

Because Lyndee will be here.

And surprisingly, that thought doesn't scare me as much as I thought it would.

I'm pouring myself a second cup of coffee when Dustin joins me in the kitchen. He's using his walker, though no obvious signs of limping like last night. "Good morning. Coffee?" I ask as he joins me at the island bar.

"Sure."

I pour him a cup. "Sugar or milk?"

"No, just black." When I set the cup in front of him, he offers a quick thanks and takes a sip. "Wow, that's good."

"It's a dark roast from South America. One of my suppliers gets it for a fancy café a few towns over and always sells me extra bags. It's my favorite. I have a hard time drinking Folgers after this stuff," I tell him, enjoying my own sip.

"I like it. So, what's going on with you and my sister?"

His question almost gives me whiplash. One minute we're discussing coffee and suddenly he's asking about my relationship with his sister. The one who slept naked in my bed last night after I did dirty things to her body.

My mouth opens, but nothing comes out. I don't really know what to say.

"Can I ask you something?"

"Sure," I reply, my throat dry and scratchy.

"Do you like her?"

I meet his gaze head-on, refusing to look away. If we're going to have this conversation, he deserves to hear the truth. "I do."

Dustin relaxes in his seat and sips his coffee. "I don't need to know details or anything, but I feel like I need to say this. Don't hurt her. She doesn't get to go out a lot and have fun. She's devoted her whole life to making sure my needs are met, and not just since Mom died. She was that way before too." He focuses on the cup in his hands. "I just want her to be happy. She deserves someone to put her first for a while."

I swallow hard and lean against the island. His words hit me square in the chest with enough force, they could knock a man down. She does deserve that, and more. I just wish I was the man who could give it to her.

"We're friends," I start, trying to find the right words. It's hard to have this conversation with him, especially since I haven't had it with her. "I don't know where this will lead, if anywhere. I like spending time with her—"

"And kissing her clearly," he retorts with a smirk.

I almost spit out the coffee I just sipped. "Yes, well, that's nice too," I reply with a chuckle.

Dustin sighs. "She's my best friend, Jasper. I don't have a lot of friends and neither does she. We have each other. I'm not telling you to figure this out now. I can tell by the look on your face, you're two seconds away from panicking," he states with a huge grin. "All I'm saying is if you want something with her, go all-in. If not, don't string her along, okay?"

I consider his words for a moment before nodding in agreement. "Deal."

He gives me a decisive nod and brings his cup to his lips once more, ending the conversation. From the first time I met Dustin, I liked him. Now, I respect the hell out of him. He's a good man and wants the best for his sister. He says she's taking care of him, but I really think that road runs both ways. I think they take care of each other, even if they don't realize it.

"What do you say we hit a Reds game this spring?" I ask, watching as the excitement fills his eyes.

"Really? I'd love that! Lyndee went with me a couple of years ago, but she doesn't know a bunt from a home run," he proclaims, a new energy filling the room. It's an excitement, like walking up to the ballpark on Opening Day.

"Sure. It's been years since I went, and I'm due. I think you're just the man to join me for a day at the ballpark. Hotdogs, beer, and maybe a pretzel with cheese."

"I'm in! Just tell me when." His energy is contagious.

"When they release their schedule, we'll take a look and see which game you think we should hit," I tell him, feeling a bit excited myself, even if Opening Day isn't for almost four months.

"Yeah, sounds good." He takes another drink of his coffee before he asks, "Do you think the other guys would want to come?"

I stop, quickly realizing who he's referring to. It's not often that all four of us are off at the same time, but it does happen. Case in point, last night. We have a great team in place, and I'm sure they'll get by without us just like always. "Walker and Jameson would be there in a heartbeat, but Isaac will take some convincing. He's a workaholic," I add with a teasing tone.

"Like you?" Dustin asks, laughing.

"Like me," I quip, smiling over my coffee cup. "Come on, smarty pants. Let's get you to the bakery."

"What happened last night?"

I glance up from the grill and find Jameson standing near me, his dark eyes assessing. The first thing to flash through my mind is Lyndee, spread wide open as I eat her sweet pussy. Then there's the image of me taking her from behind, my ears filling with the sounds of every one of her three orgasms.

But I don't tell him that. Those dirty replays are for my filthy mind only.

Instead, I shrug. "What do you mean?"

"Dustin said they had a pipe burst and are staying with you?"

I place the burger I'm grilling onto the ready bun and send the plate off to get fries. "Yeah. Should only be a few days. Why?"

Jameson's grin starts slow and spreads widely across his face. "Interesting."

"What is?" I ask, placing four freshly made patties on the grill top.

"You. Lyndee. Sharing a house," he states, his all-knowing eyes following my every move.

"It's not like that," I argue.

Oh, but it is.

Jameson barks out a laugh. "If you say so, but you should probably put your tongue away. Ever since I mentioned her name, it's been dangling out of your mouth like a dog in heat."

I narrow my eyes at my friend. "Fuck you."

He snorts. "Tempting, but you're not my type. Lyndee though..."

A growl erupts from my throat, making him laugh.

"And I rest my case." Jameson steps forward and lowers his voice so the rest of my kitchen staff can't hear. "I really like her, and I think she'd be good for you. Might even get you out of the kitchen every now and again."

"It's not like that," I argue, flipping the patties before they're ready.

"So you've said, but your eyes tell a different story, Jasper. All I'm saying is don't discount something because you're scared."

"I'm not scared," I counter.

He just gives me a look, letting me know he doesn't believe me. "Fine, you're not scared. But you're not doing what you should be doing either, which is asking her out on a date."

"A date?" The concept seems a little foreign to me. How long has it been since I've gone out on a date? A hookup, sure. Taken women home from the bar, yes. But dinner and a movie? Shit, probably since college. Maybe even high school. The women I've been with recently knew the score. Sex and fun.

"Yeah, a date. Take her out, get to know her outside of the bedroom. It's this radical new concept, you should try it."

I roll my eyes. "I've tried it. Not my thing."

"Okay, but it might be Lyndee's thing. All I'm saying is you could give it a shot. She seems like the type of woman who likes the whole wine and dine thing," he says, making me think.

Is he right? Is Lyndee a big date kind of woman? She's already said she doesn't like flowers, but what about all the other bullshit that goes along with dating someone? Fancy dinners, expensive wines, and moonlit walks under the stars?

Shit.

My mind floods with questions, but no answers. Before I go there, I probably need to decide what I want out of this. I'll admit, at first, I wanted sex, but now? After I've gotten to know her a little bit? The attraction I feel is too big to ignore, and the idea of spending more time with her, possibly even going on a date or two, has some appeal. Add in great sex, which I already know is pretty fucking phenomenal, and this dating thing doesn't sound so bad.

"Come on, Romeo. The guys will be waiting to start our meeting. Bring the food and get your lovesick ass to the bar," Jameson says, humor lacing every word, as he slaps me on the back and heads off to the door.

I finish making the burgers, but my mind isn't present. No, all thoughts are across the street with Lyndee. I wonder what she's doing right now and how her day has been. Will she be home when I get there? And why does it make my heart happy when I think about her being there, waiting?

Sighing, I plate up the food, put it on a tray, and head to the bar for our weekly meeting, doing all I can to leave thoughts of Lyndee behind.

Lyndee

"Hey, something smells amazing in here," Jasper says as he enters the kitchen, having just kicked off his shoes in the mudroom.

"I know you're the chef, but I thought I'd give it a try tonight. As a thank you for letting us stay here," I reply, pulling the chicken dish out of the oven and setting it on the potholders on the counter.

He leans against the fridge, so very close to me, and smirks. "I believe you have the same degree as I do, sweets," he states, opening the door and grabbing a bottle of water.

"True, but we took two totally different paths in our careers. I prefer to stick to the basics," I confess, uncovering the garlic smashed potatoes on the stove and sticking a spoon in the pot.

When I glance at him, I find his eyes watching me intently, the faintest hint of a smile on those lips. Lips that did very naughty things to my body early this morning. I have to turn away to hide the blush.

"Well, I'm impressed. This definitely isn't basic." Jasper watches as I plate the chicken and take it to the table. He follows suit, delivering the potatoes to the center of the set table and joining me at one of the three settings.

"Where's Dustin?" he asks, scooping a piece of stuffed chicken onto his plate.

"Right here," my brother chimes in as he enters the kitchen, a big smile on his face. "And I have news."

I can feel myself blushing.

"Tell me," Jasper instructs, scooping a healthy dollop of potatoes on his plate.

"I have a date." Dustin takes a seat and dives into the food. "Tomorrow night."

"Really?" he asks, eyes wide. "With who?"

"Daisy's older sister, Dana. She came in again today, and we got to chatting," Dustin informs Jasper.

"For almost two hours," I mumble with humor in my voice. The truth is, he worked while they visited, and I could tell there was something going on. Since my brother doesn't have a lot of friends, I stayed away and let it unfold.

When I glance up, Jasper is grinning ear to ear. "That's awesome. Where are ya going?"

"Actually, to your place. She mentioned she had a craving for the Ride A Cowboy Burger and asked me if I wanted to go with her."

Jasper slices into his chicken but meets my gaze at Dustin's statement. "She asked him?"

I nod. "It was so cute. A little awkward, but so cute. He didn't know what to say at first. He's never been asked out before," I tell him, cutting into my own meat.

"Truth. Girls don't usually go after weirdos like me," my brother says with a smile on his face.

"I think it's wonderful. I'm happy for you. I'll be sure Ross makes perfect burgers for you tomorrow night." Jasper takes a bite. "Wow, this is delicious. Tell me about it."

"Oh, it's just stuffed chicken. Nothing fancy."

"Don't sell yourself short. It's really good. Obviously, there's tomato and spinach, but what cheese is this? Gouda?" he asks, taking a critical look at what's on his fork.

"Asiago," I answer. "One of my favorite dishes is grilled tomatoes with spinach and Cheddar, but I thought I'd try something different with this recipe. I really like the nutty flavor in the cheese and thought it would really complement the tomato."

"You did well. I love it."

"Thanks," I reply, beaming with excitement and a little pride.

"You know, your grilled tomato idea might make a great burger topping," he says, seeming very intrigued with the food in front of his face.

"Really?" My excitement turns to shock.

"Yeah. I've used fresh tomatoes, but not grilled ones. And adding the zesty spinach and cheese to the vegetables, not the meat, would definitely be an interesting concept," he states, taking another bite of his food. "I'd have to try it on the hamburger, but I think you're on to something here."

I can't stop smiling as I take a bite of my food and chew. It feels good to have inspired Jasper to possibly create a whole new burger for the restaurant. What makes me grin even more is watching him dissect his food, analyzing each flavor, and studying it with a critical eye. He doesn't actually say much during the meal, but that's okay. I can tell he's in chef mode, his brain working overtime to invent.

"What?" he asks, catching me staring.

"Nothing. I'm just watching you work," I tell him, finishing up my potatoes and feeling completely stuffed.

He drops his napkin, his eyes looking contrite. "I'm sorry. I tend to get lost in my own head sometimes."

"No, don't apologize. I do the same thing when I'm in the zone in the kitchen," I reply. "It's fun to watch you go through the creative process, especially on something I might have inadvertently suggested."

He grins widely, his eyes dancing with mischief. "Pretty proud of yourself, aren't you?" he asks, teasing.

I shrug. "I am. I think I deserve more accolades."

Jasper barks out a laugh, setting his napkin down beside his empty plate. "Like a prize?" Something naughty flashes in his eyes and causes my entire body to heat with desire.

"Hey, maybe Jasper can help you tomorrow night," Dustin says, either completely oblivious to the sexual tension suddenly surrounding us or is ignoring it.

"What's tomorrow night?" Jasper asks, glancing between us.

"Nothing," I reply, but it's drowned out by my brother continuing.

"Every year, we bake Lyndee's birthday cake together, but now I won't be there."

"It's no big deal," I insist, feeling eyes boring into me from across the table.

"When's your birthday?" he asks, seeming a little surprised by this revelation.

"Oh, uh..."

"Two days."

My brother's a traitor.

Jasper's shocked eyes land on mine. "Your birthday's in two days? On Christmas Eve?"

"It's no big deal," I insist, standing to collect the dirty dishes.

"It is," Jasper argues, grabbing the pot of potatoes and following behind me. "I'll help you."

"That's not necessary," I insist, shoving the dishes somewhat haphazardly into the dishwasher.

He stands directly beside me, the familiar scent of grease infiltrating my nose and reminding me of how close he is. "I want to. What if I meet you at the bakery after I get off work? I can bring dinner, maybe those burgers you inspired."

A smile cracks across my lips. This feels like a date. Is this a date? "Umm, okay."

He grins widely, one of those breathtakingly gorgeous smiles that makes my internal muscles clench. "Excellent. I can't wait to watch you in your element this time," he says before heading over to grab more dishes.

Later that night, I'm brushing my teeth for bed, when I hear a noise on the opposite side of the bathroom door. I spit out the toothpaste and rinse my mouth before pressing my ear against the wood.

Last time I opened this door, I found Jasper practically naked, wearing only a pair of gym shorts and his body covered with sweat. A part of me wants to open this door and see what awaits me tonight. Is he running again, or will he be working with the free weights I saw along the back wall?

I consider opening the door to find out, but something stops me. What happened last night, was that a one-time thing? He hasn't so much as made a move on me tonight, so was it just sex to scratch a certain itch? He admitted before he uses sex to help him sleep.

But then there's the fact that we...snuggled. I was prepared to go back to my room, yet he crawled into his bed and pulled me against his warm body.

So what does that mean?

And am I going to get the answers standing here, listening to him work out?

No. As nice as the view would be, it would only cloud the water, because something tells me if I go in there, it won't be to talk.

Unless you consider screaming his name in ecstasy as talking.

No?

Sighing, I flip off the light and return to the guest room, making sure the door is closed securely behind me.

I go ahead and lock it too. I'm just not sure if it's to keep him out or me in.

"I'll see you later tonight," Dustin says, waving from the door as he and Dana head out to have dinner.

When the young woman arrived at the bakery, she was all smiles and dressed in a festive holiday sweater with embroidered Christmas lights around the neck. Dustin loved it, wearing his own holiday-themed tie with the Grinch and Cindy Lou Who. They walked together across the street for dinner and agreed that she would drive him back to Jasper's after they ate, so they could visit more.

Just after six, there's a knock on the back door. I pull it open without looking through the peephole, already knowing who it is.

Smiling, I open the door. "Come on in." As he brushes by me, I catch a whiff of the deliciousness in the bag he's carrying. "That smells amazing."

"I'm excited to try it," he beams, setting the bags down on the large metal island. "I was able to secure Asiago cheese from my distributor today, but I also made one with Cheddar so we could taste the difference and see which one we like best."

I can't help but grin at the way he includes me, as if I'm part of the decision-making process and not just a mouth he's feeding. "Sounds good," I tell him as he slides the first large Styrofoam container my way.

"By the way," he says, opening up the food and transferring two juicy burgers onto paper plates. He cuts them both in half, placing one of each on the two plates. "I saw Dustin and Dana before I left. I went over and said hello. She seems nice." He adds a handful of fries to each plate before sliding one my way.

"She's very nice, like her sister. A little younger than he is, but only by two years. She's a speech therapist for the county health department. She works at the schools mostly but has also been to the hospital and mental health center. She's the first speech therapist we've had in almost two decades," I tell, recalling all the details Daisy shared yesterday after her sister had left the bakery.

"That's cool," he replies, seeming genuinely interested. "I'm impressed. I bet that's a crap-ton of schooling."

I pick up one of the burger halves on my plate and examine the contents. "Seven years. Do you want me to try the Cheddar or the Asiago first?"

Jasper looks over at the food in my hand and the one left on the plate. "That's the Cheddar, so go ahead and try it first."

I bring the food to my mouth and take a bite. The first thing I taste is the juicy tomato and the tangy spinach. Mixed with the fresh ground beef patty, and it's a pretty good burger.

"Tell me what you think."

Once I swallow, I share my thoughts. "Pretty tasty," I tell him. "It's a great flavor combination, and the cheese really sets it off. The tomato is grilled to perfection, and I'm pretty sure you added a pinch of salt. I like that you melted it on the spinach instead of the patty."

His eyes sparkle as he listens, seeming to hang on my every word. When I'm finished, he finally takes his own bite and slowly chews. "I agree. The cheese is good, but I'm hopeful the Asiago is the real winner."

I eat a few fries and take a drink of water to clear my palate before reaching for the other half. I can smell the Asiago cheese, and my mouth waters. When I take a bite, the flavor explodes on my tongue and I groan in satisfaction. Closing my eyes, I savor the unique taste of the ingredients, knowing this is the winning combination. "Oh, man," I groan, quickly taking a second bite. "This is the one," I mumble with a mouth full of food.

He grins widely before taking his own bite, moaning in pure bliss. "Damn."

"Right? It's delicious," I declare. "You could even add a touch of mayo or even a thin layer of chipotle mayo for a kick, though the tomato still holds that juicy factor."

Jasper barks out a laugh, reaches into the bag, and pulls out several small containers. "Mayo, chipotle mayo, zesty ranch, and a creamy cucumber sauce I make from scratch."

We play around with the different sauces, and both agree the zesty ranch is the way to go. It adds a certain kick, while still preserving the unique flavor combinations. Once we finish our food, I toss all the containers in the trash and get ready to bake my cake.

"Will you grab that bag of flour?" I ask, getting the eggs and buttermilk from the refrigerator. I pull all of the dry ingredients off the shelf and set them beside the big, new bag of flour.

When I glance at Jasper, his eyes are dancing with eagerness. "Tell me what to do."

"Gonna let me boss you around for a change, huh?" I tease, then suddenly realize the innuendo of my words. My cheeks flame red as memories of Jasper's hot demands in bed two nights ago come playing back vividly.

He turns my way, an amused smirk on his face. "Well, if you want to...*take the bull by the horns,* sweets, you can boss me around whenever you want."

I didn't think it was possible, but my desire to have the floor open up and swallow me whole is greater than ever before. Now, not only am I thinking about what we did the other night, but so is Jasper. Clearly the bull he's referring to is his cock, and I can tell by the way his eyes devour me from head to toe, it's as if he's picturing me completely naked and recalling all the dirty things he did to my body.

A shiver rolls through my veins.

"Quit thinking about me naked or this cake will never get made," he announces, tossing me a wink. "What should I do?"

I pull out the food processor, willing my breathing and heartbeat to calm down. "How do you like cherries?"

Again, I blush.

Get your mind out of the gutter!

He smirks and pops open the jar sitting in front of him. He brings one to his mouth, tongue slipping out to catch a drop of juice before it can fall. As he chews, he whispers, "Love them."

I clear my throat and try not to think about him using his tongue on *other* things. It doesn't help, of course. "We're making a cherry chip cake with buttercream frosting."

"Excellent." He claps his hands together, heads over to wash them, and gets to work on chopping the maraschinos.

He watches me intently as I make the batter, helping add ingredients as I ask. Once the cherries are added, I divide the batter into three round, greased pans and slip them into the preheated oven.

"That's it?"

"That's it," I confirm, setting the timer. "Well, it is for the cakes. Now we get to make the frosting."

I retrieve the ingredients and toss them in the mixer. It's my favorite appliance of everything in the kitchen and the one thing I use more than anything else, besides the oven.

When it's folding together in the bowl, I glance over and find Jasper grinning. "What?"

"Nothing. It's just that you have some powdered sugar on your cheek."

I quickly swipe it away, only to have him chuckle.

"No, it was the other one."

Before I can try to wipe it off, he leans in his big, warm thumb and presses it against my cheek as he removes the smudge. "There."

"Thanks." The words are hoarse, my throat suddenly extremely dry. I'm very well aware of how close he's standing and how amazing he smells.

"You have some…" he starts, dabbing his pinky against the side of the mixer and taps it against my neck, "…thing right here."

Then his mouth descends, his warm tongue swirling around my skin before he licks and sucks the drop of icing off me. Wetness floods my panties, and it's suddenly hard to breathe. All I can think about, all I want, is him.

We move together. I turn in his arms, and he presses his lips to mine. The cold, hard steel island digs into my ass, but I don't care. I swing my arms around his neck as I lift myself up to meet his hungry mouth. He's hard, his erection firmly wedged between our bodies, and the feel of it only makes me more ravenous.

"You taste so fucking sweet," he whispers, nipping at the corner of my mouth. His hands reach back and grip my ass, gently lifting me onto the table.

I wrap my legs around his waist, rocking my hips and grinding against him. If possible, it feels like his erection grows even harder.

"If I'm being completely honest here, I was hoping you'd show up in the gym again last night," he murmurs, scraping his teeth against my jaw. "I went to bed so fucking hard, I had to take care of it in the shower."

His words—and the images they create—causes a shiver to slide down my spine. "That's hot. I'm sorry I missed it," I mutter, throwing my head back and letting him devour my neck.

"The sex or the jack in the shower?"

I lift my head and meet his gaze. "Both."

His mouth descends once more, raw and demanding as he deepens the kiss. I feel his hands everywhere. My back, my hair, my breasts. Everywhere but where I ache the most for his touch.

Just as he reaches for the button of my jeans, the timer goes off on the oven. I jerk back at the same time a loud knock sounds on the front door. I look in that direction, unable to see who it is from this angle but knowing who the knocker is.

"Shit," I gasp, sucking oxygen into my lungs. I press my hands against his hard chest and jump off the island. Retrieving potholders, I grab the three cakes from the oven and set them on the cooling rack. When I glance back at Jasper, I find him leaning against the island, a smirk on his face and his very prominent erection pressed against his zipper. "Uhh, you may want to put that away."

"This?" he asks, glancing down and taking in his tight pants. "You did that."

"Yeah, but unless you want *that* seen by my brother and his date in about four seconds, you better will that thing into submission. Think about your grandma or something."

He snorts out a laugh, adjusting his pants. "I don't have a grandma."

"Well, think of someone fast, or else you're about to scar my brother for life."

He laughs, walking over and placing a kiss on my nose. "My cock won't be scarring him nearly as much as your tousled hair, swollen lips, and nipples pressed against your shirt, begging to be sucked."

Just as I gasp and glance down, confirming that my nipples are very much a part of this conversation, my brother pushes through the back door with Dana, causing me to turn away to hide.

It's Jasper's laughter that follows me as I make a quick escape into the bathroom until my nipples decide to behave themselves.

Yeah, fat chance of that happening.

Jasper

"Hey, guys, good to see you again," I say after watching Lyndee retreat into the small employee bathroom on the opposite side of the kitchen. I lean forward against the island to cover my erection, knowing it's quickly deflating now that we're no longer alone. "How was dinner?"

"So amazing," Dana coos, her hand tucked in Dustin's arm. "The Ride A Cowboy Burger was perfect."

"I'm glad," I reply, looking at Lyndee's brother. I can tell already he's aware that something was going on in here. He's smirking, his eyes darting around, as if looking for confirmation.

"Where's Lyn?"

"Oh, she had to use the restroom. She'll be out in a minute."

"You guys baked the cake," he notices, using his walker to go over and check them out. "Cherry Chip is her favorite."

"I can't wait to try it."

"You'll be there for it tomorrow, right?"

"Wouldn't miss it," I tell him as the bathroom door opens.

"Hi, guys," Lyndee greets, a too-wide smile on her face. "How was dinner?"

"Excellent," Dana replies.

When she stops beside me, she asks, "What wouldn't you miss?"

"Cake tomorrow night."

"You don't have plans? It's Christmas Eve." Her brown eyes find mine and hold a touch of hesitance.

I shrug. I go to my folks' place on Christmas Day, but that's it. "I always work Christmas Eve. We close the kitchen down at seven and the bar at eight. I should be out around then. You don't have to wait for me, but I'd love to join the celebration when I get home."

Home.

I never thought I'd be comfortable talking about my place and a woman being there, waiting for me, but surprisingly, I am. Not the first time I've realized this, but it still doesn't freak me out.

"We usually just do takeout on Christmas Eve, since Lyn cooks on Christmas Day," Dustin informs me. "We can hold off until you get home. Seems more fitting to have you there anyway."

I swallow over the lump in my throat. "Don't wait on me for dinner, though. You should eat whenever you're ready."

Dustin glances at Dana. "Would you like to come over for dinner and cake?" Then seeming to realize it's not his house, he glances my way and adds, "If you're okay with that."

"Of course, I am. Dana, or anyone else, is welcome while you're staying with me. My place is your place."

He nods and glances at his date. "Actually, we were thinking about going back to your house and grabbing a cup of coffee...if that's okay."

"My home is your home. You don't have to ask."

"Thank you, Jasper," Dana adds, glancing to Dustin. "And I'd love to join you tomorrow, as long as you're okay with my dropping by on your birthday." She looks at Lyndee, who seems surprised to be asked for permission.

"I'd love for you to be there."

"Great. I think we're going to go and let you two decorate that cake. I can't wait to try it. It looks amazing," Dana says, moving to where Dustin stands.

"See you at home," he hollers on his way out the door, offering a wave before they disappear.

Lyndee heads over to the cakes and slips them in the freezer. "What are you doing?" I ask, completely mesmerized by her movements.

"Putting them in the freezer helps them cool faster. Plus, cold cake works better for frosting. If it's too fresh or warm, it'll peel the top of the cake off."

I head her way, dipping my finger in the buttercream as I pass. "So, what you're saying is we have a little time."

Her grin borders on shy, but quickly tips into seductive. "A little. Why, what'd you have in mind?"

I slide that finger across her lips, and then lick it off, savoring the sweet taste of the frosting and that of Lyndee's mouth. "Delicious." Then I move my hands to her head and devour. I could kiss her hot mouth all day, every day. She's seriously the sweetest thing ever.

Pinning her against the island, I reach down and lift, loving the way her legs automatically wrap around my waist once more. I can feel the warmth of her pussy permeating through her pants, and all I want to do is feel it cloak my dick.

"Are we going to be interrupted anymore?"

She shakes her head, her fingers gripping the back of my neck. "We're completely alone."

I step back, leaving her sitting on the island, and move to make sure the back door is locked. I reach down and tug my shirt out of my slacks, lifting it up and over my head before I've returned to where I left her.

"Will you remove that door stop?" she asks, pointing to the little triangle of rubber holding open the swinging door that separates the front room from the kitchen.

I kick the stop, leaving it lie where it lands, and return to the woman who has my blood humming and my dick harder than concrete. I step between her knees, her legs automatically wrapping around me. She reaches for me, her nails dragging lazily down my back as I explore her mouth with my tongue.

The kiss quickly turns rapacious, and I need more. I need her naked, riding my cock and screaming my name. I dig in my pocket and remove the condom I shoved in there earlier. No, I wasn't sure it would be needed, but a man can hope.

And I was hoping like hell.

Lyndee reaches down and removes her shirt, setting it on the cold metal behind her. Then she reaches for me, grabbing at my belt and ripping it from my pants with urgent fingers. My own hands, lacking any and all finesse, tug at the button of her pants until it pops off. "Shit," I mumble, chuckling.

"I don't care," she replies, lifting her hips as I slip down the zipper.

"I can sew it back on for you later," I tell her, catching the look of surprise on her face.

"You sew?"

I shrug, removing her panties too, as I bring the pants down her legs. "My grandma taught me when I was younger."

"I thought you didn't have a grandma," she says, setting her butt back down on the island once her pants reach her ankles. The cold steel causes her to squeal and jump.

Smiling, I tell her, "I don't anymore. She died when I was twelve. She was the one who insisted I know how to wash my own clothes, sew my own buttons, and cook my own food."

"Wow, a man who can cook *and* sew? How did I get so lucky?" As soon as her words register in her own mind, she stops, a look of panic crossing her face.

I know why. She's worried about the implication we're together.

Deciding not to let her dwell on it, I give her a teasing grin. "Well, you're not lucky yet, but you will be soon." I toe off my shoes, shove my pants down to my ankles, and sheath my cock in protection, while stepping out of the bunched material at my feet.

Lyndee unhooks her bra, scoots forward, and tilts her hips my way. I can see the wetness of her beautiful pussy glistening under the fluorescent lighting. My mouth waters. If I weren't already so crazed to get inside her, I'd take my time, teasing and licking her until she was boneless and sated beneath me.

But now's not the time.

Now, my need for her is too great to ignore.

I take my place between her thighs and stroke my cock through her wetness. Goosebumps rise on her delicate skin. They make her nipples pebble even harder. I push forward, filling her completely in one thrust. Our moans fill the space as I reach for the back of her neck, needing to feel her skin under my hand.

I set a fast, possessive pace. I can't help it. She brings out this side of me, this desire to claim. I need to have her, make her mine. Make her come around me. It's quickly becoming an obsession.

She's my obsession.

Lyndee leans back on her hands and locks her ankles behind my ass. The angle sends me deeper, allows me to drive harder. Placing my hands on the cool steel, I thrust forward, feeling the way her body starts to grip me. "Are you going to come, sweets?" I ask, mesmerized by the look of euphoria on her gorgeous face.

"Yes."

"Do it now," I direct, swiping a thumb over her swollen clit. The result causes her to clamp down on me like a vise. The squeeze makes it hard for me to move inside of her, but the feel of her tightness strangling me is enough to bring my own release to the surface.

"Ahhhh," she cries out, rocking her hips as she comes on my cock.

My balls tighten and tingles race up my spine. I rocket forward, hollering out as my release ricochets through me, completely out of control. The hand still holding the back of her neck tightens, but not enough to hurt her. My mouth descends, covering hers, as we both gasp for oxygen and ride out our orgasms. When my hips finally stop moving, all I feel is a sense of wonderment and satisfaction, both because of the woman and not just the sex.

"Well, that's something I've never done in the kitchen," she whispers, humor laced in her words.

"No?" I ask, smiling as I slide my lips across hers.

"Uh, no," she states, running her fingers across my shoulders.

"Well, me either, sweets. Probably has something to do with health code violations," I tease, remaining perfectly still to keep myself buried inside of her as long as possible.

Lyndee groans. "Oh my God, I can't believe we just did that here. In my kitchen. I'm going to have to do a deep clean and sanitization."

I can't help but snort. "You said deep."

She swats at my arm, causing me to step back, dislodging myself from her body. I reach for her hand and help her up, though her legs resemble that of a baby deer trying to stand for the first time. They're all wobbly and unsteady.

And cute.

So sexy, with wetness dripping down her thighs, making me want to fuck her all over again, location be damned.

Fuck, I have it bad.

"Let's get cleaned up so we can disinfect," I state, leading her to the small bathroom.

Inside, she grabs a towel and wets it with warm water, while I remove the condom and wrap it in toilet paper. The last thing we need is for someone like her brother to find it tossed in here. I make a mental note to take the small trash bag with me when I leave.

Once we're both cleaned up, I retrieve our discarded clothes. As I dress again, I can't help but steal glances of her. She's quickly turning my entire world upside down, and even if I wanted to, there's not a damn thing I can do to stop it. I think about her day and night, and now that I've been inside her, it's worse. I crave her, like an alcoholic needs booze. She's my hit.

My drug.

I'm dressed first and go in search of her cleaning supplies. I find the closet beside the bathroom and get to work on sanitizing the workspace we just contaminated with potential bodily fluids, all while smirking, because I'd do it all over again in a heartbeat.

Lyndee grabs the mop and Lysol, cleaning the floors until they shine. When we're done and all the supplies are put back where they belong, I pull her into my arms. "This was the most fun I've ever had baking a cake."

She giggles, resting her cheek against my arm. "I've made a lot of cakes in my time, but never like this."

"We should do it again, don't you think?" I ask, only partially kidding.

"Maybe at your place next time."

"Deal," I reply, kissing the top of her head. "What do you say we finish up so we can head out. I'm really looking forward to you sleeping in my bed with me tonight."

She glances up, her eyebrows drawn together in question. "I don't recall you asking me."

"Did you not sleep well the last time?" I ask, realizing I'm more concerned about her comfort than my own.

"No, I did," she says, a coy smile spreading across her lips. "Too well."

"Me too," I confess, reaching for the bowl of icing and giving it a stir. "I slept better those few hours than I have in years." It's not a lie, and I'm hoping tonight would have the same effect.

She gives me a soft grin that makes my heart skip a beat before turning her attention back to the cake. I watch as she retrieves the three pans from the freezer and plops them down on a piece of round cardboard that sits on a spinning tray. She trims the tops so they sit flat and fills a bag with icing. Then the real magic happens.

Lyndee moves efficiently and quickly, layering cake and icing until it's complete. "You want to do this part?" she asks, handing me a flat scraper tool.

"Tell me what to do."

She starts to slowly spin the cake, squeezing the bag and zigzagging a thick line of icing on the side. Then she does the same to the top, making circles nestled inside each other. "Gently place the spreader like this," she says, demonstrating, "And smooth the icing while it spins."

I take the spreader and step up to the tray. I give it a gentle spin and give it a try. The icing is wavy, but it's there. "Well, looks like I won't be inducted into the cake decorating hall of fame," I state with a laugh.

"It's not tt-terrible," she stutters, trying to cover a giggle with a cough.

"It looks crooked," I insist, smiling.

"Here." She takes the spreader and gets to work, righting the horrible job I did on the icing. She has the sides and top smooth in seconds like the true professional she is. Leaning against the counter to watch her work, she places a star-like tip onto the bag and adds piping along the bottom and top of the cake. "Will you cut those cherries in half?" she asks, pointing to the remaining cherries.

I grab a paring knife and slice the fruit in half, tossing the stems into the empty jar. Lyndee places the pieces along the piping and gives me a smile when it's complete. "Can we eat it now?" I ask, returning her grin.

"No," she giggles, carefully placing the cake inside a box.

"But...we can take this leftover icing, right?" I waggle my eyebrows, loving the happy little sound that spills from her lips.

She closes the lid and glances over her shoulder. "We wouldn't want it to go to waste, right?" she states with a wink, grabbing a small container for the leftovers.

"And these cherries too. I want to eat them off your tits."

She barks out a laugh, a cute blush creeping up her neck as she bats her eyelashes. "Maybe I want to eat them off you."

I groan at the thought of her tongue on me, my cock jumping to attention like a good soldier. "Let's go. We've got a date with icing and cherries."

Lyndee

"Happy birthday to Lyndee, happy birthday to you."

I lean forward and blow out the two candles in the shapes of threes on top of my cherry chip cake, smiling as I get a round of applause. Besides Dustin, Dana, and Jasper, Jameson came too after finding out at work why Jasper was in such a hurry to get home. Apparently, all you have to do is say cake, and Jameson is there.

Jasper takes the cake and cuts it into healthy slices, handing a plate to each person. "I promised Numbers I'd save him a piece, if we have some left."

"Where's he tonight?" I ask, taking my first bite of cake. Of course, I can't stop thinking about what happened in my kitchen while baking the cake, or what followed after we got back here after Dustin went to bed. Let's just say I was cleaning sticky icing residue off almost every part of my body.

"Went to Savannah's family's for dinner," Jameson grumbles, pulling a face.

"So, not a Savannah fan, huh?" I ask, teasing, though it's clear my assumption is right on.

He snorts in disgust. "She's not good for him and she strings him along. Plus, I'm pretty sure she cheated on him at least once over the last few years. I hate her." He's blunt and to the point, letting his dislike for the pretty woman known. Truth be told, I wasn't that impressed with her when I met her on Sunday. She seemed very self-absorbed, barely paying Isaac or anyone else any attention. As the other newbie in the group, I tried to talk to her after dinner, but felt like she was just trying to get away from me to return to her phone.

"Oh my God, this is so good." Dana takes a healthy bite of her cake and closes her eyes to savor the flavor. That's always my favorite part. Watching the joy on their face as they enjoy something I created.

"What do you think of the icing? Doesn't it make you want to stick your finger in the cake and lick it off?" Jasper asks, a smirk on his face, as he shovels a big bite into his mouth, looking all flirty and amused and...smug.

I, on the other hand, am not feeling as amused. I can only picture what he did with that icing-coated finger and the way I came hard as he sucked it off my body.

Is it hot in here?

Jameson snickers, as if he knows exactly what his friend was talking about, or worse, doing. Fortunately for me, Dustin and Dana seem oblivious to the thick sexual tension in the room and continue chatting, while enjoying their dessert.

When I finally glance back up at Jasper, I can read his thoughts as if he spoke them aloud. His mind has clearly gone into naughty territory. He licks his lips and gives me a very sultry look, elevating my blood pressure into stroke territory.

By the time we finish eating cake, my brother declares it present time. He wheels himself into the den down the hall and returns with a large gift bag with bright pink tissue paper sticking out of the top. "What's this?" I ask, grinning as he brings me the present.

"Open it and find out," he replies, setting the bag on my lap.

I pull the tissue paper and find a set of square canvas prints. There are four different images, all with different ingredients. "I love these," I tell him.

"I thought they'd look great in your office, since the walls are still bare."

"They're perfect. Thank you," I tell my brother, giving him a warm smile.

"Mine next," Jameson hollers, pulling an envelope out of his inside coat pocket.

"You didn't have to get me anything," I insist, taking the envelope from his outstretched hand.

"Well, it's not much on short notice, but my mama raised me not to show up at a birthday party without a gift," he replies with a grin.

I slip the sheet of paper out and read it over. "This is amazing, thank you!"

Jasper looks over my shoulder, reading the note. "Wow, pulling out all the stops, aren't we?" he states with a laugh. "Do I need to be concerned about you stealing my girl?"

My heart hammers in my chest at his question to his friend. I glance over at Jameson, who just winks. "Not at all, but if Lyndee were to discover who the better man is, well, that's on you, friend." He's clearly joking, but the statement gets a rise out of Jasper, nonetheless.

He leaps at him and puts him in a headlock. "Keep your hands to yourself," he demands, laughing, while messing up Jameson's hair.

When the guys are finished messing around, Dustin reaches for the paper. "What'd ya get?"

I hand it over and reply, "The first official beer tasting tour for Burgers and Brew, plus a variety case, once they have it ready."

"Cool!" Dustin proclaims, showing the paper to Dana.

"You're welcome too," Jameson tells my brother, trying to finger-comb his messy hair while throwing glares at his friend. "It should be ready to start producing beer next month, as long as our inspections go through."

"I can't wait to see it," I announce.

Jasper disappears down the hall, only to return a few minutes later with a wrapped box. He sets it on my lap and starts cleaning up the cake mess. Am I supposed to open this now? He's not even over here watching.

I glance up and catch Jameson's eye. He winks at me and nods, encouraging me to open the gift. I pull on the ribbon and rip off the bow before digging into the paper. Inside, I find the most gorgeous journal. When I remove the book, I realize it's not really a journal. It's a recipe book, and it's blank, ready for me to fill it in.

My gaze moves to the counter, where Jasper is working intently on sealing the cake into a container. When he doesn't look my way, I stand and head toward him. "Hey," I whisper, when I'm right beside him.

"Hi."

"Thank you," I murmur, my voice clouded with emotion. "I love it."

He shrugs, keeping his hands busy. "I just thought you could add some of your own recipes in it. I'm sure you have them all memorized, so it's probably a stupid gift," he stammers, seeming completely unsure of himself for the first time since I've known him. Jasper's always so confident, but not now.

I set the book on the counter and slip my arms around his waist. I hug into him until he stops moving. I feel him relax as he wraps his arms around my neck and holds me tight. "It's an amazing gift. Thank you," I repeat, glancing up.

He smiles softly. "So, maybe you could show me your appreciation later?" he asks, wiggling his eyebrows.

I giggle. "I think we used up all the icing."

A heavy laugh spills from his mouth. "Good thing I have a whole pantry full of supplies then, huh?"

I'm snuggled against his chest, listening to the steady thunder of his heartbeat against my cheek. My body is completely sated, and I'm not sure I could form complete sentences yet. This man does things to me I've never experienced before. Not only in bed, but outside of it too. I enjoy running new ideas by him, different flavor options, or listening to him share about his day.

But what has my attention now is his words from earlier. Twice, he called me his girl. Right before he gave me that amazingly thoughtful gift. Considering the fact he just found out it was my birthday two days ago, he did well on short notice.

"If you're able to still think that hard, I didn't do my job right," he says, a soft chuckle rumbling against my skin.

"You did your job just fine," I mutter, placing a kiss on his chest and running my fingers through the dark hair peppered between his defined pecs.

"*Fine*. What every man loves to hear," he teases with a hint of sarcasm.

Now it's my turn to chuckle. "No, that part was more than fine."

Jasper turns me on my side and faces me. "Then, what's up?"

His deep brown eyes hold a touch of concern and wonder, and even though he hasn't struck me as the "talking" type, I find myself opening up to him and saying what's on my mind. "So...tonight you called me your girl."

"I did. Twice, actually," he replies, swiping a strand of hair off my cheek and moving it behind my ear. "Does that bother you?"

Does it? I realize quickly the answer is no.

I shake my head. "It doesn't, but I guess I'm just curious as to what it means."

He takes a deep breath and places his hand against my cheek. "To be honest, I don't really know, but when I said it, I didn't regret the words. I like you, Lyndee. I enjoy spending time with you, even though we don't get that much of it. Between your schedule and mine, I find when we do actually get to share a meal or hang out, I enjoy it a lot."

Jasper sighs. "I don't date. I never have time, but with you, I find myself wanting to make time. And falling into bed with you after a long day is pretty fucking great too," he adds with a sheepish grin. "If you want to put a label on this, we can—"

"I don't need a label," I quickly interrupt.

He relaxes. "I'd give it one if you needed," he insists.

"I like spending time with you too."

"Okay," he replies, pulling me into his arms once more. "I know your condo will be done soon, but I was kinda hoping we could keep hanging out. You know, after you go back home. I have a crazy schedule, but I'd really like to keep seeing you."

I offer him a smile. "I'd like that."

He lowers his mouth and swipes it softly across mine. "Good. Now, let's go back to this whole *fine* thing."

Three weeks later, I'm just getting home from work, my legs almost too tired to carry me to my bedroom.

It's a Saturday night, so Jasper's working late at the restaurant. Dustin and Dana went to a movie, which means I have the condo to myself for a bit, and I'm grateful. My feet are killing me, as is my back from bending over my workstation and decorating cupcakes for an anniversary celebration at the furniture store down the street. It's their twenty-fifth year in business, and they asked me to bake cupcakes for a week-long sale and celebration. I was honored and spent my entire Saturday evening making dozens of special cupcakes for the client.

All I want now is a bubble bath and a glass of wine.

When I push through my door, I'm surprised to find it lit with battery-operated candles on my dresser and nightstand, as well as a bottle of wine chilling in ice on a TV tray. Smiling, I head for the note sitting on my pillow.

Lyndee,

I've been watching you work all afternoon, even after you closed for the day, so I wanted to give you a night to relax. Your brother is gone, there's food warming in the oven, and some fancy bubble bath in your bathroom. I hope you enjoy a little alone time, and if the mood strikes you, you can think of me while you're in the bath. Just make sure you take pictures...

Jasper

A bark of laughter flies as I glance around, taking in the sight. For someone who doesn't do the whole dating thing, he's pretty damn good at it.

I go to the wine and pour myself a small glass before heading to the kitchen to see what's for dinner. There's a piece of lasagna in a dish, along with bacon wrapped asparagus and thick garlic toast. My mouth practically waters.

Deciding I need to eat something first, I dive into the dish, recognizing it as one of Jasper's personal pans from his kitchen. That means, at some point today, he cooked me food. Considering he usually works all day Saturdays, that's pretty amazing. As I shovel a big bite of food into my mouth and groan, I realize he's not the only thing amazing.

So is this meal.

I inhale everything he left me before slipping down the hall and filling up the bathtub. The bubbles are lavender, one of my favorites, so I add more than enough and fill the room with the heavenly scent.

I grab my wine glass, take a sip, and search for my phone. There's a playlist for relaxation, so I fire up John Mayer and strip out of my clothes. Only when I'm up to my neck in bubbles and warm water do I finally feel myself relaxing.

I sit for several minutes, trying not to think about what I need to do tomorrow. The bakery is closed on Sundays, but I always use that day to prep for the week. I place orders, bake bread, and fill any private orders for the upcoming week. Sundays are just as busy as any other day, except I don't have the foot traffic.

But I refuse to think about that now.

I reach for my phone and pull up my camera. Making sure nothing shows through the bubbles, I snap a quick picture and fire it off with the caption "All that's missing is you."

I set my phone down on the toilet cover, knowing he won't reply for a while. It's just after seven, which means Jasper's neck deep in orders. Smiling, I picture him behind the grill, his polo shirt stretched tautly over his arms and chest, as he barks orders to his staff. I can see where some might find him hard to work for, but I find it quite the opposite. I respect the hell out of him, as a businessman and a creator, and his work speaks volumes for both.

My hand slips below the bubbles and rubs across my clit. Sparks of desire race through my veins as I imagine it's his hand between my legs. My nipples pebble as I hitch a leg up on the side of the tub and press two fingers inside of me. Pleasure takes over as I slide my fingers in and out, picturing Jasper's intense face as if it were his hand moving beneath the water.

I reach for my phone and pull up the camera. Never having snapped a picture like this before, I boldly lift my hips up so my breasts are above the water and you can see where my fingers are. It's difficult to take the photo, especially when I try to keep my face out of it, but I manage. As soon as I send it off with the one from earlier, I drop my phone on the rug and let the pleasure take over.

Being with Jasper these last few weeks has meant I've not been short in the orgasm department, but there's something so sexy and liberating about doing it myself. Especially knowing he'll find out what I've been doing when he looks at his phone. I can picture his face now. Those intense chocolate eyes and how they burn with desire and need.

When I come apart, it's only him that I see, his name I whisper. The water swallows me, as my body coils tight and then releases in bliss. Waves of pleasure ripple through my body, finally leaving me exhausted and ready for bed.

Before I climb out of the tub, I grab my phone and fire off a quick text.

Me: *Sorry you missed it. Maybe next time.*

Satisfied with the quip, I release the drain and dry off. Smiling, I head back to my bedroom, throw on an oversized sleepshirt and pants, and snuggle beneath the blankets. As I lie there, I imagine the look on his face when he sees my messages. First, the innocent one, then the dirty one.

I know I'll pay for that later.

At least I hope I do.

Twenty-Three

Jasper

I'm so fucking hard. Sitting in my office, all I can do is stare down at my phone, at the image of Lyndee in the tub. The way her nipples poke out of the water, all covered in suds and begging to be licked, and the faint sight of her fingers buried in her pussy. It's enough to make me want to lock my door and take care of myself right here and now.

Thank God I didn't look at my phone while I was still in the kitchen and surrounded by my employees.

I hear someone walking through the kitchen and know it can only be one man.

"Hey," Numbers says, poking his head around the corner.

Making sure my phone is down so he can't see the screen, I lean back casually in my chair, careful to conceal my erection. "Hi."

"Hectic night."

"Always," I reply, grabbing a stack of purchase orders and making myself busy. "I'm getting ready to head out."

"Yeah?" he asks, leaning against the doorjamb. "Hot date?"

My mind flashes to the image on my phone. "Something like that. Oh, hey, I need a favor."

"Shoot."

"I want to take Lyndee away next weekend. I'm thinking one of those bed and breakfast places over in the town with all those antique stores."

"Shipman. They have several to choose from. You need me to look into it for you?"

As tempting as it is, because we all know Isaac is the computer guy, it just doesn't feel right having him look for a room for me and Lyndee. "No, I can handle that. I was hoping you'd help Ross, if he needs it. He's not used to working Saturday nights, and well, they're a lot busier than a Tuesday. Plus, I'll have to send in our bread order Sunday morning, so I'll need help with that. I'll have it ready, you just have to send the email."

Numbers draws his eyebrows together. "You're going over a weekend? Like a Saturday night?"

I can already feel myself getting irritated with his line of questioning, because I know exactly where it's headed. "Yeah."

He comes into my office and drops down onto a chair. "Wow, never thought I'd see the day."

"What are you talking about?"

"The day where the great Jasper Kohlmann falls," he replies, grinning widely.

"Pfft!" I blurt out, rolling my eyes dramatically. "Knock it off. I haven't fallen for anyone."

Not true.

Isaac laughs. Actually laughs in my face. "If you say so, buddy. But I do recall Walker being the same way. Denied it until he was blue in the face. You see where he is now, right? Engaged and with a baby on the way," he counters, grabbing the stress ball on my desk—the one someone gave me for Christmas a few years ago as a joke—and tossing it in the air.

"That's different."

"If you say so," he repeats, pissing me off even more.

"Stop saying that," I thunder, glaring at him from across my desk. Of course, the asshole only laughs harder.

"Fine. I see we're back to the whole denial bit. I'd be more than happy to help Ross next weekend so you can take your not-girlfriend to a non-romantic weekend away."

"Thank you," I grumble, crossing my arms over my chest and relaxing in my seat. The good news is my erection is truly fucking gone.

"No sweat. I'm sure the kitchen staff will enjoy not getting yelled at too. It's a win for them as well."

He's joking, but there's a lot of truth in his statement. I'm a bastard in the kitchen. I know it. They know it. You either deal with it or you move on, it's as simple as that. "You done?"

He chuckles and gets up. "Yep. I'll stay and help Walker close."

"No plans with Savannah?"

He shakes his head. "She went out of town with girlfriends."

I contain my eyeroll, but barely. "All right, well, I'm gonna head out. Have a good night," I state, grabbing my coat and meeting him at the door. I throw the light switches and head down the back hall, stopping at the employee exit, the soft acoustical sounds of Jameson strumming his guitar filtering down the deserted hallway. "Hey, I appreciate your help. I know you're not comfortable in the kitchen, so I definitely appreciate your willingness to step in."

He meets my gaze and straightens his tie. "Actually, I don't mind helping in the kitchen at all, Jasper. I just hate dealing with your grumpiness, so I stay away. I actually like to cook."

The corner of my mouth turns up. "Really?"

"Getting yelled at by your moody ass is the reason I stay out of there," he states with a big grin.

I bark out a laugh. "I'm not moody."

I'm very moody.

Now it's his turn to chuckle. "Not nearly as much as you used to be. Yet another reason why Lyndee is good for you." He slaps me on the back and heads down the hall toward the bar, leaving me standing there alone with my thoughts.

I have been a little easier to get along with in the last month, and I'm sure he's right. Lyndee has everything to do with it.

I push out the door, making sure it's secured behind me, and grab my phone. I fire off a quick text, hoping she's still up to hear it, yet hoping she was able to get to bed at a decent hour. Every time I looked out the window today, I could see her busting her ass in that bakery, helping fill orders and restocking trays of pastries.

She's got a thriving business, and I'm so fucking proud of her.

When she doesn't reply, I climb into my Mercedes and start it up. I should definitely go home and let her rest. Even though she's closed tomorrow, she works just as hard on her day off as she does every other day of the week.

But then I think about that picture, of her in the bathtub, fingering herself, and my car turns in the opposite direction of where I live. As if completely on its own, I head for Lyndee.

To the woman I'm falling for.

"Jasper's taking the weekend off," Numbers announced to the table as I deliver our new burger selection. The one inspired by Lyndee's stuffed chicken dish a few weeks ago. I've spent weeks perfecting it and prepping it to be added to the menu. We'll debut it next week, offering the Between the Sheets burger as our featured sandwich of the week.

"What? A whole weekend?" Walker asks, his eyes wide with shock.

"Well, I'm leaving here at two on Saturday. I'll be back on Monday morning," I answer, trying to act nonchalant.

The truth is this is a big deal for me. I've never taken a weekend off like this. Never not worked a Saturday night. Even when I was a little sick two years ago, I still dragged my ass into work, masked up, and did my fucking job.

I look up and realize three sets of eyes are watching me, and they're all smiling. "What?"

Jameson leans back in his chair. "Nothing, man. Happy for you."

"Let's talk about the burger," I say, changing the subject. I hate having attention on me like this, especially when it comes to Lyndee. I don't know what we are, but I'm hoping to have the conversation this weekend when we go away. We hang out as much as we can, and the sex is fucking phenomenal. I call her my girl, but that's the only label we've put on it. I have no interest in anyone else, which is a big sign this is headed into somewhat uncharted waters.

But I'm not scared.

Worried, yes. I'm sure I make a shitty boyfriend. I'm needy and moody and often completely self-absorbed, but she knows this and still wants to be around me. She'll even put me in my place when necessary, which is exactly what I need. So as long as she's willing to work with me, I'm willing to give this whole relationship thing a try.

"What's it called?" Walker asks, eyeing the veggie combination on top with a critical eye.

"Between the Sheets. All the goodness is between two slices of Asiago cheese," I state, going through the ingredients and describing the slight changes I've made since I first cooked this burger for Lyndee.

Jameson is the first one to take a bite, not at all afraid of whatever concoction I create. "Damn, that's good," he mumbles, mouth full of food.

Walker follows suit, taking a second bite before he adds, "Delicious. Mal would love this."

Isaac just stares at his food, eyeing the green stuff as if it were to jump off his plate and bite him. "I'm not sold on the spinach. Who wants spinach on a burger?"

Sighing, I grab my own burger and take a healthy bite. "Just try it."

He does, reluctantly, and chews slowly. "It's not bad, but not my favorite. I can see it being a big draw though. The cheese and the sauce give it good flavor."

"As does the tomato and *spinach*," I reply with a clipped tone.

"You don't have to get testy. I'm just not a fan of it, and never thought I'd see it on a cheeseburger. Again, it's not bad, and I think it will sell well. I'll have my sister get on social media marketing to promote it for next week," Numbers says, making notes before diving into his fries.

"I'm not making you another one," I state, only partially kidding. "You can scrape off what you don't like."

He sighs and shakes his head. "I wasn't going to ask. Quit giving me a hard time. Did you not get laid last night? You're awfully grumpy."

I didn't get laid actually, but I'm not about to tell him that. Usually, I'd have no problems talking about sex with my friends, but not now. Not when it's Lyndee. What we do is private and not to be shared with these idiots.

"Speaking of Mal," Walker says, grinning from ear to ear as his fiancée walks toward our table. "Try this."

She takes what's left of his burger and takes a healthy bite. Her eyes widen in delight as she chews. "Oh my God, is that spinach?"

"See?" I ask, glaring at Isaac. "Someone with taste."

He just rolls his eyes and continues to eat his fries, smothering them in ketchup.

"Yes, this is so good," she mumbles, taking another big bite and leaving Walker grinning. When she tries to hand it back, he waves her off, telling her to finish it. She does, before diving into his fries too. "I should get back to work. My boss is a real PITA."

I snort out a laugh.

"PITA?" Numbers asks, glancing around the table to find everyone laughing.

"Pain in the ass. She's got Jasper's number," Jameson chimes in.

"Yeah, yeah, yeah. Get back to work or your PITA boss may fire you." I won't, she's a great server and an asset to the business.

Mallory rolls her eyes dramatically. "He wouldn't. He needs me too much. No one else puts up with his moody ass."

She's not wrong, and the guys all think so too by the way they chuckle.

"Jasper's taking Lyndee away this Saturday. They're in love," Walker sings.

There's no missing Mallory's surprise. "Really? I like her and could use another female in the group to combat all this testosterone."

Before I can reply, Isaac speaks up. "You have Savannah. I'm sure she'd love to hang out with you more."

I glance her way and notice the cringe she tries to cover quickly. Fortunately, Numbers misses it, since he's poking at the spinach on his plate. He misses the gagging face Jameson makes too. Probably for the best.

"That would be great," Mallory replies sweetly, even though I can tell she's not in the least bit interested. "All right, I need to get back over there before Marla takes my tables." She leans down and kisses Walker firmly on the lips.

A few weeks ago, I would have been annoyed by the interruption and their over-the-top displays of affection, but now, all I think about is how great it would be to kiss Lyndee right now. To have her be a part of my day, like Mallory is to Walker.

And then there's Lizzie.

Lizard.

What would it be like to have one of those little people running around? For the longest time, I would have declared it not for me. The diapers, the crying, the demand that comes with raising a child.

But then I picture the other side of parenting. How excited Lizard is when she gives Walker a new picture for his office wall and how hard she hugs him when he picks her up from preschool. The sweet way she whispers she loves him as she snuggles into her little bed before falling asleep.

Somehow, those images are more vibrant, more overpowering than the ones I always saw when I thought about having kids. It just wasn't for me. I loved spending the afternoon with my niece and nephew but am always happier when I'm back at my own place, surrounded in peace and quiet.

Now, kids don't seem so bad.

Especially when Lyndee's in the picture.

After our meeting, I head back to my office and get a little work done. I do a quick inventory and place orders, all while my mind is completely distracted by thoughts of the woman who monopolizes my every thought. I bring up my email and delete all the junk. I send a few replies and finish one I started earlier left in my draft folder, and when everything is clean and filed, I finally shut my laptop down.

Glancing at the clock, I realize it's near dinnertime. The bakery is closed, but I can't help but wonder if maybe my girl is across the street, prepping tomorrow's breads and donuts. Instead of going to the grill and getting to work, I find myself walking to the bar, to the wall of windows that faces the street.

The ones I can see directly into the bakery, to the woman who's still working away in her kitchen. She's bent over the island— the very one I took her on when we baked her birthday cake— kneading a big ball of dough.

Before I even know what's happening, I head out the door. Without a coat, I cross the street, and make my way to the alley entrance of Sugar Rush.

One kiss.

That's all I need.

One little kiss to tide me over until later tonight.

When we'll be alone, and I can show her with my body how I'm falling for her.

And maybe soon, have the balls to actually be able to tell her.

Twenty-Four

Lyndee

"So, are you excited about this weekend?" Dana asks, sitting at the table across from me.

I offer a quick grin, thinking about the getaway Jasper has planned for us. We're leaving in two days, after I close the bakery and his evening chef comes in for the night. He surprised me with this trip on Sunday, after making sure my brother would be okay by himself for the night. I know he will be, but I can't help but feel guilty. Dustin has been home by himself several times since I started seeing Jasper, but I'm usually just across town. Not an hour away.

"I am." I'm beaming from ear to ear, starting to get really excited about the bed and breakfast he booked for us. "And you two have plans Saturday night, right?"

Dustin and Dana have been spending a lot of time together. She comes over a few evenings a week and watches movies with him but has yet to spend the night. I'd be okay with it but am not really sure how to tell them that. I mean, I want him to have friends and is free to date if he wants. The fact he picked Dana, who is super sweet and encouraging for him, is the icing on the proverbial cake.

"We do. He's insisting on making me dinner. I hope that's okay," she says, taking a sip of her tea.

"Of course it is. It's his place as much as it is mine. You're welcome anytime," I reassure her, watching as she smiles the moment my brother comes through the door.

It's an unusually warm late January day, so Dustin insisted on walking the deposit down the block to get outside for a few minutes.

Using his walker, he heads our way, a tight look on his face. "Hey."

"Hi," Dana blurts out, jumping up and giving him a kiss on the cheek. I watch as the tension ebbs from his face, but only a little.

"Something wrong?" I ask, warming my hands on my own mug of tea.

"Oh, uh...I don't know," he says uncomfortably, glancing around. It's nearing our two o'clock closing time, and even though we're usually busy up until we close, it's been unusually quiet today.

Dustin sits down and sets a newspaper on the table. There's a slight shake to his hand as he pushes it my way. "I was at the bank and the ladies behind the counter were reading something in the paper. When they turned to help me, one gave me a super guilty look and shoved the paper behind her back. It gave me a weird feeling, so I stopped at the corner market and grabbed one."

I glance down, unsure what I'm seeing. The front-page article is about a food drive at the local high school, but something tells me that's not why he purchased a copy. I flip through the pages until I hit page five, and something jumps out at me. It's my name.

I scan the article, unsure what I'm reading. The words are...wrong. So wrong, I have to stop and read it again. The second time doesn't help.

I don't understand what's going on here.

"What is this?" I whisper, my throat thick with emotion.

Dustin gives me a look of pity. "It appears to be a letter to the editor."

"It has Jasper's name on the bottom." He doesn't have to confirm my statement because it's right there, in black and white. "Jasper wrote this?" I ask, my eyes clouded with unshed tears.

"It would appear so," Dustin replies slowly.

"Why?" I mutter, the question barely audible.

He reaches over and squeezes my hand. "I'm not sure. You're going to have to ask him that."

I reread the article for a third time, trying to wrap my head around what is going on. Why would he write these horrible lies? Slept with a health inspector? Was fired? Unsanitary kitchen? What in the hell?

I jump up, my chair clattering to the floor behind me, but I don't step to pick it up. "Listen, it's almost two. Why don't you two head out and enjoy the afternoon," I suggest, moving behind the counter and scrubbing at the already-clean space.

"I think I'm going to stay," Dustin says to Dana, standing up and shuffling to where I stand.

"No," I insist, tossing the cloth on the countertop. "Really, I think I want to be alone for a little while. You two go and enjoy this nice day. Tomorrow the temperature is supposed to drop again, so you might as well take advantage of it, right?" I ask, giving them a big, fake smile.

He sighs. "I don't like it."

"Please, Dust. I need to be alone right now." I blink several times, trying to keep the tears at bay. I refuse to let them fall right now. Not in front of my brother and Dana.

"Okay, but you'll call us if you need us?"

I nod and give him a hug. "I will, promise. I'm going to prep tomorrow's dough, and maybe try out that new cookie recipe I've been working on. You two go. I'll see you later tonight. Or not. Go out and have fun. Enjoy your time together," I say, practically pushing them out the door.

"We'll see you later," he insists, waiting for Dana to step out first before he follows using his walker.

Once he's down the sidewalk, I close and lock the door, only to stop and stare at the building across the street. I'm so conflicted, so confused about what is happening. One minute he's inviting me to a weekend getaway, and now he's printing lies about me in the local paper? For what?

My mind swims with questions and no answers, but that's not what hurts the most. That's my heart. The ache has become so intense, it's hard to breathe.

I flip off the lights and head to the kitchen, to the one place where everything seems right. My heart hammers in my chest as I add ingredients into the mixer, preparing my first batch of fresh banana bread for tomorrow. Flipping the lever, the machine starts to do its thing, but I don't see it.

I can't.

The tears start to fall.

I close my eyes, the pain of betrayal like an ice pick to the chest.

What am I going to do?

Why did he do this?

And why does the thought of losing him forever hurt more than the potential damage to my reputation?

Jasper

"Order up!" I bellow, pushing the plates toward my assistant. It's just after seven, and we're still hopping. The dining room is packed, even for a Thursday night. Usually, I'd have the evening off and would be with Lyndee, but since Ross is working for me Saturday, I'm taking tonight for him.

"Uh, Jasper, a word, please?" Jameson announces, approaching the grill.

"Not now. I'm busy," I reply, throwing three more patties on the grill for the next order. "Where are the fries? We're almost out of fresh cut fries!"

"Now."

There's something in his tone, in that one word. I glance up and find his angry eyes glaring at me.

What the hell?

"Uhh, Doug, can you man the grill for me for a second?" I say, setting my spatula down and following my friend toward my office.

The moment I step over the threshold, the door slams shut. "What the hell?"

"Shut up." Jameson gives me a look that would make a lesser man cower beneath the desk. I've rarely seen this side of him, never to have it directed at me. The anger rolling off him is thick and uncomfortable, but for the life of me, I can't figure out why he looks like he wants to kill me and bury my body in the woods.

Instead of arguing with him, I do as instructed and take a seat behind my desk. I expect Jameson to sit across from me, but that's not what he does. He leans over my desk, narrowing his focused eyes. "What the fuck did you do?" he growls, making me pull back.

"What are you talking about? What did I do?"

"The newspaper!" he thunders, slamming his hand down on the desk.

"What newspaper?" I demand, getting angry myself. "What the hell are you talking about."

"The letter to the editor, Jasper. What the fuck?"

My mind spins. Letter to the editor? What the hell is he talking about. "I don't know what you're talking about!" I holler back, standing up and leaning over my desk. We're practically nose to nose now, but I don't care.

"No? You don't remember this?" he asks, reaching into his leather jacket and pulling a folded newspaper from within. He slaps it on the desk between us, drawing my angry gaze down.

I read the words, but...what?

What the hell is this?

"Look familiar?" he demands, the vein on his forehead pulsing.

I look back down, trying to figure out what is going on here. It's a letter to the editor, written by me.

That article.

The one from weeks ago, when I found out Lyndee was opening the bakery across the street. I remember finding the news story about Sugar Rush and reading all about her successes. About the awards she won.

I was so pissed off.

I clicked the link and typed out all that bullshit but never sent it.

I know I didn't.

"I didn't send this," I insist, rereading the garbage on the paper for a second time.

"Not according to name at the bottom."

My lungs deflate, all oxygen seeming to evaporate from the room. I drop in my chair and try to breathe, but it's difficult. My lungs burn, my throat's dry, and my chest aches. "I wrote it, but...a while ago. I didn't send it."

"But you did."

My mind races as I try to piece together what is happening. I thought I got rid of that email. How the hell did it wind up being sent after I composed and thought I deleted it?

"I don't..." I run my hands through my hair. "I don't understand."

He snorts in disgust. "You think *you* don't understand? How the hell do you think Lyndee feels right now?"

I jump up and glance toward the door. "I gotta go."

As I fling open the door, ignoring how it slams against the wall of my office, he hollers, "You better fix this shit and fast!"

I move through the kitchen, feeling eyes on as me as I go. Glancing at Doug, I tell him to cover for me and hightail it out of the kitchen.

The dining room is full, but my focus is on the front entrance. I'm outside moments later and running across the street, a car honking its horn and slamming on the brakes to keep from hitting me.

When I hit the sidewalk, I see lights on in the back of the bakery, letting me know Lyndee's inside. I decide to take a chance that the back door is unlocked and am there a few seconds later. Twisting the knob, I'm relieved to find it unlocked as I push it open and step inside.

It only takes a moment for my eyes to adjust to the fluorescent lighting, but when they do, the scene before me breaks my heart. Lyndee's standing there, surrounded by dozens of pastries, flour covering every surface and egg splattered on the back wall.

I take a step forward, my heart in my throat. "Lyndee?"

She looks up, our eyes meeting, hers holding so much agony it causes me physical pain. "What are you doing here?" she whispers, swiping angrily at a tear on her cheek.

"I…" What do I say to fix this? "Are you okay?"

Her swollen eyes flare with fury. "Am I okay?" she repeats, sarcasm dripping off her words.

Okay, so apparently that was the wrong question.

"I just…" I stammer, taking a step in her direction.

"You just…what? What could you possibly have to say right now, Jasper?"

I move around the island, slowly joining her on the opposite side. "I don't know how this happened."

"How what happened? How you wrote horrible lies about me and my business and sent them to the local newspaper for everyone to read? How you damaged my reputation and everything I'm working for with just a few clicks of the mouse? Please, tell me all about how you have no clue how this happened."

I stop when I'm directly in front of her, those gorgeous brown eyes I love throwing daggers of venom at my chest. "Listen, I know this looks bad," I start, but don't get any further.

"Looks bad? This doesn't *look* bad, Jasper. This *is* bad!"

"I didn't mean any of that," I argue, grasping at any straw I can grab to help me plead my case.

"You didn't mean it? All those lies you told?" She laughs, but it's humorless and sounds nothing like the glorious chuckle I long to hear. "Well, thank God you didn't mean it. That fixes everything!"

I sigh, reaching for her hand, but she snaps it back before I can touch her. "I don't know what to say," I whisper, hating that she won't let me touch her.

"There's nothing you can say, is there? You wrote deceptions about me and sent them to the newspaper, Jasper."

"I'm so sorry, sweets. I didn't mean them. I was angry, and it was juvenile. I knew it after I had written it and thought it was deleted," I plea, taking a small step closer. "It must have accidentally gone to my draft folder and went out earlier this week after I was sending emails."

She closes her eyes, the tears still falling in waves, creating a hole the size of Jupiter to form in my gut.

My thumb grazes against her soft, wet skin and a whimper escapes her lips. "I'm so fucking sorry," I tell her, stepping forward once more. We're standing chest to chest, our bodies aligning perfect. She was made for me.

I lean down and brush my lips across hers. A charge of electricity slides through my body just like it does every time we touch. I want nothing more than to kiss away the pain, to take all the hurt I've caused and make it all go away.

Just as I try to deepen the kiss, she rips her lips from mine and takes a step back. I want to grab her, make her stay with me, refuse to break our connection because it's too fucking good, too fucking right to deny. But when I go to open my mouth, she's already shaking her head, the opening I saw earlier slammed shut and locked without a hint of sunlight.

"You need to go," she says, her voice trembling, yet strong.

"I'm not going anywhere. I'm going to make this right."

Those brown eyes I love so much are cold as they glare at me. "You're going to make what right? The fact I had hardly any customers this afternoon after your little fictitious letter went viral? Fix the fact I had a customer cancel an upcoming wedding cake order that I had just secured last week? Guess what, Jasper. You *can't* make this right. The damage is done. You spewed mistruths publicly, damaging my business and my reputation."

This is what a broken heart feels like.

"But do you know what's worse of all? As badly as that hurts, and believe me, that fucking blows, what hurts the most is being betrayed by the one person I thought was my friend. The one person who held me in his arms and made me feel safe and secure, who gave me the confidence I needed to push through the hardest weeks of opening my own business. The man I trusted more than anyone else, and now that's broken."

She starts to cry once more. I step forward, but she pulls back. Again.

It's like someone is cutting out my heart with a rusty butter knife.

"Please go."

I move away from her, only because I know my words won't matter. No amount of apologizing will fix this. My mind is screaming to cut my losses and get the hell out of here. I wasn't the relationship kind of guy anyway, right? This just proves I'm nothing but the self-centered asshole everyone accuses me of being. All I'll do is taint her beauty, her goodness.

This proves I'm all wrong for her.

I knew it then.

I know it now.

It's still hard though, walking away from the only woman I've ever seen myself loving. Even when I know it's the best thing for her. And for me.

But I do it. I walk to the door. I push open the screened outer one and step through it. Only when I'm over the threshold, everything I never knew I wanted standing behind me, do I stop and turn around.

And want to cry.

She looks so lost, so hurt, so devastated.

And I did that.

Me.

And because I'm the ultimate asshole, I tell her words I've never spoken to another woman, outside my family. Words I should keep to myself, knowing they'll probably do more damage than good, especially now. "I never meant to hurt you. I love you."

I walk the rest of the way through that door and don't look back. It would kill me if I did, and I'm too weak.

Love makes you weak.

Vulnerable.

Two things I hate.

So I push past the guilt, through the pain, and walk away from the woman I fell in love with. Why? Because I wounded her so intently, broke her trust so irreparably, and nothing can change or fix that.

There is no future for that kind of hurt.

Especially not for an asshole like me.

Twenty-Six

Lyndee

"That's the last one," I say to absolutely no one. With a sigh, I set my cell phone a little too roughly on the counter. But what's a girl to do? That's the final cake order I had on the books, and now it's gone like the rest of them.

Two days. That's how long it takes for a business to completely tank. For fourteen special order cakes to cancel, not even caring about the cancelation fee. I, of course, couldn't even go through with the charges, refusing to take that fifty dollars from people who would much rather listen to the opinions of an angry man.

But I understand where they're coming from. I'm the new girl in town. Burgers and Brew has been in business for more than five years, a thriving local establishment with a reputation most competitors would kill for.

Like me.

I'd kill for that kind of PR and status.

Instead, I'm left with an empty bakery, a display case full of pastries, and a loan payment coming up that doesn't care about some stupid letter to the editor.

Around noon, I hear the bell ring over the door, and I jump in surprise. When I glance up, I see Mallory and Lizzie coming in, a wide smile on the mother's face and an impending sugar coma gaze on the little girl's.

"Hi," I say, setting my cleaning rag in the bucket. "What are you doing here?"

"Well, we came for treats, but also I need to discuss a cake," Mallory replies as her daughter runs up to the display case.

"I want dat one!" Lizzie bellows, pointing to the sprinkle-covered cupcake with chocolate and vanilla swirl frosting.

"Of course you do. Pick one out for me and Walker too. We'll have them before he goes to work later," Mallory tells her daughter before turning and giving me a gentle smile.

Her kindness brings instant tears to my eyes. I cover them up by filling the cupcake box with treats, some picked by Lizzie and some by me. "Here you go, sweetie. On the house," I tell the little girl, handing over the bag with her cupcakes.

"Oh, no, I'll pay. I insist," Mallory says, pulling cash from her purse.

"No, it's okay," I reply, glancing around at the empty room.

Mallory does the same, as if understanding completely what I'm saying. "But every little bit helps," she whispers, shoving two twenties across the counter.

I give her a sad smile. "I'm not sure anything can fix this, but I do appreciate it." I slide the money back toward her.

When she takes it, she doesn't put it in her wallet, but shoves it in the empty tip jar sitting on top of the counter. "I also need a cake."

"Oh," I reply, somewhat awkwardly. Since I don't know how long I'll remain in business, I'm not sure what I should do here. "I'm not sure I'm the right person for the job," I confess, following her around the counter and joining her at a bistro table.

"What? Of course you are! You're the only person for the job. I need a wedding cake, and you're the only one I want to make it."

I smile softly, so very happy for my new friend. "Well, I appreciate it. I'd love to make it for you," I reply honestly.

"Good," she states with a nod. "We don't need a very big one, but what I'm thinking is two small tiers. I don't have a topper or anything, so just throw some flowers or something on there. I trust you."

I can't help but grin. "Okay," I reply, making a note in my notebook. "When do you need it by?"

"Valentine's Day?" she asks, offering me a smile that's both apologetic and enthusiastic.

"Wow, that's only a few weeks away! Congratulations."

"Thanks," she says. "I wanted to get married before I started to get too big with the baby. I'm not wearing a big fancy dress, just something subtle and timeless."

"I'm sure it'll be perfect."

"Well, you'll be there, right?" she insists, watching as her daughter sticks her finger inside the box of cupcakes and pulls it out covered in frosting.

"Oh, uh, I don't know," I stammer, unsure what to say. Surely she's heard all about what happened here and between Jasper and me, right?

"Listen, I know everything is a...mess right now, but I truly believe in my heart it'll turn around for you. You're too amazing at what you do to go out like this," she says, standing up. "I say you give 'em hell, Lyndee. Show this town you're here to stay. And maybe kick Mr. Kohlmann in the jingle bells on your way to the top."

I can't help but laugh. "Jingle bells?"

She leans in and whispers. "Balls. I just can't say that because then someone wants to know what balls are and why Daddy Walk likes it when I lick them." She glances over at her daughter and arches an eyebrow.

I burst into a fit of giggles and cover my mouth with my hand. "Oh my God, she did?"

"Apparently heard us one night when we thought she was sleeping. Now, she's obsessed with balls. Asked Jameson if he had them the other day," she states, collecting her daughter and reaching for a napkin to wipe icing residue off her hands. "Your daddy is going to be so happy to eat those finger-poked cupcakes later."

"I gotted him duh choccate!"

"Mmmm, you know how much he likes chocolate with Lizzie marks," Mallory says, leading her child to the door. "Don't give up, Lyndee. Men are stupid creatures, and while we love them most of the time, they do really idiotic things every now and again. Don't let his immaturity ruin you. Fight like hell."

I give her a teary nod and swallow over the lump in my throat. "Okay."

"And watch for that invite in the mail soon. I expect you to be there."

Then she's out the door, a cute little blonde girl skipping down the sidewalk beside her.

I sigh, taking note of the full display case and grab one of those chocolate cupcakes Lizzie picked out. I take my treat over to one of the small tables by the window and watch as happy patrons walk out of the restaurant across the street, smiling with bellies full of delicious food.

I remove the paper from the cake and take a healthy bite, catching a taste of the creamy fudgy filling. "These are damn good," I say to no one. "You all are missing out," I add, glancing at the groups walking down the street.

Finishing off my treat, I start to form a plan. Mallory's right. I'm not going to let what Jasper did ruin my business. I'm going to fight. If I go down, it's going to be swinging.

I spend the rest of my Saturday and Sunday coming up with a plan, and Monday executing. I deliver what was left from the case on Saturday to the local nursing home. They gladly accepted the treats for their residents. If they had read the article in the paper last week, they made no indication.

When I return from my delivery, I'm happy to see a few customers taking advantage of my new offer. A free cup of coffee or tea with the purchase of a pastry. Dustin and Daisy are friendly, without being overly so, and refill cups once they are halfway gone. It wasn't part of the plan, to give refills too, but they went with it and I didn't complain. The longer the customers stay, the more likely they are to maybe leave with something else, like a slice of pie for later or fresh bread to go with their dinner.

By Wednesday, business remains at a small trickle, but at least it's better than nothing. Some are repeat customers, while others are new. I can tell by the way their eyes dart around suspiciously, as if they'll looking for piles of trash or other uncleanliness lurking in the corners, but am relieved when they realize it's not at all what the article claimed.

Speaking of article, I have yet to see Jasper. Not since he walked out of my bakery last Thursday evening. The rest of the crew, Jameson, Isaac, and Walker, have been in, buying up way more goodies than any of them could eat, but I appreciate their efforts, nonetheless. They all offered me their apologies, vowing to help give my business the boost it deserves after the train wreck their friend caused.

I've had to cut Daisy's hours a bit, to make up for the lack of income. I hate it, but she insisted it was fine. Her schooling keeps her plenty busy, and she's able to give a little more time to that. It still killed me to do, but I promised to return her hours as soon as I can.

If I can.

On Thursday afternoon, the bell rings over the door. I'm in the kitchen, baking a raspberry cream pie, when my brother hollers from the front counter. "Lyndee, can you come up here a minute? There's a gentleman who'd like a word with you."

I wash my hands at the sink and dry them off on my apron before heading up front to see who my visitor is. A bubble of hope explodes in my chest at the thought that it might be Jasper standing there, and then I chastise myself for even entertaining the thought. I don't want to see Jasper.

Not today.

Not ever again.

Right?

I round the corner, ignoring the disappointment I feel when I find a tall, older man smiling at the counter. "Miss Gibson?" he asks, reaching out a hand to shake.

"Yes."

"I'm Dwayne Jordan. My mom is a resident at the Stewart Grove Care Facility, and I believe you've been delivering pastries and things there the last few days." He offers me a friendly grin. "I was there visiting yesterday when they brought a tray to our table. They were delicious."

I return the smile, feeding off his relaxed demeanor. "I'm glad you enjoyed them."

"Enjoyed them? They were simply amazing. I took one home for my wife, who raved about your chocolate croissant. Miss Gibson, I have a proposition for you."

Twenty-Seven

Jasper

I slam the empty container of sliced onions down on the table. "If you can't do it right, I'll find someone who can! That goes for all of you!" I bellow, feeling the eyes of my stunned staff on my back as I storm away.

Shutting the door with force, I plop onto my desk chair and drop my head into my hands. A loud sigh slides from my lips as I close my eyes in exhaustion. I'm so fucking tired. I haven't slept for more than a couple of hours each night since it happened. For weeks, I've been an aggravated zombie, going through the motions and so short fused, even my closest friends don't want to be around me.

Who'd blame them? Not me.

I'm an absolute bear who deserves to be alone.

I get up and leave my office, needing to escape the four small walls that continually close around me. I don't make eye contact as I walk through the kitchen and down the hallway, pushing open the employee entrance and stepping out into the sunlight. I feel like that damn Kid Rock song about not seeing it for three days, but not because I'm drowning myself in booze and drugs. My excuse is I'm working myself to death, day and night.

Hating myself a little more with each passing minute.

The sun is warm against my skin, even if there's a cool February chill in the air. I embrace the sting of the dampness though. It's a welcome reprieve from the darkness that's surrounded me.

I drop down on the picnic table and take a deep breath. It burns my lungs, but I don't care. I revel in the pain.

My mind continually replays the same scene, over and over again like a broken record. It invades my thoughts all day, but worse, at night. When I close my eyes, all I see is her tears. They stream down her lovely cheeks, each one a burning poker to the chest. Tears of betrayal, that's what they were, and I can't get them out of my head, as much as I've tried.

And I have.

I've drank way more than I should to try to forget her, but it hasn't helped. I've worked out until I was so bone-achingly tired I was sure I'd pass out from exhaustion. Only to still see those tears after I closed my eyes.

Worse, I hear her words. How each one dripped with the pain of deception.

My deception.

"Thought I'd find you back here," Jameson says as he walks through the back door and drops down on the bench across from me. He pulls out a cigarette and lights it, only to offer me the pack before he puts it away. I take one, even though I'm not a smoker, not since my younger, dumber college days.

"What are you doing out here?" I ask, lighting the cigarette with the offered flame.

"I drew the short straw," he announces, taking a deep inhale and looking much cooler than I do.

I snort out a laugh. "Pity for you."

He leans back, extending his long legs out in front of him. "It is. No one wanted to be the one to come out here and deal with your bullshit."

"Tell me how you really feel," I grumble.

"You don't want to know how I really feel, Jasp."

I sigh and close my eyes. "You know what, maybe I do. Let me have it. It can't be anything I haven't already thought myself these last few weeks."

When he doesn't reply right away, I open my eyes and meet his gaze. "You're scared."

Okay. That's not what I thought he'd say.

"What?"

"You're scared, because she made you feel things you've never felt before and it was easier to run from them than to face them head-on."

"I'm not scared," I argue, even though it's fruitless. I am.

"Bullshit. You may have done that newspaper thing accidentally, but in the last couple of weeks, you've had every opportunity in the world to fix it. But you haven't. You know why?"

I stare at him with a blank expression. "Because I'm scared?" I ask, deadpan.

"Exactly."

"So, tell me, oh wise one, why am I scared exactly?"

He just smiles. "Because you love her, and you think you're no good for her."

I blink, trying to wrap my head around his surprisingly astute assessment. "I don't love her," I whisper, but the words sound hollow, even to my own ears.

"You do, and that scares you. But the truth is, you two are better together than apart. She brought out this whole new side of you, and you didn't know what to do with it. It's like you were sitting back, waiting for the other shoe to drop so you could turn tail and run at the first opportunity.

"Well, you did that, and look what happened. You're miserable and so fucking grumpy no one wants to be around you. Your staff is on the verge of quitting, but you're too stubborn and stuck in your own head to see it.

"But do you know what's worse? She loves you too, and you're too wrapped up in your own head to even see it." He takes a long drag from his cigarette and stares at me.

I close my eyes and picture her standing in the kitchen of her bakery. "I told her I loved her. It was selfish, because I was walking out of her life, but I had to say it. For myself. Not to hurt her, even though I'm sure it did. Because I'm a prick. A fucking dick who had to say the one thing I should have said before everything blew up in his face. A coward."

He nods slowly in understanding, but also in agreement. "You're right." I can't help but laugh, smiling for the first time in forever. "You're a dick. Always have been. But you're also the first guy to jump in and help if one of us needs something. When all that shit happened last fall with Walker and Mal? You were right there, despite having a job to do. You're a good friend, Jasper. You don't give yourself enough credit.

"You made a mistake. Out of frustration or anger or whatever that was. We know you didn't mean to send that bullshit to the newspaper, and deep down she knows it too. You'd never willingly hurt someone you love. That includes us. And her."

He takes another long drag. "So, now the question is, what are you going to do about it? Let her go, to live her life? You gonna be content to see her come and go across the street without saying hello? What happens when she starts to date, and they come into the restaurant for dinner? That okay with you?"

I pull at the collar of my polo, even though it's not tight. Suddenly, I can't seem to get enough oxygen into my lungs.

"That's what I thought. Listen, Jasp, if you don't love her or don't want to see her again, fine. I won't say another fucking word. But you still owe her an apology. You did her wrong, and that's not okay. Fix that because it's the right thing to do. She's not our competition and doesn't deserve what's happening to her."

My chest aches. "What's happening to her?" I ask, even though I don't think I want to know the answer.

He sighs and puts out his cigarette, only to retrieve a second one. "Business sucks. Dustin said she lost all her cake orders and had to donate a bunch of product to the hospital and nursing home."

Again, I close my eyes and try to hide from the humiliation and shame. "What if I do love her?" I whisper, putting my cigarette out.

He smiles and stands up. "Then, don't stop until she forgives you."

I watch as one of my best friends walks away, leaving me outside in the cold. But this time, I'm left with something else too. Hope. The truth is I'm probably all wrong for her, but Jameson's right. I'd rather be with her, spending my life proving to her I'm worthy, than spending it without her.

Now, I just have to figure out how to apologize.

The right way this time.

Lyndee

"Are those cakes packaged and ready to go?" I ask my brother, who's carefully stacking mini chocolate lava cakes onto a large tray for easier delivery.

"Almost done," he says, placing the final few small boxes onto the pile and giving me a satisfactory grin. "There. Perfect."

I return his smile before it drops away with apprehension. "Do you think the chocolate is a good choice? Too much?"

He pats my hand, reassuring. "It's perfect, Lyn. Really. Nothing says Happy Valentine's Day like warm, gooey lava fudge cake."

I exhale deeply and nod. "Okay. Good. I'm going to get these loaded up. You'll be good here while I'm gone?" I ask, slipping on my coat and grabbing my purse.

"I'll be fine," he insists. "Besides, you'll be back soon."

I glance around, making sure I have everything, and lift the heavy tray in my arms.

"Let me get the door," Dustin hollers, stepping outside and making sure there's enough room for me to slip out without fumbling the tray stacked with mini cakes.

Once they're loaded in the back seat, I tell him goodbye and throw him a wave. It only takes me a few minutes to get to the restaurant across town. Jordan's is a great little family-owned place that serves a wide variety of entrées. I pull up to the back door and prepare to unload my goodies for this weekend's big Valentine's Day promotion.

"Hey, Lyndee, good to see you!" Dwayne says, meeting me outside.

"You too. I have four dozen lava cakes for you," I tell him, carefully pulling the tray out of the car.

"That's perfect! These are going to be a hit," he insists, helping me carry the tray into his kitchen.

When Mr. Jordan stopped by my bakery, it was to offer me a deal I couldn't refuse. A partnership, if you will. It turns out, their dessert selection wasn't selling, so Mr. and Mrs. Jordan thought it would be great if I provided the desserts for their restaurant, and in return, they promote my business with signage and mentions. After all, word of mouth is the best form of advertisement, right? It's my first weekend as their exclusive dessert provider, and it's a big one.

Valentine's Day weekend.

"Lyndee, these are amazing," Mr. Jordan announces, glancing inside one of the boxes. "The perfect dessert for two."

I smile proudly. "Thank you. I hope they're a success for you."

"And for you," he replies, closing the lid on the box. "We have you listed prominently on the menu as the dessert provider for the weekend. Plus, every time one of the servers offers the dessert, your name will be mentioned."

"I appreciate this. Thank you," I state again.

"No, thank you. I think this partnership is only a small step for you. Plus, that big write-up in the paper won't hurt either," he adds with a chuckle.

"Write-up?" I ask, confused as to what he's talking about. That letter to the editor was weeks ago, but I definitely don't see it as helpful.

He looks at me with surprise in his eyes. "You don't know? The newspaper printed a retraction today."

"What?" I ask, my chin practically unhinging from my jaw.

He turns around and grabs a newspaper from a table along the back wall and hands it to me. There, on the front page, is my business name and a photograph of my front window. The headline reads, "Sugar Rush is Here to Stay. Local Business Owner Apologizes for Letter."

I skim the article, only to stop and reread the entire thing a little more slowly the second time. It's a retraction, written by Jasper Kohlmann. He talks about how amazing the pastries are and explains why he said the things he did. When I get to the end, my heart feels like it's trying to claw out of my chest.

"Oh my God," I mutter, glancing up and trying to wrap my hands around what I just read.

"Right? I didn't know you and Jasper knew each other."

"We went to school together," I mumble, even though he already knows that, since he read the article.

"I just hope we can still work together, even after you get bigger," he says with a chuckle.

"What?"

"Well, this is going to do wonders for your business, and I'm sure you'll eventually get so big you won't have time to make desserts for my little ol' restaurant anymore."

I reach over and squeeze his arm affectionately. "Not going to happen. You took a chance on me when everyone else was running the other way. You helped save my business, Mr. Jordan. You and your wife will have desserts for as long as you need them."

He smiles softly and pulls me into a hug. "Thank you, Lyndee. I'm happy to do business with you."

"Likewise."

After a few more minutes of chitchatting, I head back out to my car and drive to the bakery. When I turn down the block, I'm shocked to see people. Tons of people, lining the sidewalks, coming and going from my business. I quickly pull around back and run inside.

"Thank God you're here," Dana bellows. "All of a sudden, this place just got crazy. We're almost out of pastries!"

I glance up front and find every table full and a line from the counter to the door. Daisy and Dustin are up there, filling white paper bags with treats and paper cups with coffee. I grab the tray of scones and muffins I had already prepared for tomorrow and take them up front.

By the time we close at two, there isn't a treat left in the shop.

I flip the closed sign and drop into the first chair I come to. "Holy shit," I mutter, still trying to process what just happened.

"I don't want to complain, but what the hell was that?" Dustin asks, transferring himself into the extra wheelchair we keep in back.

I laugh and grab the newspaper sitting on the counter. I don't have to open it, just hand him the paper with the front page on display. "*This* happened."

Dana and Daisy lean over Dustin's shoulder and read the article. I catch their gasps of disbelief, and their eyes wide with astonishment. "Holy crap!" Daisy proclaims.

I sit back down, my legs tired, and glance across the street, still trying to wrap my head around what I've read.

What he did.

For me.

"What does this mean?" I ask to no one in particular.

"You mean his very public apology? The fact that he not only admitted he was wrong, but that he made it up?"

"Yeah. That."

Dana starts to laugh. "It means he loves you."

Tears cloud my eyes as I look back out the window. The door opens and a young couple walks out, his arm thrown over her shoulder as he guides her down the sidewalk. I can't help but feel envious of them. Of their public display of affection. Of the way he seems to shield her from the cold breeze behind his coat.

"What do you need?" Daisy asks, setting a cup of tea in front of me.

"Nothing. You guys all have plans tonight," I remind them. Dustin and Dana are having dinner to celebrate Valentine's Day tonight, since Mallory and Walker's wedding is tomorrow night, and Daisy is going out with girlfriends. "I have some work to do now to get ready for tomorrow." You know, considering I sold all of the pastries I had prepped for Saturday.

"But you have the wedding cake to finish," Dustin reminds.

"It won't take me very long. It's already made, I just have to decorate it."

After thirty minutes and a lot of convincing that I was indeed fine, I'm left alone on a Friday night, with a to-do list a mile long. I glance around, trying to figure out where to start.

Donuts, muffins, and scones.

Plus, pies and cookies.

Well, it's not going to bake itself.

I might as well get busy.

Jasper

I've been standing outside the bakery on the sidewalk, watching her work, for a while. There's something so calming, so soothing about the way she moves, how she works efficiently and quickly to prepare whatever she's working on.

She places a tray of cookies into the massive oven and grabs something from the refrigerator. It's a two-tiered cake, the bottom layer chocolate and the top white. It reminds me of a wedding cake, and to be honest, for the first time in my life, I can picture myself in front of one.

With Lyndee beside me.

But let's not put the cart before the horse. Right now, I just need to get her to talk to me. I assume she saw the article, or at least, I pray she did. Otherwise, my plan will go completely to shit in a matter of seconds. No, it won't. I'll just have to back up and start at the beginning.

The way I should have the last time I was here.

I know this door will be locked, so I move around to the alley behind the building. The moment I reach the door, I'm overcome with the familiar scents of sugar and cinnamon. It reminds me of her, of my sweets. I take a deep breath and knock on the door.

My heart literally climbs into my throat while I wait.

A few seconds later, the door opens, and there she is. A beautiful breath of fresh air, like the first spring rain to wash over you. It's glorious, refreshing, perfect.

Like her.

"Hi."

"Hey," she replies, glancing around and clearing her throat. She looks so small, as I tower over her, yet so unbelievably gorgeous with sugar granules on her cheek and flour in her hair.

"May I come in for a minute?" I ask nervously, trying to play it cool. I'm sure the last thing she wants is for me to burst through the door like the Kool-Aid Man and take her in my arms.

"Uhh, sure," she replies, stepping back and granting my entrance.

I glance around, noticing the canvas photos she got for her birthday hanging on the wall and mountains of ingredients all over the island. "Those look great there," I tell her, nodding toward the photos.

She nods slowly, hanging back and waiting. After a few very long seconds, she finally asks, "Is that what you came here for? To approve of where I hung my art?"

"No," I insist immediately. "I came here to apologize the way I should have weeks ago."

"You did apologize," she reminds me, referring to the lame excuses I threw at her the day she discovered that letter.

"I did, but not the right way." I take a step in her direction, and I notice she doesn't back away. I take that as a good sign. "I shouldn't have just told you how sorry I was, I should have showed you. But the truth is, I was afraid. I was terrified of not being what you really wanted or needed. I was scared of falling for you, and you realizing you can do so much better than me. I'm a jerk. A complete asshole more often than not, but the truth is, you made me want to be better. You brought color into my black-and-white world, and I'm a hell of a lot better with you than I am without you."

Deep breath.

"I don't know if you'll ever forgive me for what I did, but I pray someday, you will. I never should have said those things, even in a stupid email, but worse, I didn't even mean them. Because the truth is, you're the best thing that ever happened to me, and I fell in love with you, and if I have to spend the rest of my life trying to earn your trust again, then I'll do it, because I'd do anything for you."

She starts to cry, and it kills me—literally, I feel my heart breaking in half—to see her tears. Especially knowing I'm the asshole who put them there.

I move toward her before I can even stop myself. "Please don't cry, sweets," I whisper, cupping her jaw in my hand and wiping away the wetness on her cheeks. "I hate to see you cry."

"These are good tears," she insists, offering me a small smile and a sniffle.

"No tears are good ones," I tell her, pulling her petite body into my own.

She sighs, reaching back and clutching my shirt in a death grip, as she hugs me. I feel my own tension release, my body starting to relax for the first time in weeks. "Thank you for the retraction."

I rest my chin on the top of her head, and just breathe her in. "I'm sorry it took me so long to write it. You deserved it immediately, and for that, I'm truly remorseful."

"But you did it now, and I'm grateful. I was completely packed today," she says, sniffling and glancing up at me. Her eyes finally shine like chocolate diamonds, brilliant and stunning.

"You should have been all along," I add, still hating the fact she took a hit to her business because of me.

She shrugs. "I was working my way back up. Mallory told me not to give up or to go down fighting, so I was trying a few things."

"Like what?"

"Well, Jordan's and I partnered to use my baked goods at his restaurant. Tonight's the first night they're available with dinner," she says, giving me a proud smile.

My heart drops to my shoes. "Jordan's?"

"Yeah," she says, giving me an uneasy look.

"The place with the rubbery chicken and lumpy mashed potatoes?"

Instead of getting upset at me, she just shakes her head and grins. "Stop it. Just because it's not Jasper-prepared perfect, doesn't mean there's anything wrong with his food or his menu. In fact, when I was there this afternoon, he mentioned they have almost a full house worth of reservations tonight and tomorrow."

I grumble, but not much. Even though it's not my taste of food, mostly because they cook more blandly, I can appreciate what ol' Dwayne did for Lyndee. Joining forces with her was probably one of the best business decisions the guy could ever make.

I'm just pissed I didn't think of it first.

"You're right," I tell her, pulling her back into my chest and just breathing her in. "I'm just jealous he thought of it before I did."

She chuckles, it floating to my ears as the most beautiful sound in the world. "I'm sure you'll survive."

I pull away and meet her gaze. "You're right, I will. As long as I have you by my side. I'm sorry I was such a dipshit, sweets. I love you."

She grins, her eyes watery once more. "I love you too."

And then I kiss her. Finally. Our lips meet slowly, tasting and savoring the feel of the other, as if it had been too long since we'd felt the other against our mouths.

And it had.

Too fucking long.

That was my fault, and you'll be damn certain I'll never make that mistake again.

Before the kiss can deepen, a timer sounds. "Shoot," she mumbles, pulling away. "My cookies." She turns and runs to the oven, pulling out the large tray of freshly baked cookies.

I glance around, really noticing how much baking she's been doing and how much she still has to go. "What can I do?"

She gives me a questioning look before a smile spreads widely across her lips. "How are your baking skills?"

I walk to the sink and scrub my hands. "Excellent. I do believe the last cake I baked, I earned a gold star." I throw her a wink and a smirk over my shoulder and finish washing up. When I turn around, I add, "I'm all yours. Put me to work."

And she does.

We work side by side for the next several hours, slowly crossing everything off her list. While I'm taking muffins out of the oven, she finally sits down to work on the cake.

"That's a pretty fancy cake for the front case," I observe, watching as she quickly smooths a layer of icing over the outside of the cake.

"It's a wedding cake. For tomorrow." She moves to the refrigerator and pulls out a tray of gorgeous flowers made of fondant.

"Tomorrow, huh? I happen to know of a wedding happening then. Across the street, actually," I reply, placing the final tray of muffins in the oven to bake. Setting the oven mitt on top of the island I turn to face her.

She's smiling. "So I've heard," she murmurs, concentrating on adding intricate details to the side of the cake.

"You know, I can take a date. If I want."

"I already have plans tomorrow night. A wedding," she quips without breaking concentration.

I can't help but grin. "Yeah? So you can go with me."

"Nope," she states, popping the P. "I already have a date."

My blood runs cold as I meet her gaze over the top of the cake. Jealousy slides effortlessly through my body, rendering me unable to move. "You do?"

"Sure." She shrugs. "Dustin and Dana are coming with me."

When she smiles, the anxiety is replaced with serenity. "Interesting."

"What is?"

"Well, you're going to be there. I'm going to be there. Jameson's gonna play music, so there'll be dancing. If you're lucky, I'll save you a dance or two." I lean against the island, watching her every move.

"Only a dance or two?" she jibes, her eyes dancing with laughter as she feigns anger.

"Well, how many do you want?" I ask, stepping up and taking her in my arms. "I do have a busy night."

She gazes up at me and grins. "All of them."

And then I kiss her, reveling in the rightness of feeling her in my arms. The one made for me.

Sure, we're not perfect. Lord knows I'm definitely not, but with her beside me, I feel confident I can be the man she needs.

And maybe even get her all riled up every now and again, because there's nothing cuter than seeing fire in her eyes and a smile on her lips.

Maybe getting her mad every now and again isn't so bad.

Besides, the making up is proving to be well worth it.

Lyndee

I've never seen Burgers and Brew look like this. The place is empty, closed to the general public, on the busiest night of the year. Valentine's Day. There are gorgeous white and red linens covering the tables and dark red rose centerpieces adorning every flat surface.

In the bar are chairs, all facing the small stage where I once saw Jameson play. Right now, that's where Walker stands beside a minister from a local church. The room contains family and friends, all here tonight to witness the union between husband and wife.

Jameson sits off to the side, strumming a gorgeous melody on his guitar as the rest of the small group takes their seats. I'm here, with Jasper on one side and my brother and Dana on the other. Isaac sits directly in front of us, while the rest of the staff are scattered behind.

When the song he's playing transitions to the wedding march, we all stop and turn, glancing toward the back hallway. We all stand as Mallory and Lizzie make their grand entrance in soft ivory satin and lace. My eyes immediately tear up as I witness the moment Walker sees her for the first time. He smiles so widely, his own eyes filling with wetness as he watches her slowly make her way to him.

I feel Jasper's big, warm hand wrap around mine, squeezing it gently before he slips his fingers into mine. Together, we watch as mother and daughter make their way to where Walker stands, waiting.

"Daddy! Wook at my dwess!" Lizzie yells when they're barely halfway down the makeshift aisle, making everyone chuckle.

Walker steps down and meets them, dropping to one knee in front of the little girl. "You look like a princess," he tells her.

"I tolded you it was pwitty."

He scoops her up and places a kiss on her cheek before standing up in front of Mallory. She's crying, but they're definitely tears of joy. "I've never seen a more beautiful woman in all my life," he whispers, smiling so fondly and proudly.

He takes her hand and leads her up to the altar, where they repeat vows and make promises to spend the rest of their lives together. I've been to a handful of weddings, but this is the one I truly love. It holds you tight and refuses to let go. Maybe it's the holiday, but I don't think that's entirely it. It's this couple and the love they share. It's a living, breathing thing. Something everyone strives for.

By the time Walker kisses his bride, my makeup is good and truly screwed. I spent the entire wedding weeping, as if I've known them longer than just a few months. Perhaps it's because they welcomed me into their circle so swiftly, so easily. And not just me, but Dustin and now Dana too.

As everyone starts to mingle in the bar, Jasper and I slip off to the kitchen. He spent the afternoon preparing tonight's meal, even though Walker was prepared to have it catered. Jasper refused, stating no one but him would ever cook in this kitchen or serve meals in this restaurant. I guess they just realized it was easier to relent than to argue.

We slip inside the kitchen and find it coming to life. Jasper and his team quickly go to work, finalizing the plates of fresh salmon and filet mignon, roasted potatoes, and grilled tomatoes covered in spinach and cheese. That one made me giggle.

I stand back and watch as he moves in the kitchen, commanding the space with his expertise and precision. If I'm being honest, watching him work gets me a little excited, if you know what I mean, and if the way he grins at me from across the room is any indication, he knows it too.

But what's a girl to do? I have the most gorgeous, infuriating man on the planet, and his eyes are set on me. I'm not strong enough to fight it or him, not that I want to. I choose him. From the moment I read his words in the newspaper yesterday, I chose him. We may not be perfect, but we're real and committed to making this work.

It won't be easy, of that I'm sure.

Not when you're dating a man who has a natural ability to push all your buttons and get under your skin.

But I must say, the make-up sex is even better than I thought it could be.

I learned that fact last night.

Twice.

Jasper

"May I have this dance?" I ask, extending my hand to the most stunning woman in the room.

Lyndee smiles and places her smaller hand in my larger one. I lead her to the dance floor and pull her into my arms. Together, we sway in beat to the music as Jameson plays guitar and sings about finding love. I hold her against my chest and rest my chin on the top of her head. Walker gives me a wink, as he slowly spins his new wife and daughter around the dance floor. I've never seen him smile so much in my entire life.

I'm so fucking happy for my friend.

"Did you get a slice of cake?" she asks, dark brown eyes meeting mine.

"I didn't. I was going to sneak a piece back for later, but I caught Lizard shoving her finger into a few slices and licking the frosting off. I thought better of it," I state, recalling the mischievous grin the little girl gave me when I busted her on it. The chocolate smeared on her chin let me know she'd probably been at it awhile.

"Oh, well, it was pretty good. I was able to get a piece without finger marks," she replies with a chuckle.

I glance over and see Dustin and Dana. They're sitting together at a table, their heads very close in conversation. "What's going on with those two?" I ask.

Lyndee sighs. "He asked me if I was okay if he went back to her place tonight. It's the first time he's ever stayed out all night. I feel bad though. I don't want him to not feel welcome in his own house."

"I'm sure that's not it, sweets. He just wants to be alone with her. And do all the alone things you don't want to think about him doing," I state, wiggling my eyebrows and making her laugh.

"Gross. Stop. That's my brother."

"You should hear about all the dirty things I did to his sister this morning in the shower. There were all kinda naughty impressions left on the glass door," I reply, earning a slap on the arm.

"Stop that. Someone will overhear you," she says.

"Someone did," Numbers grumbles, quickly spinning Savannah away from where we're dancing.

"See? You've scarred him for life," she teases.

I glance over to Lyndee's brother, who catches my gaze. He gives me a chin lift, letting me know he sees me. There's also a hidden message that says I better treat his sister right, or else. At least that's the message he gave me loud and clear earlier this morning when I went to make coffee and found him standing in their kitchen. I've never been more honored to hear one of those brother speeches than I was at seven o'clock this morning.

"You about ready to blow this Popsicle stand?" I ask, kissing her forehead.

"You don't want to stay? The party's just getting started," she insists.

I shake my head and pull her flush against me. My hard cock rubs against her stomach as realization settles into her eyes. "No, I was hoping to take this party somewhere else. Somewhere a little more private."

"Why, Mr. Kohlmann, you sure have a way with words," she quips, batting her eyelashes.

"You know it, baby," I reply, spinning her out and pulling her back into my chest.

She settles her cheek against my chest, her warm hands holding my back as we sway to the music. "One more dance."

"You got it, sweets," I tell her, completely content with dancing, as long as she's my partner.

And we do. Until the very end of the celebration, I dance with the woman I fell in love with. The one who owns me, heart and soul. The one I look at and can picture in a white dress, our own family and friends gathered around us.

Not now, but someday.

Until then, I'll keep trying to prove she made the right decision in forgiving me. That nothing is too big of an obstacle to overcome, as long as we have each other. My goal is to keep her happy and smiling for the rest of my days.

Well, maybe having the occasional argument isn't so bad. After all, I discovered making up with Lyndee is greater than any sex I had before her.

Plus, my girl's a tiger in bed after she's been upset.

Maybe making her mad every now and again isn't so bad after all.

The End

Don't miss a single reveal, release, or sale! Sign up for my newsletter.

http://www.laceyblackbooks.com/newsletter

Books by Lacey Black

Rivers Edge series

Trust Me, Rivers Edge book 1 (Maddox and Avery) – FREE at all retailers

> ~ *#1 Bestseller in Contemporary Romance*

Fight Me, Rivers Edge book 2 (Jake and Erin)

Expect Me, Rivers Edge book 3 (Travis and Josselyn)

Promise Me: A Novella, Rivers Edge book 3.5 (Jase and Holly)

Protect Me, Rivers Edge book 4 (Nate and Lia)

Boss Me, Rivers Edge book 5 (Will and Carmen)

Trust Us: A Rivers Edge Christmas Novella (Maddox and Avery)

> ~ *This novella was originally part of the Christmas Miracles Anthology*

BOX SET – contains all 5 novels, 2 novellas, and a BONUS short story

With Me, A Rivers Edge Christmas Novella (Brooklyn and Becker)

Bound Together series

Submerged, Bound Together book 1 (Blake and Carly)

> ~ *An International Bestseller*

Profited, Bound Together book 2 (Reid and Dani)

~A Bestseller, reaching Top 100 on 2 e-retailers
Entwined, Bound Together book 3 (Luke and Sidney)

Summer Sisters series
My Kinda Kisses, Summer Sisters book 1 (Jaime and Ryan)
~A Bestseller, reaching Top 100 on 2 e-retailers
My Kinda Night, Summer Sisters book 2 (Payton and Dean)
My Kinda Song, Summer Sisters book 3 (Abby and Levi)
My Kinda Mess, Summer Sisters book 4 (Lexi and Linkin)
My Kinda Player, Summer Sisters book 5 (AJ and Sawyer)
My Kinda Player, Summer Sisters book 6 (Meghan and Nick)
My Kinda Wedding, A Summer Sisters Novella book 7 (Meghan and Nick)

Rockland Falls series
Love and Pancakes, Rockland Falls book 1
Love and Lingerie, Rockland Falls book 2
Love and Landscape, Rockland Falls book 3
Love and Neckties, Rockland Falls book 4

Standalone
Music Notes, a sexy contemporary romance standalone
A Place To Call Home, a Memorial Day novella
Exes and Ho Ho Ho's, a sexy contemporary romance standalone novella
Pants on Fire, a sexy contemporary romance standalone
Double Dog Dare You, a new standalone
Grip, A Driven World Novel
Bachelor Swap, A Bachelor Tower Series Novel

Burgers and Brew Crüe Series
Kickstart My Heart
Don't Go Away Mad

Co-Written with *NYT Bestselling* Author, Kaylee Ryan
It's Not Over, Fair Lakes book 1
Just Getting Started, Fair Lakes book 2
Can't Get Enough, Fair Lakes book 3
Fair Lakes Box Set
Boy Trouble, The All American Boy Series
Home To You, a second chance novella

Acknowledgments

So much work goes into a book, and this is my opportunity to say THANK YOU to those who helped along the way!

My editing team – Kara Hildebrand, Sandra Shipman, Joanne Thompson, and Karen Hrdlicka. You ladies are THE best! I couldn't do it without you!!

The book team - Photographer, Wander Aguiar; Model, Lucas Loyola; Cover Designer, Melissa Gill; Graphics Designer, Gel with Tempting Illustrations; Formatting, Brenda with Formatting Done Wright; and Promotions by Give Me Books. You each make this entire process easy!

Kaylee Ryan, Holly Collins, Lacey's Ladies, and my ARC team, thank you for listening, for your encouragements, and for your constant support.

To my husband and kids, thank you for always standing by my side and forgiving me when I submerge myself into my book world. It's not easy, but we make it work together.

To all the bloggers and readers, thank you, thank you, thank you. I hope you enjoy this story as much as I loved writing it.

Lacey Black is a Midwestern girl with a passion for reading, writing, and shopping. She carries her e-reader with her everywhere she goes so she never misses an opportunity to read a few pages. Always looking for a happily ever after, Lacey is passionate about contemporary romance novels and enjoys it further when you mix in a little suspense. She resides in a small town in Illinois with her husband, two children, and three rowdy chickens. Lacey loves watching NASCAR races, shooting guns, and should only consume one mixed drink because she's a lightweight.

Email: laceyblackwrites@gmail.com
Facebook: https://www.facebook.com/authorlaceyblack
Twitter: https://twitter.com/AuthLaceyBlack
Website: www.laceyblackbooks.com

Sign up for my newsletter so you don't miss a single sale, reveal, or release!
http://www.laceyblackbooks.com/newsletter

www.ingramcontent.com/pod-product-compliance
Lightning Source LLC
Chambersburg PA
CBHW070632260626
47161CB00007B/2674